WHAT

DATE DUE

OTHER TITLES BY ANDREW E. KAUFMAN

Twisted
While the Savage Sleeps
The Lion, the Lamb, the Hunted
Darkness & Shadows

WHAT

SHE

DOESN'T

KNOW

ANDREW E. KAUFMAN

Text copyright © 2018 by Andrew E. Kaufman
All rights reserved.

Published by Thomas & Mercer, Seattle

www.apub.com

Amazon, the Amazon logo, and Thomas & Mercer are trademarks of Amazon. com, Inc., or its affiliates.

ISBN-13: 9781477809082
ISBN-10: 1477809082

Cover design by PEPE *nymi*

Printed in the United States of America

To those who stood at my side during the battle

The ultimate aim of the human mind, in all its efforts, is to become acquainted with Truth.

—*Eliza Farnham*

1

On a Thursday afternoon, beneath a hearty spring downpour, Riley Harper walks out of Glendale Psychiatric Hospital a free woman. But she might as well have PSYCHOTIC MURDERER stamped across her forehead, because that's how many will always see her.

If you were to ask why she was committed in the first place, Riley would contend her breakdown was the product of bad timing and a lousy memory. The press and public would disagree. They'd argue that her supposed mental illness was an elaborate scam to avoid community disdain and the threat of a retrial.

Shortly after Riley and her sister, Erin, emerge from the hospital entrance, a wave of reporters rolls across the wet tarmac, blocking their path, shooting photos, and shotgunning questions. Erin gave fair warning that the press was camped out in the parking lot, but Riley had no idea there would be this many of them. She pulls down her raincoat's hood to shield her face from the cameras, and the two women dash for the car.

"Ms. Harper!" hollers a local TV reporter, wagging her microphone as if it were a trophy with a large white 5 affixed to it. "How does it feel to be free?"

Riley ignores the reporter as Erin strides briskly by her side, trying to navigate the driving Northern California rain and a thick storm of aggressive newshounds. As they continue rushing to Erin's car, the press keeps coming, feet clacking, shutters snapping, jaws flapping.

"Do you still claim you can't remember what you were doing during the murder?" asks a reporter with an ugly green-and-red tie that makes Riley think of Christmas. Odd, since it's the middle of April.

"We've heard the investigation might be reopened," another newsperson shouts. "Are you worried your arrest could soon follow?"

But ignoring questions from the reporters only seems to urge them on. Now they form a human barricade between the sisters and Erin's Jeep Cherokee. A news copter swoops in from high above, battering the darkened, pathless sky while trying to grab aerial shots of Riley's departure.

"Move it!" Erin says to the press with a sharp snarl that's barely audible beneath the thundering copter. Dragging Riley by a hand, she shoves through the crowd and shouts, "I said, *move* it!"

But the mob pushes back, and Riley loses her footing. She slips on slick ground and falls to her knees. The cameras continue to roll, following her mishap to its bitter end.

"What the hell's wrong with you people?" Erin shrieks with pink-faced anger while she helps Riley up.

"Ms. Harper, did or *didn't* you kill her?" says a reporter, jockeying beside them.

Riley pulls to an abrupt stop and battles a ferocious urge to lash out, but if eyes could shoot lightning bolts, this guy would be lying belly-up on the pavement. The reporter must sense she means business, because he shuffles a few preemptive paces backward.

She's about to turn away when her limbs go weak. Demetre Sloan slinks through the crowd, watching Riley's every move. For a fleeting moment, the two women's gazes connect, then Erin steps up just in time. She yanks open the car door and helps Riley inside before slamming it shut, then fights her way around to the driver's side. Erin is not by any means a large woman, but she's tough. Determined, too, as she rams her way through the microphones and cameras and flailing hands so she can grab the car door handle.

They make it safely inside the vehicle, although to Riley it feels like a fishbowl. Erin takes a moment to catch her breath, until a jarring palm slap against the window interrupts the effort. Riley flinches. A reporter mouths something indiscernible from behind the glass, obviously last-ditching it for a parting comment.

This time, Riley manages to remain composed. Once more, Erin saves the day—she affords the crowd a long, ear-shattering *honk*, leaving it little time to clear out before she shoves the car in gear and flies into reverse. Seconds later, they escape the media mayhem, hightailing it away from Glendale and down the road.

2

"She was there," Riley says. "Demetre Sloan was there."

"I know." Erin sucks in a fitful breath. "I saw."

"Just a few minutes out of Glendale, and already that bitch with a badge is coming after me."

Neither says anything for a good five minutes. Riley needs these moments to settle her nerves. To decompress. She looks down, runs a hand over her torn and soiled jeans.

"Shit! You're hurt!" Erin says, splitting her attention between Riley's bloodstained knees and the road.

"It's no big deal. Just a few scratches."

"Damn it! Things weren't supposed to go like this." Erin shakes her head. "They were not . . ."

"How did the press even find out I was being released?" Riley checks the side-view mirror to see if they're following. "Aren't there rules against giving out that kind of information?"

"There are supposed to be."

"But?"

Erin sighs. "A few months back, an unnamed source from inside the hospital leaked that your condition was improving and you were due for release. It was all over the news."

"I suppose that same source also told them today would be the day."

"Probably, yes."

Riley stares blindly out her window. In a perfect world, she would have looked forward to this day, but for obvious reasons, she's been dreading it. This past hour was only the beginning, a watered-down version of what lies ahead. People have been watching TV. They've read things. So has Riley, and she can tell which way the wind is blowing. Suspicion has wrapped itself around her like a rancid stench, and she's being thrust into the hostile community without a lifeline. The resentment toward her that's been incubating outside the institution walls feels more threatening than anything that could have happened inside them. At least Glendale's most dangerous were kept under restraint. But who will protect her now?

Though she doesn't look, she can sense Erin keeping a watchful eye on her. Gaze leveled ahead, Riley works hard to maintain a stoic expression, shedding not a single tear. Then she tastes blood, realizes she's chewing her bottom lip, and makes herself stop.

"It's going to be okay, sis," Erin tries, sounding a shade too measured to pass for believable. "I promise. It will."

Riley nods. Not because she feels comforted but because it seems like the right thing to do at this moment.

But things *aren't* okay.

Erin opens her mouth to talk, hesitates, then stops, and an obstinate silence broadens between them. This was not their norm before Erin had her committed. But then, so much has changed since that day when Erin walked in and found Riley lying on the kitchen floor.

The river of red, snaking its way across tile.

Riley, begging Erin to let her die.

The ambulance. The hospital.

The crushing disappointment and heartbreak.

Riley examines the four-inch scar that runs up her wrist, then squeezes her lids shut and tries to wrestle away those buffeting memories.

The car rounds a corner, and her emotions take a nosedive. They're passing through Meadowview, the old neighborhood. She didn't expect this. After being away for a while, it's a shock to her system. This is where it all happened. The beginning of the end. Where time stopped and life turned inside out.

Her spine hitches ramrod straight. Her tongue feels as gritty as dirt. But she tells herself it's okay, that she can handle this. In an attempt to derail the gnawing anxiety, she strikes a deal with herself to pull away, to observe how much life in the neighborhood has changed since her public descent into insanity. New buildings have sprung up. Old ones have been renovated. And the general population seems younger—either that or she is growing older. What was once her favorite little movie theater has been converted into a trendy thrift shop called Frock 'n' Roll Fashion. The video store is now a café, an abundance of Gen-Y boomers lounging outside, gazes glued to laptops while they sip coffee.

Her distraction works for a little while.

Until it doesn't.

More wind. More unremitting rain. An unforgiving combination that bullies the windshield and assails it with water. Rain that drives her memories deeper into the chaos that spun her world off its axis. Deeper into her private hell. She clutches the armrest and squeezes. Soon, her fingernails are digging into leather.

The car hangs a right and lands them near the one patch of earth she doesn't want to revisit: Greenday Cemetery, the place where her mind betrayed her. Images and sensations from when she regained consciousness on the side of the road cut through her mind like a filthy, jagged razor blade. The chuffing wind. The rain that stung the back of her neck. Her banged-up forehead.

The bloody sneaker.

This no longer feels like an awful memory. She is there again, somersaulting down the rabbit hole.

"Son of a bitch!" Erin says.

Riley flees from the darkness and pops into the moment.

"I'm so sorry!" Erin pounds her palm against the steering wheel. This time *she* appears shaken. "I didn't even think about—I should have gone a different . . . Oh shit."

Riley clears her throat and, in a voice rough and crackly, says, "It's okay."

"It *isn't* okay." Erin slows her car to compensate for the slippery road. "You just got out of Glendale, and here I am, taking you on a drive through Misery Lane."

More of that uneasy silence. More rain.

"I'm fine," says Riley in a final attempt to repair the discomfort, but her dull affect strains credibility, making this moment between them that much worse.

She's not fine.

Because instead of moving away from the hurricane, she's flat-hatting directly into it.

3

As it turns out, the old neighborhood won't be a problem, because that isn't where Riley will live. But her new neighborhood raises an entirely different host of concerns.

The comfortable middle-class community in which she grew up, then created a family, no longer meets her budgetary constraints. Thankfully, Erin stepped in—as Erin always does—by petitioning Glendale to put Riley on the fast track for its Hospital Release Housing Program. HRHP will pay 50 percent of the rent, and the rest will be up to Riley. Erin has taken away some of that financial pressure by fronting Riley enough money to survive until she can get on her feet. That said, her housing options are limited to a designated area.

About thirty-five minutes from the old neighborhood, Rainbow Valley may be the most unbefitting name ever: gray skies shelter a dismal collection of apartment buildings, warehouses, and convenience stores.

Erin pulls the car up to Riley's development.

"This is it!" Erin says, working hard to show enthusiasm as she points past the flip-flopping windshield wipers.

Riley gets out and sees two police vehicles parked against the curb, blue and red lights twirling, and grapples with her stinging uneasiness.

Fighting the downpour, the two women trek toward a pair of bruised and battered doors, then Erin inserts a key to open them. The inside entryway is a cramped space, barely big enough to house rows of dented, dirt-smudged mailboxes. Overhead hangs a square light fixture constructed of filmy gold-colored glass, the brass housing broken in several spots.

They climb the stairs, and Riley works hard to school her uneasiness. This place is dark. And depressing. Dusty light sconces cling for their lives to peeling wallpaper. Even the sprayed-on popcorn ceilings look cruddy, an occasional spiderweb bridging the lumps. Halfway down one hall, a door stands wide open, the apartment beyond it empty, a carpenter's bag resting on the kitchen countertop.

Riley's got no right to complain. In all honesty, she signed up for this. Moving in with Erin wasn't an option. There's no way she'd be willing to disrupt her sister's life—not with all the chaos from the press and public. Besides that, more than ever, she needs privacy.

Get out. Stay strong. Trust your truth, she thinks, reciting her survival plan. She'll find a job, save some money, and, after wrapping up loose ends, make tracks out of this town. There's a better life waiting elsewhere, if she can just stay on course.

"This is all part of a whole gentrification project!" Erin exclaims, clearly trying to find light in a situation where there is little of it.

Riley half smiles as an attempt to appear on board with the concept.

"No, really," Erin goes on. "From your window you'll be able to see the brand-new building that recently went up, facing the rest of downtown. It's quite lovely, and I've heard there are others on the way. This will eventually be one of the hottest neighborhoods in town."

Eventually, Riley thinks, studying the hideously patterned low-pile carpet, but she'll be lucky to see it in her lifetime.

"And here it is!" Erin says when they near the hallway's midpoint.

She inserts a key into the door and pushes it open, and Riley braces herself. The combined fetor of dirty bleach and scouring powder rushes out to greet them. Riley forces back tears as she covers her nose and peers inside, but with the blinds pulled down, it's hard to make out much. When Erin lets in some sunlight, the view doesn't improve: the only things to see are heaps of boxes stacked throughout the living room.

"I didn't have a chance to finish everything I wanted to," Erin says, turning on a few lights, "but I did get the bathroom unpacked. I also made sure your room was in order. Hope you don't mind that the bed came from my guest room."

"Thanks, Erin," Riley says, trying her best to sound grateful for a new life that already feels as if it belongs to someone else. In spite of that, she truly is grateful. Erin has made significant efforts to soften Riley's landing in the real world.

Erin places a hand against her forehead and winces.

"What is it?" Riley asks.

"Oh . . . one of those stupid migraines."

"Have they been acting up a lot lately?"

"These last few days." Erin has been plagued with them since her teens. "It's the stress. You know, work and stuff. I've been getting ready for a murder trial, and it starts next week."

Riley can't help but feel that she's the one responsible for this particular onset.

"Help you start unpacking?" Erin offers.

"Thanks, but you should go home and get some rest. You've already done more than enough and—"

"I really don't mind."

"—and I'm too exhausted to do much right now anyway. You go take care of yourself, okay?"

Erin nods. She presses a key onto the countertop. "I also had spares made. They're in the kitchen drawer. And—oh." Erin points to her. "I can drop your car off tomorrow after work, then help unpack."

"Thanks again." Riley smiles her acknowledgment. "For everything."

Erin goes in for a goodbye hug, but Riley instinctively deflects the move, crossing her arms and turning her body sideways.

Erin's expression falls flat.

Again, a wall of silence drops between the two women, but this time the reason feels more tangled, weighted down by unspoken words and unresolved issues. A wall bigger than both of them. A wall that neither knows how to break through.

"I—I guess I should go," Erin says, voice wavering, hands stuffed in pockets.

Riley's gaze darts around the room because she doesn't know where to look.

Erin pulls a small gift box from her purse and says, "I almost forgot. Here."

Riley opens the box. Inside is a delicate gold bracelet, and between the links sits an infinity symbol with Sisters engraved on it. With mouth opened wide, she looks up at Erin.

A tenuous shrug. "It's a welcome-home gift."

"Erin, it's absolutely beautiful."

Now she feels guiltier.

"Thanks," Riley says, putting on the bracelet and holding her focus there. "Things are just overwhelming for me right now. But I really do apprec—"

"It's okay," Erin says, but she looks injured. "One more thing. If you need anything around here, the office is downstairs off the lobby. Aileen Bailey is the manager."

"Aileen Bailey. Got it."

Midway through reaching for her car keys, Erin adds, "One word of caution about her. She's a bit on the disagreeable side."

"Meaning . . . ?"

"With all the news coverage and negative attention, she was undecided about renting to you. I talked her into it, but she made me promise there wouldn't be any problems and you'd keep a low profile."

In an effort to seem unfazed, Riley starts loading silverware from an opened box to the washer.

Erin takes reluctant steps toward the door. Halfway there, she looks back and says, "Be sure to lock up after I'm gone. Okay?" Her voice resonates with heedful warning, and Riley can't determine if it's prompted by the lousy neighborhood . . .

Or an angry public on the hunt for justice.

4

Riley's lids flicker open, and it takes a few seconds for her mind to square with reality, to recognize that she no longer lives at Glendale, to become acclimated to the idea that this new apartment—in this rocky new world—is now home.

She's not sure which is worse.

Then she looks at the ceiling sprinkler heads, rusted and dirty, and feels her affection lean an inch toward Glendale. It's not that she loved her life there, but even the hospital was in better shape than this place.

The grass is always greener?

"Debatable," she says to nobody at all while swinging her legs toward the bed's edge. But if she's going to be truthful, the lawn looks scrubby and brown on both sides of the fence.

From the medicine cabinet, she pulls down her meds, which Erin thoughtfully placed there. She studies the labels:

OLANZAPINE

TAKE TWO TABLETS BY MOUTH IN THE MORNING AND TWO IN THE EVENING.

Lexapro
Take one tablet by mouth in the morning and one in the evening.

She shakes into her hand two round, white Olanzapine tablets and one of the round, white Lexapro tablets.

Depression with psychotic features. The diagnosis came shortly after Riley's arrival at Glendale. But her life had been skidding off the rails for about five years before then, illogical thoughts and strange voices already in full swing. Looking back through the fissures of insanity, all she sees are splintered fragments of a life blown to pieces by tragedy. A life left forever in ruins.

After she steps into the shower, her thoughts drift to yesterday's clumsy encounter with Erin. Neither mentioned the tragedy. Neither had to. Both felt the tension. Both knew where it came from—the thorny events that, through the years, have become harder to skirt.

Though Erin, in her late thirties, is Riley's younger sister, she acts like the older one. It's been this way since they were kids, one of those sibling role reversals that take root early on. By the time anyone notices, the dynamic is already hardwired and irreversible.

Growing up, Riley constantly found herself walking in Erin's shadow. During grade school, she was the awkward one—a shy child who always stood somewhere along the fringes, who sat in the back of the class and chewed on her hair. The observer of life rather than the participant. The outsider, endlessly searching for a place to belong. And Erin was always the leader—the prettiest, the smartest, the most socially adept.

It went like this: Erin takes first place in the Franklin Elementary Art Show. Erin wins each event at her middle school's track-and-field championship. Erin single-handedly captures both the homecoming and prom-queen titles. And, of course, Erin effortlessly secures her spot as the magna cum laude of her law school.

Riley got a paper route when she was twelve.

For a while, the distance between them grew and grew, most of it—okay, probably all of it—coming from Riley. Then adulthood came crashing in. Differences were settled. Blood became thicker than water. And she and Erin began to discover commonalities they'd never known existed. As a result, they experienced what—if there were a name for it—might be called a latent sisterly connection. They became closer than they'd ever been, and Erin reinvented herself as Riley's advocate, her animal spirit of sorts.

It was all so lovely. Then Riley's life capsized.

Today, their relationship is similar but more complex. Erin is a successful defense attorney, and Riley is the alleged wack job, the outcast, the suspected murderer.

During Erin's first visit to Glendale, the staff had to make her leave after Riley's hallucinations produced an explosive and violent outburst. After that, Erin stayed away for a while and returned once her sister became lucid, but the circumstances had driven an intractable wedge between them. It didn't take long for Riley to wonder if Erin doubted her innocence. But she never asked, and Erin never offered to share her thoughts. With no memory of the murder, even Riley didn't know what had happened. But she wasn't so sure Erin believed that part, either, so the topic became off-limits.

This, she suspects, is how their relationship will always be: stuck with an immovable concrete divider between them.

Riley takes her morning shower, then puts on her bathrobe and treads to the kitchen coffee maker. After starting the machine, she begins to walk away, but her feet stop moving.

The front door is unlocked and slightly ajar.

She rushes to open it, looks up and down the hallway, but nobody is in sight. She closes the door, locks it, and goes straight to the bedroom—the only room she can't see from her entryway. At the threshold, she comes to a shaky halt, and it takes several seconds for her mind to fully absorb what it sees. Then the blood drains from her face, and black dots dance before her eyes. Two words glare at her.

Ugly words.

Scratched into her bed's headboard.

Vile enough to give her an appalling chill.

CHILD KILLER

5

Riley takes faltering steps toward the headboard, then runs an unsteady hand across the letters' grooves.

They're real.

And in that moment of awareness, the hairs on her arms flick up, allowing fear to surface.

Someone was here while I was taking my shower.

She checks the rest of her apartment, wondering how long the intruder lingered, violating her space. Back in the bedroom, her peripheral vision catches something lying on the floor, something shiny: a construction nail. She picks it up, presses the pointy tip into a deep indentation on the first letter. It's a match, and her fear ratchets up.

The feeling doesn't endure, because her mind goes into a fast flip. Fright changes to anger, which quickly morphs into determination. She puts on some clothes and, with the nail in hand, bounds out her door, then marches toward the apartment under repair.

She stomps in and scans the room. A box of nails lies on the counter next to the carpenter's bag. After pulling one out, she holds it next to the one from her apartment: another match. With the door open, anyone could have grabbed it. Her hands quake while she roots through the bag. She digs out a sheet of sandpaper, then she's out of there.

CHILD KILLER. CHILD KILLER. CHILD KILLER.

The revolting words poke, prickle, and refuse to leave her.

Inside her apartment, she vigorously scours away at the writing. She wants to make it disappear. To take away the pain. To shake herself loose from this world that's again trying to hijack her mind—not with insanity but with the poison of persecution and torment.

"YOU WON'T BEAT ME DOWN!" she shouts, berating the wood as if it's to blame for all her problems, sanding harder, sanding faster. "YOU WILL NOT!"

Her arm is sore from rubbing, her breath is out of control, and tears roll down her cheeks, but none of that matters. She's angry. This is personal. It's taken too much to fight her way back, and there's still more at stake. She won't give in to the waspish harassment that has followed her into this hellhole. She'll stay here as long as it takes to carry out her plan, and only then will she leave on her own terms.

About forty-five minutes later, her riot of agitation starts to settle. She examines the bare spots on her headboard, knowing they'll endure as a constant reminder of the unvarnished truth that she's at a disadvantage when it comes to defending herself.

She drops the sandpaper, walks to the bedroom window, and stares out at the new building across the way. Moving a finger along the glass, she traces the structure's sleek outline, and her tears again start, but this time they're different, no longer fueled by anger but by the ruins of frustration. Beds can be fixed, but her life? That's another story. She wonders whether she'll ever be able to fit her square-peg self into this round-holed world instead of constantly having to fake it.

6

Among the brazen artillery of thunder, Riley stares at her door and catalogs every squeak, rattle, and thud that travels through the apartment.

Figure this out . . . I have to figure this out.

Calling the police about this morning's break-in isn't an option. They're the enemy. Asking Aileen to change the locks on her door isn't an option, either—not after Erin's warning about making waves. So, instead, she takes matters into her own hands, going with the *easier to ask for forgiveness than permission* plan.

She calls a locksmith.

A few hours later, she's got a new lock in her door and a new set of keys in her hand. Hopefully, nobody will even notice.

She weaves through the labyrinth of cartons piled tall in the living room—full of belongings Erin packed and put into storage after Riley lost her house—then goes on a hunt for the one box she herself packed long before that. It's marked *Blue Bed Linens,* a special code that only she understands, with special items inside. It takes some unstacking and restacking, but she finds the box, carries it into her bedroom, and rips the flaps apart. She looks inside, closes her eyes. She opens them. And a hybrid of nostalgia and sadness stirs within her.

With great care, she removes two piles of folded garments and places them on her bed. She separates the layers, pulls out a pair of faded blue jeans and a pink-and-white shirt. She holds them up side by side to the light and nods in approval, then lays them across the bed.

The rest will go into her closet until she picks a new ensemble to leave out for tomorrow.

7

Riley slips between the boxes and toward her living room window, then looks out through the rain-soused glass at the new building across from hers, which offers a stark contrast to this place. Modern and slick, the Pointe at Canyon Hill boasts sexy lines and glass, screaming loud and clear that Riley has been sequestered to a land different from that one. She studies the six-foot wrought iron fence that separates them, how the building stubbornly faces away toward the downtown skyline, practically insisting that it wants nothing to do with this place. She allows her gaze to linger for a few moments longer, then shifts her weight, crosses her arms, and lets out a pained sigh.

Abrupt movement from the new building draws her attention in time for her to see someone snatch a pair of drapes shut.

The phone rings.

She jumps.

Her racing pulse settles. Since nobody else has her landline number, it's a good guess that Erin is checking on her.

"Hey, sis. What's going—"

"Sorry, not your sis. Stacey Freelander, Channel Five News. We'd love to set up an interview. Will you be around to chat? Say, about one?"

"No."

"When, then?"

"Never."

She hangs up, and a new worry swoops in, one she hasn't yet considered—this could be the first of numerous calls from the press. Then another concern: reporters may be camped out around her apartment. She considers the door for a moment, takes long steps toward it, and looks through the peephole. Nobody there, but they could be lurking somewhere out of view. She knows they won't give up easily. In the years before being committed to Glendale, she put on quite the public freak show, and the press lapped it up like a pack of starved wolves. Before long, Riley Harper had become a household name for all the wrong reasons.

It doesn't matter, she decides. She can't let that keep her from leaving this apartment. She doesn't want a repeat performance of the mess outside Glendale, but staying here would feel like being locked away all over again.

Get out. Stay strong. Trust your truth.

She has plans to make. Required appointments to schedule. She needs to fit in. Abide by the rules.

Grabbing her release papers from the kitchen table, she plucks off the business card fastened to them, then stares at the name.

PATRICIA LOCKWOOD, PSYCHOLOGIST.

She dials and sets up an appointment.

After taking a second shower to wash away the day's stress, she gazes into the full-length mirror but doesn't much love what looks back at her. There was a time—a long-ago time—when she finally felt comfortable in her own skin, but heartbreak stole those feelings away and in the process levied a physical toll.

It's as if she blinked and everything went south.

She's lost too much weight. Her eyes, once light brown with brilliant flecks of green, have faded. Her strawberry hair, once shimmering with blonde highlights, is accented only with streaks of gray. And her face . . . what a mess it's become. Dark circles cradle her eyes, and she no longer needs to smile to see the laugh lines—they're etched into her skin, harsh reminders of good times gone bad.

In the bathroom, she shakes her head in defeat after remembering that any makeup she had was left behind at the hospital. Out of hopefulness—or maybe blind desperation—she opens the top drawer and finds new packages of foundation, lipstick, and eyeliner.

Erin.

She applies the makeup, but even that can't fix the damage caused by a life wasted, a life destroyed. Then a tear—the kind that expresses what words never could—rolls down her cheek.

8

Riley is making her way down the hall when, up ahead, an apartment door starts to open.

Groan.

She lurches back against the wall just as a lanky outstretched arm snakes its way across the floor, trying to grab a newspaper tossed several feet from the doorway. She guardedly paces closer. She lowers her gaze through the door's narrow opening, and a pair of wide, panicky eyes peer up at her from behind a set of stringy blonde bangs. She slowly picks up the paper and extends it toward the woman, whose bony and poorly manicured fingers reach out and latch on to it.

Cousin Itt is my neighbor. Awesome.

Not that it surprises her—at this point there isn't much that can.

She offers her neighbor an iffy smile. The woman does not return anything close to one; instead, she gives her a scalding up-and-down inspection.

"Thanks," Cousin Itt allows, then pulls her paper through the narrow gap. "Now get the hell away!"

The door bangs shut.

"Ingrate," Riley says.

"Bitch," she hears from behind the door.

The dead bolt snaps into its housing.

Riley goes storming down the hallway. She takes the dank stairwell to the lobby.

But trouble waits outside. As soon as she steps into the rain, a reporter perks up and runs toward her, his photographer trailing close behind.

Gaze fixed ahead, Riley keeps moving, but contempt chisels away at her patience. First, she lost her family, then these people transformed her tragedy into torment. Now here they are, trying to pick up where they left off.

"Ms. Harper!" he shouts. "Can we talk?"

Before he can speak another word, Riley pivots, aims a palm at the camera lens, and says, "No. We're not doing this. We are not!"

The mechanized *whir* of the camera zooming in sends her nerves into a roaring buzz. She takes off, a line of sweat rolling down the center of her back, then stumbles forward into a trot. After gaining enough distance from the reporter, she bails around a corner, but in the process, Erin's bracelet catches on the rough side of a light post and breaks from her wrist.

She hears feet advancing as she drops to the ground and scrambles to retrieve the broken pieces. She tries to pick herself up, but the wet sidewalk has other ideas. She falls, clambers to a stand, then takes off running again, her tears mixing with rain.

9

The cell phone store clerk scratches her temple while inspecting Riley's driver's license. The name tag on her blue-and-maroon company shirt says she's Kristen L.

"Is there a problem?" Riley asks.

"You'll need a current form of ID to establish an account with us," Kristen L. informs her, then hands back the license. She flicks a restless glance toward the next person in line.

"I'm sorry . . . I . . ." Riley pushes a thatch of hair behind one ear and studies her ID, which appears to have lapsed while she was in Glendale. "I guess I didn't realize it was expired."

The clerk tips up Riley's paperwork to examine it, then asks with a rumpled brow, "It says here you've only been at your current residence for . . . a day?"

"I recently moved in."

"Oh. Okay," Kristin L. says, then points to a spot on the form. "You can go ahead and add your prior residence right here."

Glendale Psychiatric Hospital won't cut it and will likely bring unwanted recognition, so Riley adds her Meadowview address instead, then looks up at the girl.

"A current ID?" Kristen L. says. "I still need one."

Riley's cheeks warm with frustration. She's been off the map for too long, hadn't considered how difficult it would be to throw down new tracks. This phone was supposed to be the first step in her plan. She needs it, has to find a way to make this happen, so she looks at the application, trying to figure out her next move. The DMV is several miles away. Erin would need to drive her there, but even then, a new license would take weeks.

The clerk is waiting.

Riley says, "This is all I've got. Is there anything else you can do for me?"

Kristen L. points to an endcap with a display of burner phones and says, "Next customer, please?"

But when she looks back at Riley, her expression changes: budding realization, interrupted by a flashing red alert. She reexamines the name on Riley's application, glances up at her, then back at the application. Then her expression sharpens and becomes more recognizable.

Startled recognition.

Kristen L. raises a hand to her lips and staggers backward, and Riley's heart skips. The girl zeros in on a television hanging on a wall across the room. Riley reels around, looks there, too, and sees video of her chaotic departure from Glendale. She can't hear the anchorman, but it's not necessary. The words crawling across the screen say it all:

FORMER TEACHER SUSPECTED OF MURDER RELEASED FROM GLENDALE PSYCHIATRIC HOSPITAL AMID COMMUNITY FEARS

"That's her! That's the psycho killer!"

Riley swivels in another direction. A guy in his twenties, wearing a backward baseball cap and loose-fitting shorts, pokes a finger in her direction. She no longer feels her heart skipping—it's bongoing against her chest, and all she can think about is getting out of there. Before Riley makes it to the door, she glances over her shoulder at the gawking crowd. Some are pointing while others whisper.

"Good riddance, you crazy bitch!" a woman, blistering with hostile contempt, shouts from a different corner of the room.

Riley doesn't wait to field further insults. She bursts through the door and out into the rain, her only companion a blustering wind.

"Ms. Harper!"

She jerks her view toward the parking lot. A stray newspaper reporter comes hustling toward her, shouting, "Got a moment to chat? It won't take long."

"Get away from me!" she says, flustered and changing direction.

"I just want your side of the—"

"GET THE HELL AWAY FROM ME!"

The reporter falls back as Riley quickens her pace. In an effort to seek safety, she lopes through the downpour toward one end of the shopping center. Leaning against a wall, she hunches over and grabs hold of her knees. Rain soaks her hair, her face—everything—while she tries to slow her racing thoughts and keep from hyperventilating.

Footsteps approach.

She jolts, lifts her head. Some teenage boys stroll by, joking, chuckling, and splashing through the puddles. They take a look at Riley, and one of them says, "What the hell's *her* problem?"

The boys break out into laughter, and she watches them disappear into the distance, for once craving the privacy of her desolate apartment. Anywhere would be better than here.

She starts walking and tries to collect herself. Several feet later, a door swings open, nearly slamming her in the face, and out races a beautiful woman. Mid-twenties. Black business suit, flawless complexion. Raven hair that falls past sculpted cheekbones before tumbling onto slender shoulders. The dark-haired stranger breezes past Riley without even looking at her and flippantly says, "Sorry," as if it were an afterthought. She opens her umbrella, then rushes toward a red late-model Mercedes-Benz.

Within seconds the woman is gone.

That's the psycho killer!

Good riddance, you crazy bitch!

Those harsh comments swirl through Riley's mind like a virulent band of smoke.

She shoves her key into the apartment's lock and opens it. After slamming the door shut, she leans against it, then stares up toward the ceiling and waits for her mind and body to unruffle.

She glances down at the puddle gathering around her shoes, slips out of them, and on her way to the bathroom grabs a towel. She manages to take her hair from soaked to damp, but her clothes are a completely different story. She peels them off and throws them over the shower bar to dry.

Trembling, she reaches up and pulls the pieces of Erin's bracelet from her pocket to examine them.

The links are severed beyond repair, the infinity symbol barely dangling off one end.

Maybe our kind of infinity is bound to be nothing more than a never-ending wish.

10

Evening is on the approach, and life feels a little less chaotic.

Riley removes the clothes she laid out on her bed this morning. After folding them with the greatest of care, she takes one last look at them, puts them away, then goes to the bedroom window and gazes out at a shimmering, silvery dusk.

Rain. All I see is rain. This miserable damned rain.

Abrupt movement distracts her.

She locates it in time to catch someone practically jumping out of view at that same second-floor apartment across the way. A brambly sensation batters inside her stomach. Either whoever lives there is extremely high-strung, or someone is watching her.

Don't be paranoid. People move about all day long.

The curtains across the way snap shut.

The dead bolt on her front door jiggles in its housing.

Her heart hurls a triple whack against her chest. She's halfway to the door when three solid knocks strike.

"It's me." Erin's voice booms from the hallway while she unsuccessfully tries to unlock the door again.

With life running circles around her all day, Riley forgot her sister was coming over to drop off the car and help unpack boxes. Her pulse slows.

Everything's okay.

She tries to stabilize a few nerves before opening the door.

"Why isn't my key working?" Erin asks, examining the dead bolt and repeatedly flipping the lever from side to side.

"Oh, that. It's nothing." Riley wheels around and walks away. She doesn't want her sister to know about the apartment break-in. Erin would demand she call the police, which Riley is adamantly against. She can't trust law enforcement, and the less she sees of them, the better off she'll be.

"What do you mean, *nothing*?" Erin challenges, then again asks, "Why isn't my key working?"

"I changed it out." Riley tries to affect casual. "You know, with the press hounding me and all."

"The press?" Erin says, looking down the hallway as if searching for logic. She slings her gaze back to Riley. "Have any of them tried to break in?"

"Well, no. Not yet. But you can't be too careful."

"Have they even been inside this building?"

Riley tosses up a shrug. "Not that I've actually seen."

Erin's head falls into a wary slant that speaks her doubt. Riley busily searches through a random drawer for nothing, but she can practically feel the fire of Erin's gaze heating up the side of her face.

"I put your car in the lot," Erin says, her tone suggesting confusion as she slowly lowers her purse onto the countertop.

"Thanks, but it looks like I won't be able to drive it yet. Turns out my license is expired." Riley contemplates how to dodge the next quandary charging down the pike. Erin doesn't need to know about the driver's license fiasco at the phone store, either, not to mention the subsequent hate-fest. She's already unnerved by Riley's flawed lock explanation—no need to snap the tension rip cord with that particularly unpleasant narrative.

She changes topics. "Can you find a way home?"

"I'll catch a cab," Erin replies. She looks at her phone's planner. "I've got court next Monday and Tuesday, but we're in recess on Wednesday, so how about if I take you to the DMV then?"

"Yes. Perfect. Thank you."

"Also, before I forget, I figured you might need this," Erin the Mind Reader says, pulling a brand-new cell phone from her purse.

"Oh wow . . . I—you really didn't have to do that."

"All I did was change to a family plan. That's what we are, by the way."

"Huh?"

"Family."

"I know that."

"The only one either of us has. And I'll always be on your side. No matter what."

Riley abandons the conversation. They're treading on delicate terrain, stumbling once again toward the elephant in the room. She busies herself by tearing open a large carton, then parks her attention on the contents.

"Hey," Erin says.

"Yeah?" Riley pulls out an item wrapped in newspaper, studies it.

"Are you okay?"

"Sure . . . fine." She finally finds enough moxie to meet Erin's gaze and tries her best to smile off the edginess.

"Because you seem awfully overwound tonight."

Riley's laugh is dry. "Well, I *did* recently leave a mental hospital." She returns to her unwrapping. "So there's that."

"I know . . . but is there something else?"

"Oh, look!" She pulls away the paper and holds up a doll for Erin to see—a small rag doll—a girl—expression part sad, part pensive. "I almost forgot about this. Do you remember it?"

Confusion flattens Erin's expression like a steamroller. She shakes her head.

Riley grins at the memory. "Clarissa hated this doll so much as a kid that she'd constantly hide it. Her favorite place was on the floor behind the living room drapes. I'd see this tiny pair of Mary Janes sticking out. I'd laugh, then put it back in its place, but not long after, *poof!* The doll would be gone, and I'd have to search for it all over again. It became a game with us."

Erin responds with a penciled-in nod.

In this case, at least, Riley is grateful for the silence. She sits the doll on a side table, then with hands on hips takes in all the boxes and says, "So. Guess we should get busy with the rest of these, right?"

"Right . . . ," Erin says, consternation so apparent you could drive a spike through it. "Do you have something for me to open these with?"

"There's a box cutter in my bedr—" She stops to think about the headboard, then says, "Wait. It's a mess in there. I'll go."

But Erin is already cruising toward the bedroom. She pulls to a cold halt and stares blankly, silently, at those bare patches marring the headboard.

Oh. Shit.

"I decided to refinish it," is the only answer Riley can come up with on such short notice.

"Now. You decided to do it now."

"Yeah. Uh-huh."

"One day after moving in. Before you're even fully unpacked."

"I just wanted to make it my own," Riley says, going in for the save. "You know how I am once I get an idea to do something." In an attempt to draw Erin's observation away from the headboard, she points to a box cutter on the top of her dresser and says, "Go ahead. Take that. I'll grab a knife from the dishwasher."

Riley practically runs toward the kitchen, pulls open the washer's door, then spins out another change of topic. "I met one of my new neighbors yesterday. Well . . . kind of met her. A rather interesting character, to say the least."

Erin's silence from the other room seems to indicate her bewilderment over having to follow this erratic, quickly shifting discussion.

"The woman is nasty," Riley goes on, talking toward the bedroom hallway as she reaches down for the knife. "I don't think she ever leaves her apart—"

She stops after feeling a sharp prick to her finger. Looking down, she suppresses a gasp. Her butcher's knife has been flipped over in the wash basket, green handle facing down, business end aimed directly up at her.

Like a threat.

And she didn't put it in that way yesterday. She never would.

"Riley? Are you okay?"

She slams the dishwasher door shut, spins toward the hall where her sister stands, looking at her.

"Riley," Erin says through broadening bafflement, "what's going on with you?"

11

The two make progress in their unpacking efforts.

As the evening wears on, Erin's mistrust fades some, and they're on good terms when she leaves—well, for them, anyway. The moment the front door closes, Riley immediately hurries back to her dishwasher.

The knife has changed positions.

Again.

The green handle faces up, the sharp, menacing tip aimed down.

What's going on?

She knows for sure she didn't flip that knife back over. There wasn't enough time. Erin came up on her so fast that she immediately closed the dishwasher door.

The bitter taste of dismay coats her tongue. Her body feels weak.

Hold it together. Think this through.

She puts a hand up to each temple, looks down, and tries to think: she loaded the silverware yesterday, then changed out the lock this morning—which means nobody got in this afternoon while she was away, which means the incident with the knife had to have happened last night while she slept. She thinks about those awful words on the headboard, and her blood pressure spikes, followed by a biting chill that can sever flesh.

Someone could be stalking me.

She hurries to the window, sends her wary gaze into the thick, impenetrable darkness—darkness that, in this instant, seems more ugly and threatening than ever before.

The sound of squealing tires erupts from the parking lot.

What if they're still out there?

She can't call the police, can't tell Erin, and the building manager, Aileen Bailey? Forget about that. She has to take care of this herself. On her way out the door, she grabs a hammer resting on top of a box and her keys from the kitchen table.

Outside in the rain, with senses on high alert, she rounds the building and looks for anyone suspicious or loitering on the premises. Reaching the rear of the building, she spots a plain, dark sedan parked several feet from the entrance. Its lights are off, but someone is definitely in the driver's seat. She narrows her focus, but the dense night forms a blue-black barrier between them, denying an opportunity to clearly make out a face. But one thing is certain: the person is looking her way.

That could be the one. That could be the same one who's been inside my apartment.

Another sound, the combination of a palpitating engine and crackling asphalt. Riley swings around in time to catch a different car as it wheels into the lot of the new building across from hers.

A red Mercedes. Driven, improbably, by the raven-haired woman who nearly bowled Riley over outside the shopping center today. She watches while the woman disappears into the slick and opulent building.

When Riley looks at her own parking lot, the sedan has vanished.

More people disappearing.

12

She wakes to a forceful thunderclap.

The storm is getting worse, and Riley's body doesn't feel right. She looks down at herself and . . .

What the—?

She's still wearing her clothes. A hangover of confusion ensues. She doesn't even remember getting into bed.

I . . . I don't understan—

The clock says it's 6:00 a.m.

Was she so exhausted from all the turmoil that she passed out and slept through the night?

A downpour slaps against the window, startling her. She rocks her body away from the gray and muted light. She sits up, swings her legs to the edge of the bed. She pulls herself into a standing position. *Unsteady.* That's how she feels but is nevertheless determined. Determined to turn her stumbling leap from Glendale into a sprint past the finish line.

Get out. Stay strong. Trust your truth.

Vision bleary, she staggers into the kitchen in search of coffee. She opens the dishwasher for a cup, then instantly releases the handle and flies into reverse.

The butcher's knife is gone.

Gone?

She looks deeper inside, wondering whether her morning fog is to blame for what she sees—or doesn't. Then her head swivels toward the front door. Did she forget to lock it before running outside last night? She didn't check the knife after coming back. Did someone sneak into her apartment while she was gone and take it?

Not again. This can't be happening again . . .

Determined to grab hold of reality, she scrambles from room to room on the hunt for her knife. She checks the closets, looks underneath furniture, scours the carpet.

In the bedroom, those bare spots in the headboard laugh at her. They mock her sensibilities. She drops into a seated position on the bed, and through her peripheral vision, a thin shimmer of light twinkles at her side. When she looks, her skin flashes hot and cold. She lifts her pillow, and with trembling hands reaches for the butcher's knife.

The one that, all night long, lay inches beneath her head while she slept.

This is no mistake. No flight of imagination.

This is real.

13

Patricia Lockwood looks much as Riley imagined during their phone conversation. Silvery hair drops into a short, crisp bob that barely grazes her chin. Her smoky-blue silk blouse almost perfectly matches her eyes. And although she appears pleasant enough, her expression falls a few notches below the welcoming point. Too professional. Too intense. It's the Therapist's Stare, which Riley grew to know well during her time at Glendale.

With one leg crossed over the other, Patricia repeatedly flexes her foot, causing the heel of her shoe to snap on and off. Riley finds the action—and the sound—grating. She does her best to ignore it and instead focuses on the blue folder that rests in Patricia's lap.

"So," Patricia says, settling back a few inches into her chair, "how are you feeling?"

"Fine." Riley dishes out an affable smile after telling one whopper of a lie.

Patricia's eyes dart back and forth between Riley's as if she's trying to measure the veracity of her statement. But it appears she quickly figures that one out. "You say you're feeling fine. Can you give more details?"

Riley lifts a shoulder. "Well, you know . . . considering."

"Considering . . . ?"

"That I've recently been released from a mental hospital."

Patricia reaches for her glasses atop a side table, puts them on, and opens the folder. Skimming it, she says, "Have you been taking your medications regularly?"

Riley tells her she has.

"Good," Patricia says, then goes back to her heel clicking.

Riley's left hand jerks with irritation.

"How do you feel being back in the community?"

"Strange . . ."

Patricia grabs for a notebook, also from the side table. She flips a page, presses her pen against the paper, and gives Riley her full concentration.

Riley scoffs. "I'm not exactly the town's favorite daughter."

"Have you encountered difficulties because of that?"

"The press has been after me," she answers, steering clear of her recent troubles: the nasty message on her headboard, her magical dishwasher knife, the dark sedan, and the onslaught of public hatred since she left the hospital. Lockwood reports to Glendale. Bringing up anything questionable has the potential to create additional complications.

Patricia looks over the tops of her glasses at Riley and says, "I'd like to discuss what happened to your family."

Riley blows out a tense breath and feels the cords in her neck pull tight.

"It started with my husband's death and ended with my daughter's."

"Let's begin with your husband."

"Jason brought my daughter and her friend on a camping trip." Riley's throat closes around the words—saying them is enough to plunge her back into the ache. The wrenching torment. "Clarissa lost her father, and I lost the love of my life."

"What happened?"

"Jason went with Clarissa's friend, Rose, to gather wood for the evening. There were signs everywhere warning people to stay away from the cliffs. But Jason could never resist a beautiful sunset. He walked toward the edge to take a picture but didn't notice a rock in his way. He stumbled, lost his footing, and went over the edge."

"How did you find out?"

"The evening after they left, I opened the door and . . ." Riley's heartbeat becomes uneven. She tries to steady her trembling words. "And right away I knew my world had caved in on itself." She looks off to one side, rolls her collar between two fingers. "A pair of police officers stood on the stoop with Clarissa, and her face was stained by dirt and tears. After that, everything seemed a blur."

"What ended up happening to the friend?"

"When Clarissa got to the cliff, Rose was in shock and unable to speak. It took several hours before she could give authorities the details."

"Did she ever recover from the trauma?"

Riley doesn't want to open that door, doesn't want Patricia to start prying. So instead, she only says, "I don't know."

"Why not?"

"Because she and her father moved away after . . ." Riley looks out through the window, rubs the heel of a hand against her chest, and tries again. "After . . ."

Helping her along: "Clarissa's murder."

Clarissa's murder.

New territory, and just as bad. She looks back at Patricia. "My family had been ripped away from me. It was . . . I . . ." Riley swallows hard, choking on her next words as they fight their way up. "Everyone said I did it, that I killed Clarissa, but with no memory of the incident, I couldn't explain what had happened, couldn't defend myself."

"Did you eventually get the memories back?"

Riley shakes her head.

"That had to make the situation feel even more impossible."

"*She* made it more impossible."

"Who did?"

"Demetre Sloan." She says the name as if it's rancid on her tongue. "The detective assigned to Clarissa's case. She was after me from the start."

"Losing your child and then being blamed for it. I can't even imagine."

"No, you can't *imagine*. You cannot." Riley angrily swipes away a tear, takes a tissue from the box Patricia extends.

"I was under investigation for a while before they made the arrest. Then, as everyone knows, there was the hung jury and the mistrial."

"But no retrial."

"The DA decided there wasn't enough evidence to pursue it again."

"That must have felt like a relief."

"For about a minute."

"Why do you say that?"

"My life, my whole reputation, was destroyed. The hung jury didn't mean innocent. The hung jury meant undecided, so the public made its own decision. They still believed I murdered my daughter. Try living like that for a while and you'd go crazy, too. I spent the next five years living on the streets and going in and out of County Mental Health."

"But why the streets when you had a home?"

"Because I couldn't quiet Clarissa down while I was there."

"You mean the auditory hallucinations," Patricia confirms. "She spoke to you."

"No, she *screamed out* to me. It was like having to hear her being attacked over and over and over, but I couldn't help her. Then one night, the noise got so unbearable that I ran outside, and that was the first time she talked to me, and I realized it was our house that upset her. She didn't like us being there anymore."

"So that was when you took to the streets."

"It was the only way to keep Clarissa talking."

"What would she say?"

"Lots of things . . ." Riley looks down at her empty palms, feels her chest growing heavy. "But it always hurt the most when she said, 'I'll never leave you.'"

"Still, you found the streets more peaceful."

"Not exactly."

"Why not?"

"That's sort of complicated."

"Life can be complicated."

"It's just that . . . things kept spinning faster. I became a public nuisance and started following strangers around town."

"Why did you do that?"

"Because I was crazy?"

Patricia grins. "Even crazy people have their reasons."

"I thought they were Clarissa—I'd tap them on the shoulders, but when they turned around, it wasn't her. Other times, I saw people I thought could lead me to her."

"Did you ever get to see Clarissa through these hallucinations?"

Riley hesitates, then, "Not until after I arrived at Glendale."

"How did you finally end up there?"

"I went back to my old house to kill myself. It had foreclosed and gone vacant, so I figured nobody would look for me there. But I was wrong. Erin, my sister, did. She figured it out just in time, then had me committed."

"Do you think it was a cry for help?"

"No, I wanted my life to end. I wanted out of that torture."

Patricia glances down at her folder, looks up at Riley. "You were there for about two years."

"I was catatonic for a while, so they were unable to treat the psychosis. Once I came out of it, I spent my time hallucinating, getting into fights with other patients, and trying to hurt myself by banging my head against doors."

"Do you ever feel the urge to harm yourself now?"

"No. I've had enough pain."

Patricia studies her but says nothing.

Riley asks, "What is it?"

"I'm just wondering . . . does life seem better after leaving Glendale?"

"I guess I'm finding there's not much difference between being in or out." She pauses to think about that for a moment. "They're just two different sides of the same hell."

14

There's a certain look Riley is quickly becoming accustomed to seeing.

A creased brow. A leery stare. Narrowed eyes with a gaze that lasts longer than it should. The look of recognition. Of suspicion. Contempt, even. A look that followed her into Glendale and has followed her out.

Then there's the other part.

A gnawing, almost tactile feeling in her bones that someone is watching her.

On her morning return from the neighborhood hardware store to pick up a portable door jammer for added nighttime security, she hears someone walking on the sidewalk behind her. It makes her scalp tingle. Maybe it's the soft, distant footfalls or that she's extra cautious after the knife incidents. Maybe it's because during her stay at Glendale, she developed an instinct for staying alert, sniffing out danger. Whatever the case, it doesn't much matter how she knows, just that she does. She speeds up, and the footsteps do the same.

Someone's following me.

In an attempt to increase the distance between them, she breaks into a fast clip and hears the footsteps gain momentum.

She makes it to her building, ducks inside, looks out onto the street, but nobody is there. Icy needles poke beneath her skin. In her apartment, she goes straight to the window and looks out for someone suspicious.

Nothing.

Still not satisfied.

She fishes an old pair of binoculars from the kitchen drawer, drags a chair to the window, then surveys the lot and beyond for anything out of the ordinary.

Just as she pulls away the binoculars, her vision lands on that red Mercedes parked in the same spot as last night. Her mind jumps tracks, jetting into thoughts of the young woman who drives it. The same woman who almost ran into her at the strip mall, who now also seems to be her neighbor. Heck, she's probably trailing Riley, too. Why not? Seems like practically everyone else is these days.

Several minutes pass, and the parking lot remains uneventful. She's about to go back into the kitchen and fix a cup of tea when the *chirp* of a car alarm sounds. She lifts her binoculars and zeros in on the young woman walking to the Mercedes. Minus her business suit, she instead sports a pair of faded blue jeans and a white T-shirt, her ebony hair pulled neatly into a ponytail. Insistent curiosity takes hold of Riley. She slides the chair closer to the window and continues watching.

The woman has the walk of someone who's just won a million bucks, her stride bouncy, her chin held high, all of it projecting an unmistakable air of infallible confidence.

I know that walk. Clarissa used to walk like that.

She wonders where this young woman found all that confidence, then switches her scrutiny to the large portfolio bag she carries made of black, expensive-looking leather. She opens her trunk, places the bag inside. Then, a few beats later, the red Mercedes leaves the lot.

Riley checks the clock: it's 8:45 a.m. She does the math, surmising that Ms. Confident likely has to be somewhere by nine, maybe work? She wonders where, and whether the portfolio bag might provide a clue. Is she an architect? An artist? The car certainly isn't cheap, so she must have a well-paying job.

Either that, or she was loaded to begin with.

A flash of envy strikes when she thinks about how wonderful Ms. Confident's life must be, the kind Riley can only dream about. A possibility taken from her. Stolen.

The kind she will never have a chance to live.

15

Riley and Erin are about to wrap up their visit to the DMV when the clerk behind the counter squints over her glasses at Riley. She looks at the name on the paperwork, looks at Riley, then looks back at the paperwork.

"Is there anything else you need?" Erin asks.

In her sixties, the woman has a wolfish face. Her flat, elongated nose hangs beneath a pair of pointy, wide-set eyes. In an accusatory tone, she says, "Aren't you the lady who killed her girl?"

Erin jumps in. "Aren't you the lady who's supposed to be doing her damned job?"

"Excuse me, *madam*. I was just asking a question."

"And I was just responding to it." Erin leans forward to check out the woman's signature on the form, then in a whippish tone adds, *"Maggie."*

Maggie glowers.

Erin says, "And nobody says *madam* anymore. Not unless they're an early-century model that fell off the production line."

Maggie doesn't seem to enjoy that remark, either. She raises Riley's paperwork high in the air like stinking roadkill, then lets it drop into a wire basket.

"Be still, my heart," Erin mutters as they walk away. "Another angel just got her wings."

Riley chuckles. Her sister joins in, and before either knows it, they're holding their sides from laughing so hard.

But as they travel home, the emotional climate shifts when Erin notices Riley's empty wrist.

"I forgot to put it on today," she says before Erin can ask about the bracelet. Telling her it was destroyed will only upset her.

Erin makes no outward response, and it gets quiet, too quiet.

"Looks like the press is finally starting to die off," Riley throws out purely as a conversation starter.

"They may rebound," Erin says, nodding in agreement with herself. "They often do, so be on the lookout."

More quiet for a good five minutes.

Then Riley asks, "You doing okay?"

Erin doesn't answer.

Riley says, "Tell me what's wrong."

Erin breathes in through her nose. "Ever since you got out of Glendale, you've been distancing yourself from me."

"What are you talking about?"

"Like at your apartment the other day. When I said you were family? I was trying to offer comfort, but you completely skirted away from it. Why did you do that?"

"Jeez, Erin. Where's this coming from? We were laughing a few minutes ago."

"It's been bothering me. Is that okay?"

"Of course, and I'm sorry. I didn't mean to offend you."

"There's no need to apologize. Just tell me what's happening."

"I'm having—" Riley turns her gaze out the window. She closes her eyes, pinches the bridge of her nose. "Adjusting to life outside of Glendale . . . It's like I . . . It's making me really edgy."

"What's making you edgy?"

Riley hesitates. She can't tell Erin the truth. She seldom can, so instead: "You know . . . the everyday stress."

"See?"

"What?"

"I'm trying to help here, and all you can give me is some vague, catchall answer?"

"It's not a vague, catchall."

"Riley, for once, can you be straight with me? I don't know where to go with this any longer. It's like the more I give, the more you push back."

"I'm not doing that at all."

"Really? Have you forgotten I cross-examine people for a living? Do you think you can just omit information—lie, even—and I won't notice?"

"But I'm telling you the truth!"

"Decided to refinish your headboard a day after moving in? For heaven's sake, you weren't even unpacked yet. And that new lock? Since when do the press conduct home-invasion interviews?" She scoffs. "Honestly, Riley, you're not even a good liar."

Riley's got nothing. She stares out the front windshield and shakes her head.

"There's something else," Erin insists. "Tell me what it is."

Riley doesn't know how to disentangle herself from this gnarled mess. After all, what can she say? That her butcher knife appears to have gone on tour inside the apartment? That someone is stalking her but she has no proof of it? Erin would have her thrown right back into Glendale. Riley can't let that happen, but her sister also has her BS detector cranked up high. Riley's cornered. Busted.

Erin is still waiting for an answer.

Riley decides to tell the lesser truth—at least some of it. She draws a breath, holds it for a moment. She releases it. "Okay, you're right. I withheld information, but only because I was afraid it might upset you."

Erin spares her a glance, deep, parallel worry lines surfacing between her brows.

She lets the information out fast. "Someone broke into my apartment."

"What? *Holy* . . . Riley! You should have told—"

"Those sanded-off places you saw on my headboard? They were there because I'd removed a message. A very angry one."

They stop at an intersection. Erin searches Riley's face—Riley redirects by pointing through the windshield at the traffic light, which has changed to green.

Erin hits the gas pedal. Pushing well past the speed limit, she says, "Tell me the message."

"Please don't make me repeat it, but that's why I changed the lock. It seemed like my only option."

"What about calling the police? Was that ever an *option*?"

"Absolutely not."

"Why?"

"You know why."

"Oh, for crying out loud. Are we really doing this again? The thing with the cops? Listen to me. Someone broke into your apartment. You have to report this."

"No." Riley is adamantly shaking her head. "No, I don't."

"You can't let this go!"

"I can, and I will. The cops will just get in the way."

"In the way of what?"

She fumbles to speak. "Do I have to spell it out for you? Look at what they did to my life, what Demetre Sloan did. I spent all that time behind bars before and during the trial, all because of her. Time I'll never get back. Now I'm supposed to ask the cops to help me? Nope. I can handle it myself. You'll have to trust me on this."

"*Trust?* How can I trust you when this whole conversation is built on a lie?"

They pull up to Riley's apartment.

"The answer is still no," Riley says. "I don't want to draw any attention to myself. I already have enough of that."

"I can protect you from it."

"You couldn't then, and you can't now."

"That's not fair." Erin frowns at her. "I did protect you. I got you the best lawyer I could find. A lawyer strong enough to get a hung jury. A lawyer strong enough to prevent the DA from refiling charges!"

"Not that. I meant from everyone else."

"I couldn't do it all!" Erin looks injured. "But I damned well tried. You know I did."

"I'm—" Riley throws both palms against her temples and rapidly shakes her head. "I—I'm sorry. I didn't mean it like that. I'm upset . . . Can we . . . Can we just leave this alone?"

Erin's expression says it all. Exasperation. Aggravation.

Disappointment.

Nothing new.

"Look, I'll call you later," Riley says as a way to cap the conversation more than anything else.

She opens the car door, steps out, and walks away, once again leaving so much unsaid between them.

It's a lonely trip to her apartment.

Inside, she sits at the kitchen table, concentrating on her coffee cup while repeatedly rotating it in its place.

She messed up.

Why does everything I do drive a wedge between us?

Erin isn't the enemy. She was trying to help, and what did Riley do? She became flustered. She flew off the handle.

I'm such an ass.

She's never been quick on her feet, acts even slower when she feels trapped. The past several years are unmitigated proof of that, her disagreement with Erin only piling on more evidence.

She grabs her phone and dials Erin's number but after only one and a half rings gets dumped into voice mail.

Rejected.

"Hey, it's . . . it's me . . . Look, I'm sorry for overreacting. I know you were only trying to help—you're always try to help—and I didn't mean to . . ." She lowers the phone, stares at it, then tries to figure out how to undo damage levied on a relationship that has already taken too many hits.

She lifts the phone and, through a cracked whisper, says, "This is so hard to say . . . I feel lost, *really* lost. Like everyone is against me. Well, everyone except maybe you . . . Wait. Not *maybe* you. I didn't mean it like that. What I meant was . . ."

I'm rambling.

"Never mind . . . Anyway, I just want you to know how much I appreciate everything you've done. And I'm sorry . . ."

She clicks off the phone.

That didn't go so well. Nothing is going well.

She takes stock of her front door, the jammer she recently bought for it.

And calls the locksmith again.

16

On her return from the grocery store, Riley walks by the shut-in's apartment and notices another newspaper tossed out of reach.

She's about to move on when an unexpected surge of empathy washes over her. She can certainly understand what it feels like to be trapped in a world you can no longer tolerate. And to be completely honest, lately she, too, has had an urge to hide inside and never come out.

She gives further thought to the woman who keeps herself imprisoned behind a closed door, wondering if she's perhaps found a peaceful moment in an otherwise unsettled life. She moves closer to the door, thinks about what horrible event might have happened to make her neighbor give up on the world. To lose all faith in it, to crumble beneath its crippling weight.

She raises a hand to knock on the door. She stops, swiftly withdraws the hand, then transfers a few food items from one bag to another. This time, she follows through with a knock.

No answer.

Riley places the newspaper inside the shopping bag. She ties it to the doorknob.

Then walks away with a deep ache in her chest.

17

It's 8:16 p.m., and Riley has been to her living room window three times to see if Ms. Confident, with her privileged car and her privileged life, has come home for the day.

Make that four.

She grabs the remote and clicks on the TV. She tries to shift focus, but somewhere between a documentary about penguins in Antarctica and a dog show in New York City, she again finds herself looking out her window at the lamplit blacktop.

Still no sign of the Mercedes.

The woman was already home by this time last night, so she obviously doesn't leave work at the same time every day, maybe even likes to do a little partying afterward.

Riley sticks by the window and considers another possible explanation. Could Ms. Confident have come home earlier and parked someplace else in the lot? Maybe the spots aren't even assigned and she has a preference for that one. Had she been parking there only out of convenience to unload her large portfolio made of expensive-looking leather?

She scans the rest of the lot through her binoculars but sees no sign of the Mercedes elsewhere.

She goes back to the couch and starts flipping through channels. Nothing catches her interest, so she again goes to the window.

And the spot is still empty.

This back-and-forth window watching is starting to feel a bit obsessive.

Outside near the parking lot, she decides, would be a much better vantage point from which to assess the situation.

Riley splashes through puddles on her way to the other lot, keeping mindful of her surroundings and her potential stalker, who could be spying on her from somewhere between the folds of a rain-soaked night.

I'm not doing the same thing, she argues to herself. *It's not like I plan on playing games with her butcher knife.*

At about twenty-five yards in, she runs directly into an obstacle she'd forgotten about: the six-foot wrought iron fence that divides the two lots. She walks along the fence line, and a few minutes later spots a gate.

A locked gate.

She examines the keypad, which holds a secret combination that will grant entry into Ms. Confident's fairy-tale world. It looks pretty high tech. She circles her vision through the lot as if some solution may be waiting for her. Through the gate, she sees an older well-dressed woman leave her car, then start toward the building.

"Excuse me!" Riley yells to her. "Ma'am?"

The woman glances over her shoulder at Riley, who meets her gaze with an innocent, frustrated expression. She points to her building and says, "I recently moved here and was helping an elderly friend at the apartments across the way. I must have dropped that slip of paper where I wrote down the entry code. Would you mind?"

The woman looks at Riley's grungy building, looks at Riley, then appears to be thinking, probably attempting to make the connection work.

She comes to the gate and punches in the keypad numbers.

Riley steps through and with a grateful smile says, "Thank you so much."

"Not a problem. The code is eight-six-three-four. Make sure to put it in your phone this time so you don't lose it."

"I absolutely will," Riley says, committing the numbers to memory.

The woman takes off.

Several feet into the lot, Riley spies an underground parking garage. She can slip through if someone opens the security grille to drive in. But as she turns back around, distant headlights blind her.

The red Mercedes drives by and proceeds to its regular outside spot. Ms. Confident exits her car, then hustles around to the trunk. She looks much the same as before—still wearing blue jeans, still wearing a T-shirt, and still with her hair pulled into a ponytail. She must put in long hours if she's not partying after work. But where would she work in such casual attire? The Gap? Not with the expensive-looking portfolio bag she carries, and certainly not with her fancy car and apartment.

The woman scurries through the rain and toward her building, and Riley's curiosity urges her to follow at a safe distance. Another keypad waits at the main entrance. She punches in some numbers. A mechanized lock disengages, the double doors swing open, and she glides through.

Riley wants to see what the woman's extravagant, beautiful world looks like inside and hopes the entryway code matches what she's already memorized. She gives it a try. The doors open. She's in.

As expected, the building's interior is lovely—no, it's beyond that. Multistory, hexagonal mezzanines surround a stony waterfall on the main floor, complete with tumbling greenery.

She definitely doesn't work at the Gap—not unless she's the CEO.

Riley watches a resident punch in a code that opens her door, while another exits, allowing his to automatically lock upon closing.

"Good evening, Ms. Light."

Riley switchbacks to the left and finds her target. Ms. Confident greets the man who, judging by the gold tag on his blazer, works in the building.

Ms. Light. A last name.

The woman enters a room filled with mailboxes. About a minute later, she walks into a glass elevator, which swiftly floats toward the upper levels. Riley shifts positions for a better view and sees the elevator stop at the ninth floor. Light strolls out, then moves along the mezzanine. At her apartment, she pauses for a moment and, without warning, looks over the balcony. Riley freezes. Although it's difficult to tell, the woman seems to be looking directly at her. Riley dodges for cover behind a six-foot planter with plenty of girth. A few moments later, she peers out, but the woman has disappeared into her apartment.

She hurries toward the mail room. Inside, she takes a gander at the rows and rows of shiny, gold mailboxes. Residents breeze by in the lobby. Her luck could run out if someone discovers she doesn't belong here. She spots a trash can, waits for the hallway foot traffic to slow, then shovels through a sea of circular ads. After fishing out a blue envelope, she holds it up to examine the label.

Samantha Light

A first name.

A grumpy-looking middle-aged man walks into the mail room, sees Riley studying the envelope, and gives her a suspicious look. She tries to disarm him with a smile. It doesn't work. Time to get out of here, so she fast-tracks out into the lobby and through the exit doors.

Outside, she inspects her immediate surroundings, then approaches the driver's side window of the red Mercedes. On the slight chance that it was left unlocked, she gives the car door handle a gentle tug.

It was not. The alarm protests with a scream, and she breaks into a fast clip, fully aware that running will only make her stand out. After gaining a safe-enough distance, she looks over her shoulder in time to see a security guy rolling his golf cart toward the red Mercedes.

But even worse is the vague human figure she sees on her way back to her building, ducking into the formless night.

18

Riley wakes with a start.

An alarm wails. A thin layer of smoke crawls across the ceiling. At first, she doesn't recognize the sound or the smell, then her senses kick in.

She hurtles from bed and grabs clothes on her way to the living room. Between the alarm's bleats, she hears the frantic pounding of feet and mad shrieking in the hallway.

The moment she opens her door, her faculties are overloaded. The alarm is deafening. People run through black, soupy smoke spilling out of one of the apartments. Riley is about to join the escape downstairs when her conscience niggles at her. She spins around, rushes back down the hall.

At the shut-in's apartment, she places an ear against the door and hears the woman's quiet whimpers. She starts pounding.

"Open the door!" she shouts, banging harder. "You have to get out!"

She glances down the hallway—it's almost completely clear of people, smoke growing thicker—and all at once, she knows time is at a higher premium.

But the woman behind the door still doesn't respond, and those quiet whimpers have metamorphosed into pleading sobs. Even a deadly fire can be no match for an agoraphobic's paralyzing terror of the outside world.

"Please!" Riley shouts, coughing on smoke. "*Please!* At least come to the door! I won't make you do anything you don't want to. I promise! I only want to help!"

Firefighters burst from the stairwell, then plow through a dense wall of smoke. Another follows behind—she takes one look at Riley and shouts, "Hey! You! Out of this building! Right now!"

Riley ignores the order, pounds harder. A few seconds later, the peephole flickers with light. Pushing a strand of hair away from her face, she tries to tame her out-of-control panting and yells, "Can you hear me okay?"

"Yes . . . ," the shut-in says, voice so tiny that Riley can barely hear it.

A crashing noise—the firefighters breaking down a door.

"Okay." Riley swallows back against her own rising panic. "Look, I know how hard this must be for you, how scared you probably are, but you can't stay here. Do you understand? You have to get out."

"I can't!"

"You *can*. If this fire spreads, you'll die! I'll help you. I'll be there the whole time."

No answer.

"Listen," Riley tries again with firmness. "I can be a horrid bitch when I want to. I won't let anyone hurt you. I promise! Okay?"

A four-second pause, then quietly, through tears, "Okay."

Progress.

"I'm Riley."

"W-Wendy."

"What do you say, Wendy?" Riley angles her head away to cough. "Are you ready?"

The lock sluggishly jiggles, and Riley steps back, using this opportunity to size up what's going on down the hall. The smoke has turned white. One firefighter comes around the corner, but before she can see what he's doing, Wendy's door cracks open.

"I'm right here," Riley assures her, extending a hand. "Come on out. Go ahead . . ."

The door opens about six inches farther to reveal a trembling woman in her early fifties, skin the shade of a peeled potato and smoky-blue eyes that launch in every direction.

Riley gives her a fast nod of encouragement. The two women's gazes connect, and Wendy's expression changes. It's the look of fading fear, or thankfulness, or—

"The flames are out!" a firefighter shouts to someone at the bottom of the stairwell. When Riley looks back, Wendy's expression has again changed, this time falling into a burdened state of relief.

Riley offers Wendy a consoling smile—she appears grateful before slowly regressing inside her apartment.

The door closes.

19

Morning.

The air tastes and smells like burned lumber. The hallway carpet is still damp from the emergency sprinklers and covered in a flurry of scattered ashes. But the situation could have been much worse.

Riley's section of hallway suffered a fair amount of smoke damage and will require new paint and carpeting. As for the other half, it didn't fare nearly as well. After the flames were extinguished, she went outside to speak to a firefighter, who told her the apartment where the blaze started needs to be gutted. Management has moved fast: the remaining residents in that wing are being relocated until the mop-up is complete and the apartments are restored to livable states. As if this place wasn't bad enough, there's the weighty and stubborn odor of scorched soot to further bring down the mood.

She stops at Wendy's place to check on her, studying the crack beneath the door. There's no sign of movement, no sound coming from inside. She leans against the wall and slides into a seated position on a less dirty section of carpeting—maybe it's because this spot seems reassuring. Maybe it's because she's starting to feel this woman's pain in a visceral way. Much like Wendy, she understands that life here on the outside can be very frightening.

"I'm feeling you," she mutters, face planted in hands, fortitude wearing thin. "I was trying to rescue you, but I'm starting to think it's me who needs to be saved. You might have had the right idea all along. It's better inside."

"Don't be so sure of that."

Her head jerks up.

Wendy continues speaking through her closed door. "I'm thinking you're the one who got it right."

"What do you mean?"

"My phobia nearly killed me last night. I'd give anything to be where you're standing."

"Then what's stopping you?"

Wendy pauses for a few seconds, then softly says, "Fear."

"Of what?"

"Don't want to talk about it. But you're different than me. You don't have that fear, and I keep being a damned slave to it."

Riley's laugh is rueful. "You probably wouldn't say that if you knew me."

"I already do."

"No . . . No, you don't."

"Maybe not completely, but I've seen what I need to."

"We've hardly spoken, and you rarely open your door." Riley runs her finger along a dirty scratch in the wall. "What could you possibly see?"

"Well . . . during the ten or so years I've been trapped inside this apartment, you're the only person who's bothered to notice I exist."

"And here's me, wishing people would forget that I do."

"Why? Are they doing something to hurt you?"

Riley stands, straightens her shirt, and says, "Don't want to talk about it."

"Touché," Wendy says, unable to conceal her stifled laugh.

20

It's been a few days since Riley left her sister that apology message and still no response. Obviously, Erin hasn't heard about the fire; low-rent blazes rarely garner much media coverage. That said, it's anyone's guess when she'll be back in touch—once she is, they'll move on to the next phase. Erin will call and ask some random question to test the waters, Riley will play along, and that will be that.

She slides the phone into her back pocket in case Erin decides to call, then begins laying out Clarissa's clothes for the day. She likes doing this, enjoys the way it makes her feel, how it affords her the opportunity to reminisce about better times. Somewhere between twelve and thirteen, Clarissa began fighting her on it, arguing that she was old enough to pick out her own wardrobe. Jason—the consummate family mediator—had laughed about the disagreement.

"Our little girl is growing up," he'd gently reminded Riley, explaining that it was time to let her make her own decisions.

"Oh, sweetheart," she says. "What I wouldn't give to go back to those days when you were young."

She releases a lengthy, regretful sigh and takes out another pair of blue jeans, plus the green-and-white blouse with three-quarter-length sleeves, a front keyhole accent, and a tie closure. This was always one of Clarissa's favorites. Riley spends considerable time arranging and rearranging the outfit on her bed just so, sharp and tidy, smoothing out every wrinkle. She takes a step away for a final examination, feels satisfaction over the presentation, then leaves.

She goes to the living room window and checks out Ms. Confident's red Mercedes in its parking spot. The rain has diminished into a light drizzle, but she still wonders whether the sun will ever again shine on her dreary world.

The phone rings. She takes it out of her pocket: Erin calling. She answers.

As if the two had hung up only minutes ago, Erin says, "I was just wondering, do you have enough bedsheets at the apartment?"

Predictable as an atomic clock.

"Um . . . yeah?" Riley says.

"You sure? 'Cause I found a box filled with a bunch. I know they can't be mine."

She's about to move away from the window when she sees Samantha Light exit her building. With a new accessory—her briefcase—in one hand, she flips her umbrella open with the other but doesn't go toward the parking lot; instead, she heads for the sidewalk, then stops to answer a phone call.

"Hey, sis," Riley interrupts, still distracted by Samantha, "I'm kind of busy. Can I call you back in a few?"

"What are you doing?"

She forgoes giving details; Erin doesn't need to hear that Riley is spying on Samantha Light through the window, so she says, "I'm in the middle of a thing."

"What's the *thing*?"

"Nothing major. I'll explain later."

"Wait. I—"

"Gotta go."

She hangs up, moves in closer toward the window, and gazes with interest.

Where's Ms. Confident going now?

Riley doesn't know, but she's interested enough to find out. She grabs her raincoat and umbrella.

She's out the door.

21

Samantha Light is still standing on the sidewalk and chatting on her phone when Riley arrives; she stops at just the right distance to eavesdrop on the conversation.

"Oh, sure. I can definitely have it done by then," Samantha says with a southern drawl that heightens Riley's interest. Cradling the phone between her ear and shoulder while balancing the umbrella on an arm, she digs through her briefcase. "Can you have someone leave it there for me?" She nods so fast that it nearly jars the phone loose, then adds, "Okay. Got it."

The call ends, then Samantha is on the move, and Riley follows at a slow pace from several feet behind. They leave the complex, end up on a side street. She continues to secretly observe Samantha, still with that confident stride, still looking as if she's on top of the world. But she doesn't go far. Samantha hooks a right and marches through the doors of a small café located just a half block from her complex.

By the time Riley catches up and walks inside, Samantha is already on her way to a table; she checks her watch, then with flawlessly manicured nails taps a beat while waiting for the menu.

Riley waits at the hostess's station, using this opportunity to study the young woman at a closer range. She looks more polished today with her trendy tortoiseshell-framed eyeglasses, her pretty tan blouse, and her black skirt with a slit running up the side. Black stockings cling to a pair of well-toned Pilates legs, complemented by shoes that do not look cheap.

"Would you like a table, ma'am?"

Riley startles.

The hostess stands before her. She considers Samantha, now looking over her menu.

Why not?

"Sure," she says.

Riley takes her seat at a table close enough to continue observing. Samantha removes papers from her briefcase. Riley wants to know what Samantha is reading, but because of the distance between them, she can discern only that they're drawings of some sort. Samantha flips through the pages, then looks up and catches Riley peeping at her; she politely smiles. Riley pretends she was daydreaming and unexpectedly noticed Samantha, then smiles back. A connection. And relief: Samantha doesn't seem to recognize Riley from the night she spied on her at the apartment building.

She tries to exercise discretion while keeping watch over Samantha. During the course of her meal, the woman fields two phone calls, both of which seem to be work related. In one she shuffles through pages from the document and appears to be discussing them—either that, or she's keeping herself occupied while the caller goes on. For the next discussion, Samantha seems pensive, as if she's trying to solve a problem. Riley's curiosity jumps a notch. For someone so young, she sure seems extremely important and successful.

Halfway through her meal, she decides a trip to the restroom might afford her a glimpse at that document, but just as Riley passes, Samantha returns them to her briefcase.

Damn it.

Inside, she checks her appearance and reapplies makeup. But when she's about to hurry back to the dining room, Samantha enters. She walks up to Riley, holds out her hand, and says, "I think you dropped this by my table."

Riley takes the photo. Feeling her face warm, she puts the picture inside her purse and says, "I—I didn't even realize that I . . . It must have fallen out. Thank you."

"No worries," Samantha says, then lets out a diminutive laugh, clearly aimed at easing tension she doesn't quite understand. Her drawl becomes thicker. "You should see me. I've actually thought about hiring a personal assistant to follow behind and catch everything I drop." She takes a tube of lipstick from her purse, looks into the mirror, and while applying the makeup asks, "Is that your little girl? In the photo?"

Riley's only answer is a faltering half nod.

"She's absolutely beautiful," Samantha says, pulling away from the mirror for a final inspection.

Riley is tongue-tied.

"Are you okay?" Samantha asks.

"She was killed." The statement comes flying out. "My daughter was. About ten years ago."

Sliding two fingers down a gold beaded necklace, Samantha says, "I'm so sorry. I didn't—" She looks at Riley's wrist, then quickly averts her sight.

Riley glances down. Her sleeve has hiked up several inches, exposing the scar. She feels her ears becoming red, then her face, then her neck. In a panic, she yanks down her sleeve and rushes out, leaving Samantha alone in the restroom.

By the time the young woman appears in the dining area, Riley is already on her way out the door.

22

"Just a little two-alarm fire is all," Riley says while she and Erin walk through the hallway.

Erin looks at the black-stained ceiling, looks at her sister. "Who on earth is responsible for all this?"

While opening the door, Riley steps in front of Erin to block her view of the new lock. Inside, she throws her keys onto the counter. "It wasn't intentional."

"Well, *that's* a huge relief."

"Not so much for the guy who started it. Apparently he hadn't finished his smoke break but decided to pass out anyway."

"Oh, dear Lord."

"I'm told there have been other similar incidents. Only not with this much firepower."

"Don't tell me it was the same guy."

"Other residents." Riley opens her fridge and grabs two cans of soda. She offers one to Erin. Erin shakes her head, and Riley puts the extra can back. "But here's a silver lining. One of the neighbors told me Aileen wants to launch a campaign to educate people on the hazards of smoking in bed."

"Like they actually need to teach people this? Not to fall asleep with a burning butt?"

Riley shrugs. Her smile is drenched in sarcasm. "At the very least, it's an opportunity to bring this blossoming community closer together."

"Sad that it took a tower of flames to do it," Erin remarks, ignoring Riley's sarcasm, then she clumsily changes topics. "Hey, did you have a chance to check your sheets yet?"

Riley resists the urge to roll her eyes and says, "Yep. I'm all good."

"I can bring the others over, you know. Just say the word."

"Got it. Thanks," Riley says, trying to wind up the conversation.

Erin's scrutiny wanders to the lock on Riley's door, which is a different color than before. Riley managed to dodge that bullet on the way in, but it appears to have boomeranged back. Erin blinks a few times, then says, "Riley, did you change out your lock again?"

"Uh-huh." She avoids looking at Erin. "I didn't like the other one. It wasn't secure enough."

Erin considers the lock again. Riley lowers herself into a chair and does a double take at the doll on her side table—it's been moved. She leaned it against the lamp's base the night they unpacked, but the little girl now sits an inch or two away, head slumped forward.

"Riley?"

She comes back to her sister.

"Is something wrong?"

"No, why?"

"You got quiet all of a sudden."

"I'm fine," Riley says, trying to fake buoyancy while slipping in a vigilant glance around the apartment.

Erin nods, but everything about her body language is screaming *no*. She excuses herself, goes to the bathroom.

And Riley can't stop looking at the doll. She tries to reason: There was a lot going on the night she and Erin unpacked, and the change is barely significant. Is it possible she bumped into the table and hasn't noticed the movement until now?

Am I being paranoid?

As she leans the doll back against her lamp, the bathroom door opens. She jumps into the chair, waits for Erin's return, but Erin doesn't make one. Riley leans over to glance down the hallway and finds her sister peering into the bedroom. But from the look on her face, she's not checking out the latest furniture-refinishing project.

Oh hell.

She's staring at Clarissa's clothes laid out on the bed.

Erin catches Riley's gaze and doesn't speak, but her dropped jaw and dazed expression demand an answer. Riley rushes to the bedroom and hastily closes the door. "Relax," she says, faking nonchalance. "I just like taking her clothes out to look at them."

"Your deceased daughter's clothes—you like looking at them. Ten years after her murder."

"I know it might seem kind of strange, but I've been so lonely lately, and it helps me feel closer to her. It's really no big deal."

Erin mouths, *No big deal.* Riley follows her into the living room. Erin lowers herself onto the love seat, then stares straight ahead as if gathering her thoughts.

"Riley . . . ," she at last says, tempering her tone with kindness, "I know you've been through so much . . . but this isn't a healthy way to grieve. It's like denial."

"It's not that at all. Clarissa was murdered. I'm well aware of it."

"But laying out her clothes isn't normal. You realize that, right?"

"Since when is there anything normal about losing a child?" Riley feels a firm emotional tug in her chest. "I'm doing my best to cope."

"I know that. I really do. But have you discussed this with your counselor?"

"No, why?"

Discomfort apparent, Erin shifts her body. "Maybe you should."

23

Riley finishes ironing Clarissa's clothes for the day—a navy skirt and white chiffon blouse—then holds the garments up side by side to admire them.

She smiles.

She can still remember the first time Clarissa wore this ensemble. There was a big debate at school that day, and as a good-luck gesture she'd surprised her daughter with the new outfit. Clarissa got so excited that she threw her arms around Riley.

"You're the best mom ever," Clarissa had said.

"You're the best daughter ever," Riley says out loud, remembering her reply.

She lays down the clothes, skirt beneath blouse. Placing a finger against her lips, she studies them.

Something is missing.

The gold cross Riley gave Clarissa—she wore it with this outfit to the debate.

Riley goes to her bureau, opens the top drawer, takes out the cross. She smiles again.

She brings the necklace to her bed and drapes it over the blouse. *Perfect.*

Riley spends several hours pounding wet pavement and fighting the rain on her hunt for a job, but so far the effort has proved futile.

The folks at Glendale have been kind enough to offer information on their website about how to transition from a psychiatric hospital to the outside workforce. Sadly, they fail to mention what to do when your face has been plastered all over the television and newspapers and you're labeled an accused killer. Of your own daughter, no less.

For painful and obvious reasons, her former job as a school-teacher is out of the question. Today, at the establishments where she applies, employers either blow her off after recognizing her face and name or have no available openings. She even tries for a few low-profile positions like telemarketing sales, but those employers don't seem interested, either.

She's doing her best to push forward, but life keeps pushing back, and she wonders how much longer she can endure this discouragement before it swallows her alive. Though Erin set her up financially for the month, she can hear each tick of the clock, every day taking her one step closer toward running out of funds. Independence was what she wanted, and independence she has, but the price is steeper than she first imagined.

At least there's one reason to feel grateful. For the time being it seems as though the media has still backed off, probably having moved on to the next big thing. If she can remain under the radar, hopefully they'll stay gone.

The rain comes down harder, and she decides it's time to call it a day on this useless job search. She's about to walk back toward the car when Samantha Light crosses her path on the way into Urbana Grill.

Riley moves closer to the restaurant window, looks inside, and continues studying Samantha, who is now chatting it up with the hostess. A few moments later, a handsome young waiter passes by and smiles at Samantha over his shoulder—she flirtatiously smiles back at him, then continues talking to the hostess.

A charmed life, indeed.

Riley considers the fancy white tablecloths, the beautiful decor, the well-dressed staff. She's never walked into a place this fancy, can't afford it.

But she simply cannot resist.

24

Samantha sits at a table, casually skimming the menu.

Riley waits for the hostess and tries to be discreet while keeping an eye on the young woman. Today, she wears the tortoiseshell-framed glasses, and she's let her hair down. Her bright kelly-green blouse is made of fine-spun silk and almost perfectly matches her shiny patent-leather pumps: Samantha pays attention to the finer details.

Riley requests a table in the adjacent dining room, which offers a clear view of Samantha as the waiter delivers a glass of red wine. Samantha orders her lunch, and the waiter moves on to Riley's table.

Her stealthy position provides an opportunity for another detailed examination of Samantha Light. Riley is surprised to find that her first impressions were slightly off. Samantha's hair is dark, yes, but Riley missed the subtle mahogany highlights, a combination almost identical to Clarissa's.

Samantha's phone goes off. She grabs it from her purse, answers, then starts talking. Riley tries to overhear, but the conversation at a crowded table nearby grows louder, making it impossible. Samantha ends the call, places her phone on the table, then glances around the room until she lands on Riley.

Riley pretends to be pleasantly surprised.

Samantha seems to be as well. She smiles and waves.

Riley waves back.

But Samantha looks as if she's deliberating over a thought. A few seconds later, she rises from her chair and walks to Riley's table.

"So," Samantha starts, "I'm not the kind of person who likes to let false impressions stand, but you left in a hurry the other day, and I didn't get a chance to apologize."

Riley shakes her head.

"About your daughter's photo. I upset you and feel awful about it."

"No, it wasn't your fault." Riley looks down at the table. "There's more to it. I . . . I lost my husband in an accident shortly before Clarissa died."

"Oh no . . ." Samantha touches a finger to her lips and says, "I'm so sorry . . ."

"The reason I'm telling you this is because my life is really complex, and it's hard to come up with a good explanation for why I feel cornered when new people express sympathy."

"I don't know what happened, and I can't begin to imagine what you've been through . . ." Samantha pauses as if deciding what to say next, and a line etches its way between her brows when she says, "This isn't the same thing, but my mother killed herself when I was a girl."

Riley slides a finger beneath her sleeve. She rubs it across the scar on her wrist, realizes what she's doing, then clutches her chest.

"Yes, it's exactly like that," Samantha says, "like having someone reach into my chest and rip the heart right out of it. I guess what I'm trying to say is, I can understand some of what you went through the other day when I asked about your daughter. People would innocently make comments, ask questions, but each time it would take me back to that horrible place. The one I so badly wanted to escape.

Eventually, the pain took on a life all its own . . ." Samantha's voice trails off as if she's leaving her horrible place. "I think you know what I mean."

Riley nods. "You've described it perfectly."

"The point is, in my own way—and through my own experiences—I sort of get it."

"I imagine you might."

"So, what do you think about a redo from before? Join me for lunch. It'll be my treat."

"That would be lovely," Riley says, knowing she can't afford this place and thrilled by the prospect of moving further into Samantha Light's world.

"Great. I'm Samantha Light, by the way."

"Riley Harper."

"Very pleased to meet you, Riley, even if it was through an unexpected accident."

25

Lunch is served, and the two women relax into quiet, comfortable conversation.

"So, what brings you to this part of town?" Samantha asks.

"I've been out looking for a job—or trying, anyway."

"Not much luck?"

"Not much at all."

"Hmm. That really sucks." Samantha gazes upward, and her drawl becomes thicker. "I may be able to help. What kind of work are you looking for?"

"Well, I used to be a teacher, but I'll take whatever pays the bills. I can't afford to be picky, and I'm a fast learner."

"I'm new here, but let me put out some feelers and see what I can find."

"You'd do that?"

"Absolutely. I love helping people." She beams. "It's my favorite thing."

"Wow. I'd really appreciate that. Where do *you* work?"

"Right now, I'm working on my life," Samantha laughs. "Also not so easy."

"Having problems?"

"Yes, but they're remarkably underwhelming, and I'd rather not bore you with them."

"But we've done enough of me, so let's do you now."

"Okay, here's me." Samantha straightens her posture and grins. "I came north from LA. Been there for the last several years but finally got sick of it. So glad to break out of there. Those crowds. And don't even get me started on the ridiculous freeways. Too many of them, and too many cars. It's like trying to drive through a jammed parking lot. Add to it the failed relationships—seems I'm always picking the wrong people to be close with—and I knew it was time for a new start."

"LA seems like another world to me. I've never traveled far from this town. Hopped around a lot through the years, but I always manage to stay in the general area."

I even hopped right into the nuthouse one of those times.

Samantha sips her wine, then abruptly stops to look at Riley. "Hey, I just got an idea. My car's navigation system confuses the hell out of me, and I'm still having a difficult time trying to find everything. I was fixing to check out Google Maps to get a feel for where everything is, but would you be up for showing me around town?"

Riley brightens. "Absolutely. I'd love to."

"Awesome. I *did* figure out how to find a Starbucks, though. You know, priorities and all. I can make it there in four minutes flat from my place." A wink and a smile. "That is, if I pretend not to know the speed limit. Don't come between me and my coffee," Samantha says in playful forewarning. "I can turn bitch in a hurry. Caffè mocha's my drug of choice."

"Well, coffee does make the world go 'round."

"Okay, now I like you even more." Samantha laughs. "But, seriously, coffee is one of my obsessions."

"And the other?"

"Others," Samantha corrects. "But let's not go into those."

"Got it."

"I will say that the good stuff can give me a religious experience."

"That must really be something."

Samantha flips her wrist to check her watch. She perks. "Oh wow. I've been enjoying our time together so much that I didn't realize how late it is. I've got an appointment in, like, three minutes."

"Then you'd better get going."

"Here. Hand me your phone."

Riley does. Samantha punches in her number, texts herself, then hands the phone back. Riley looks up at her and smiles.

"Well, that's the happiest face I've seen all day," Samantha says.

Riley shrugs. "I'm just glad we've crossed paths again."

"Right back at you," Samantha says. Now she's smiling, too.

A few minutes later in the parking lot, Riley is still reflecting on her and Samantha's conversation, but several feet from the car, her blood runs cold. She stares vacantly, mind unable to fully absorb the sentence keyed into her passenger's side door just above the handle.

DIE MURDERER!

Chilling words, biting words.

She allows the fear to own her only for a few seconds, then her body locks up with rage—rage that sears its way into indignation. Using her key, she scratches out the letters, then spins around and at the top of her lungs shouts, "QUIT HIDING AND BRING IT ON, YOU COWARDLY ASSHOLE! I'M READY. DO YOU HEAR ME? I'M SO READY!"

Riley looks around. People are stopped on the street and staring at her.

Flustered by the sudden onslaught of unwanted attention, she squirms, wipes her brow, and jogs to the driver's side door, acting as if nothing happened.

26

"How are things going?"

"They're going."

Patricia Lockwood has a different look today. She's taken the once-whimsical gray bob to a new and exciting place, blowing it forward. And the color of the day is purple—lots of it. Purple blouse, purple pants. Even her shoes are purple.

Riley realizes she's been goggling and averts her gaze to the opposite end of the room.

"Have you found work?" Patricia asks.

"Not yet."

"Have you been looking?"

She swings back to Patricia. It sounded like a challenge rather than a question, and Riley's tone is a shade too curt when she says, "As a matter of fact, I did. All day yesterday."

Patricia's approving nod seems like an effort to smooth the situation over. "And? How did it go?"

"Well, let's see . . . awful?"

Patricia's head tilts to the left. "What happened?"

"It's what didn't happen. There's not much demand for a suspected murderer who just crawled out of the loony bin—especially one whose face has been all over the news."

"I'm sorry you had to go through that."

"Not nearly as much as I am."

Slap, slap, slap.

Riley snaps her eyes to Patricia's foot.

Patricia stops. She leans forward and concentrates on her steepled hands. A transition of some sort. She waits a beat or two longer, then looks up at Riley and says, "I'd like to talk about Clarissa today."

"I'd rather not."

"I know it's difficult, but difficult is what we try to fix here."

Riley's jaw clenches. "What about her?"

"Well . . . everything came down on you pretty hard after the murder."

Patricia is stating the obvious, and Riley's not sure how to respond, so she doesn't.

"With all that happening," Patricia continues, "did you ever have the opportunity to mourn her death?"

"Not much."

"Not much or not at all?"

"I guess not at all."

"Why do you think that is?"

"Everything happened so fast. I was too busy trying to defend myself to the cops, then I got thrown in jail and put on trial. Then, after that was over, I started to crack and fall apart."

"What about while you were at Glendale? Did you do any grief work there?"

"A little toward the end, but they spent much of the time trying to get my mind stabilized."

"And now?"

"Now it's about trying to put my life back together."

Patricia raises her chin. "It's never too late, you know. To grieve."

"I've tried, but it seems like I can't even get that right."

"Why do you say that?"

Riley scrubs a hand across her face as if the act might wash away her frustration. "I got in trouble the other day with Erin. She saw that I'd taken out some of Clarissa's old clothes and left them on the bed."

Patricia's probing expression asks the next question.

Riley answers it. "I don't feel like it's that big of a deal. It's not like I'm hurting anyone. Do you think it's wrong?"

"I think we each find our own way to grieve."

"So it's okay."

"Considering you've only recently had a chance to begin that process, I'd say it's a step. Externalizing those feelings—talking about them—here would be the next." Patricia pauses, looks pensive, then, "Did Erin explain why she had a problem with what you were doing?"

"She thinks it's denial."

"Do you?"

"There's nothing to deny."

"Did you tell her that?"

"I tried. She didn't buy it."

Patricia's smile is sad.

And Riley can't stand to look at it. She focuses on her fisted hands, but when she comes back, Patricia has a hard fix on her.

"What?" Riley asks.

"I'm wondering why you avoided looking at me. Was it something I said?"

"It was your expression."

Patricia asks her to explain.

"The sympathy," Riley says. "It makes me uncomfortable. I don't like it, don't need it."

"Why not?"

"It hurts too much."

"Interesting response . . ." Patricia pauses. "Sympathy is used to comfort people. Why do you suppose it has an opposite effect on you?"

"I don't know." Riley locks both arms across her chest and feels it rumble with something scalding and raw.

"Could it be because—"

"Because I needed that sympathy then." The statement bursts from Riley's mouth. Her eyes start to burn, but she fights the tears. "Because nobody would give it to me, and getting it now only reminds me of how lonely I felt, how hated I became. Because now it just makes the pain hurt harder."

"How about your sister? Didn't she offer the sympathy you so wanted?"

"She doled it out sparingly."

Patricia pulls her head back. "How come?"

"It's complicated."

"Life can be complicated."

"Why do you always say that?"

"Because it's always true."

Patricia silently holds Riley's gaze, waiting for the answer to her question, and the room is thick with tension.

Which makes Riley blurt out, "I don't think Erin believed I was innocent, okay?"

"Really?" Patricia asks, broad eyes going broader. "Why do you say that?"

"Because she never told me."

"But how do you know that means—"

"I—I think I've had enough for today." Riley grits her teeth. Her emotions are raw, and Patricia is pushing too damned hard. "I just—I need a break from this. I'd like to go."

Patricia nods.

Riley practically sprints toward the door.

27

Riley is still reeling from her session with Patricia.

She watches her tired feet straggle down the hallway, then a buckle breaks free from her shoe, causing the strap to fling off to one side.

Great. Just great.

Inside the apartment, she goes directly to the window. She's aware her preoccupation with Samantha is a bit over the top, but watching her has become so routine that she hardly even thinks about it anymore.

She looks out and blinks a few times. The red Mercedes is parked in its spot. She checks her watch, then looks back at the car. She checks her watch again. It's only 4:00 p.m.

This isn't the regular pattern.

Everything feels out of whack today.

I could use a distraction.

She grabs her cell phone and, without thought, dials Samantha's number.

"Hey!" Samantha answers.

"Hi. I hope I'm not bothering you," Riley replies, recognizing her impulsivity and feeling a little awkward about it.

"Not at all. Glad to hear from you. What's up?"

Riley gulps. She hadn't thought about that one, either, so she randomly throws out, "I was just following through on my promise to give you a tour of the town. Are you still up for it?"

"Yeah. Absolutely!"

"I'm heading out to grab a bite." She tries to figure out why she had to lie. "I thought maybe you could join me. I can point out some things along the way."

"Gosh, I'd love that—I really would—but I already have plans. You know, personal stuff. So boring."

"It's okay." Riley holds a palm to the back of her neck and rubs, knowing in retrospect that her sudden, improvised invite was presumptuous. "It's no big deal at all, really. It was just one of those spur-of-the-moment thoughts."

Actually, there was no thought.

"How about tomorrow?" Samantha suggests. "I'm free after two."

"Great time for an afternoon pick-me-up. Coffee?"

"God, I love you for that. Absolutely. Text me your address, and I'll pick you up."

"No," Riley immediately volleys back.

Samantha doesn't speak.

"Sorry. I meant to say that I won't be home then." She cringes at the thought of Samantha seeing this place, even more at the thought of her finding out it's the dump located directly across from her swanky building. "I have to drop something off at my sister's. I'll be coming from there."

"You have a sister? Cool. What's her name?"

"Erin. Why?"

"Nothing. Just didn't know you had one. A sister."

"Can we meet somewhere in town?"

"Sure! So check this out. I stumbled upon this little gem of a coffee shop. They serve an awesome cup. It's on Sixth and Falcon. Meet me there?"

"Yes," Riley says. And already starts to feel better.

28

On her way to meet Samantha, Riley stops at a gift shop and finds the perfect conciliation present for Erin: a glass cube with an orange-and-yellow sea anemone inside. She loves anything to do with the ocean and is thrilled when Riley drops by to deliver the offering. Erin is happy, and Riley feels good about making her sister smile.

Reset button hit. Lingering resentment over. Everything fine.

"In a hurry to go somewhere?" Erin asks when Riley tells her she has to shove off.

"I've got a few errands to do," Riley says, smiling through yet another lie.

Samantha comes to the table with two large caffè mochas. She passes one over.

"I've really missed a good cup of coffee," Riley says.

"Missed it?"

"I went on the decaf train for a while. It crashed."

"Welcome back to the Heavenly Kingdom." Samantha lifts her cup in a toast. "We've missed you."

Riley regards her with quiet amusement.

"What is it?" Samantha's smile slowly builds. "What's that look for?"

"Nothing, really. It's just that you remind me so much of my daughter right now. She had a quick sense of humor, too, could toss out the lines so effortlessly."

"I would have loved to have met her."

Riley becomes distracted when a mother and her teenage daughter walk in. They're joking, laughing with each other. Having a great time. When Riley lands back in the moment, Samantha wears a compassionate expression.

For a time, neither says anything, the quiet between them feeling a bit thick.

Eventually, Riley draws a grounding breath. She looks down at her coffee cup. "Clarissa was fifteen. I was driving her home from school, and we had an argument. A bad one. Things got out of control, and I . . . I lost my temper." Riley hears her shoe tapping a nervous, erratic beat against the wood flooring. She shakes her head and looks Samantha in the eye. "I made her get out of the car and walk the rest of the way home." Her voice cracks as she repeats herself. "I made her walk the rest of the way home. Those are the memories that haunt me every damned day."

Samantha lets out a heartbroken sigh as though the ache belongs to her as well. She takes Riley's hand from across the table and cradles it inside hers.

"We were only a few blocks from home," Riley continues. "I thought she'd be safe. How could she not have been safe? It doesn't make any sense. But it was stupid of me. Because . . . because . . ." Her breathing picks up, and her words tumble out in broken bits. "Because twenty minutes went by . . . and . . . and she still wasn't home. I got worried and went out looking for her. Then . . . later—I don't know how much later—a horrible storm came in. But I stayed outside. I did. I kept running, running everywhere she might be, screaming out her name. I couldn't find her . . ." Tears fill her eyes. She can almost feel the wind in her face, the hysteria rushing through every living cell in her body. It sounds like a pleading whimper when she says, "Samantha, I couldn't find my baby . . ."

Samantha takes a tissue from her purse, gives it to Riley, then takes one to wipe away her own tears.

"Next thing I knew, I woke up lying beside the road with no idea how I got there. The rain was stinging my arms, my neck, my forehead. My head was throbbing. Then I felt something in my hand. I was holding Clarissa's sneaker. At first I thought the blood was coming from me, but there was none there, then . . ." Her throat constricts around the last word, strangling it. She presses a fist to her lips, closes her eyes.

Samantha waits, giving Riley the time she needs to gather herself.

"And all of a sudden, I knew something horrible had happened to my child. I panicked. I took off running, screaming out her name. But my mind was so hazy, and I didn't even know where I was running to. A few minutes later the police found me."

"What did they do?"

"They ruined my life," Riley says, tears of sadness changing into angry ones. With anyone else she'd struggle to hide the emotion, but right now she has a powerful need to let Samantha see it. "When they questioned me at the station, I tried to explain that I hadn't hurt my daughter, that I never would, that I was trying to find her, but I could see suspicion all over the detective's face, and right then, I knew I was in trouble. In theory, I could see how my story sounded questionable. A witness saw us arguing in the car, and a neighbor reported seeing me arrive home alone, then a few minutes later leave in a panic. Of course, when the blood on the sneaker I was holding ended up matching Clarissa's, it didn't help matters. About a day after the storm passed, investigators found my scarf snagged on a tree branch at the cemetery right next to where I'd woken up."

Samantha frowns and shakes her head. "How did it end up there?"

"I have no idea, can't remember, but by then the detective in charge—Demetre Sloan was her name—had formulated her own theory and was determined to make it stick. That while passing the cemetery, I stopped, made my daughter get out, and killed her, then came home, then left again to dispose of the body."

"And you still can't remember what happened?"

"No."

"You're sure? Not even tiny bits?"

"None of it. I wish I could. I've tried."

"But you weren't the one who killed her."

"No, I was not." Riley looks squarely at Samantha, rage brewing in her gut, voice hitching when she says, "Nobody believed me. *Nobody.* They had their suspect and were too damned lazy to search for anyone else."

"Did they arrest you?"

Riley nods. "The evidence was circumstantial, and it ended with a mistrial, but that hardly mattered. To this day, the public, the media, everyone still believes I did it."

Samantha gazes down at the table as if some form of rationale might be waiting there. She puts two fingers against her temple, shakes her head. "Like losing your daughter wasn't horrible enough? Then this?"

"The only thing I was guilty of was kicking her out of the car, and believe me, I've paid for it every living day and sleepless night since. There was no way out. No way to escape so much pain, so much regret. What you saw in the restroom that day?" Riley pulls up a sleeve to reveal the scar that runs along her wrist. "I jabbed a pair of scissors in and kept cutting. Right after that, Erin had me committed to Glendale Hospital, but there wasn't a medicine or treatment on this earth that could take away my pain. And the worst part? They never found the monster who killed my child."

"What about Clarissa? Did they find her?"

"At the cemetery. Apparently, it's one of the oldest tricks in the book. The killer found a spot where a grave had been dug for a funeral, then pushed Clarissa's unconscious body facedown into the hole and covered it with dirt, leaving her to suffocate and die." Riley feels a little winded just thinking about it. "The next day, a coffin was supposed to go on top of her, and that would be that. But the rain continued overnight, and the grave began to cave. Work crews found her the next day while trying to repair the damage."

Samantha doesn't say anything—it looks as if she can't.

"But you know what?" Riley smiles through her tears. "After all I went through, and after all of the drugs and therapies that were supposed to magically repair my broken life, it was actually my daughter who saved me."

Samantha silently questions Riley.

"Clarissa didn't leave me. Not really." She sounds stronger, more steady and clear. "Each day, without fail, the daughter I lost still lives on."

"Of course she does, and she'll always stay in your heart," Samantha says with the saddest of smiles.

29

Riley already feels wobbly, but at the parking lot, a different kind of distress knocks her off balance.

Oh no . . .

She hadn't given thought to what a huge embarrassment her outdated, beat-up Toyota Camry would be. She cringes at the large dent in her front bumper, the unadorned, mismatched spare tires she never replaced after Clarissa's murder. Then there's the new scratchy mess she made of the driver's side door. Good Lord, she could have at least washed it. Compared to Samantha's slickly polished late-model Mercedes, Riley's car screams poverty in the worst possible way. She'd crawl under the vehicle and hide, but its ugliness would just draw attention.

"I—I'm still getting back on my feet again," Riley says.

Samantha looks at the car, places a hand on Riley's shoulder, and says, "Believe me, your car looks like a dream compared to the clunkers I used to drive. This is not a problem. Don't even worry about it."

Riley tries to appear amiable in light of the goodwill gesture but feels as if her body has shrunk to about half its size.

"It's not about the car, anyway—it's about the company. But if it really bothers you, we can take mine." Samantha points to her Mercedes, then tosses Riley the keys.

Riley runs her fingers over the soft, warm leather that covers the weighty and pristine key fob. She shakes her head and says, "I don't know, Samantha, I'd be too nervous—"

"Have you received any driving convictions?"

"Well, no, I—"

"How about any accidents?

"Not in a long ti—"

"Then we're good." Samantha walks to the passenger's side, opens the door, and says, "Now get in the car and show me around this place!"

Going from Riley's car to Samantha's is like going from a pudding pack to crème brûlée. Riley loves the soft, supple seats, loves the intoxicating smell, how the leather generously gives way to the human form, how it feels so smooth and cozy against her skin. And the dashboard. *Goodness, this dashboard!* She's never seen anything like it. So richly appointed. No gauges covered in aging, cloudy plastic, no clunky dials, just lovely screens and brushed steel buttons and a sexy steering wheel, also gussied up in leather. In this moment, Riley can almost imagine what it must feel like to be Samantha, to enjoy the spoils of a life blessed with affluence, with privilege.

Samantha looks out through the windshield, appearing content, as if she hasn't a care in the world, as if leaving this expensive machine in Riley's hands is as easy as lending out a pair of shoes.

Riley hangs a sharp left, and her purse flips over next to Samantha's feet.

"Oh dear," Riley says, hitting the brakes to slow down as they approach the straightaway. "Sorry about that. Guess I'm not used to driving a car with this much power."

"Don't even worry about it," Samantha says, righting Riley's purse on the floorboard. "I take corners on two wheels all the time."

"Well, I don't. Not in an expensive Mercedes that doesn't belong to me."

"What's this?"

Riley turns her head toward Samantha, who is now retrieving an appointment card from the floor. She examines it.

Riley shoots her flustered gaze back out the windshield, feels her ears gathering heat, then her cheeks, and sounds mousy when she says, "It's my therapist. I'm seeing a therapist, you know, to help me with everything."

The conversation drops for a few seconds, which feel like a thousand.

Then Samantha takes on a light, disarming tone. "Of course you're seeing a therapist. Who in the world wouldn't after what you went through?"

Riley coerces a smile from herself, and they drive on.

They've already covered all the grocery stores, a few of the top shopping areas, even a park or two along the way. Then Samantha asks, "So where's the best burger joint around here?"

Riley chuckles. "You make being a tour guide easy, not to mention letting me drive your fancy car."

Samantha shrugs. "I'm just common folk like everyone else."

Riley takes her focus off the road to give her a dubious look.

Samantha breaks out into laughter and says, "What? You're not feeling me on that?"

"To the burger joint we go," Riley brightly says, letting her avoidance answer the question.

Samantha is still laughing. "Damn, woman. You're harsh!"

Now they're both laughing.

About a mile or so away from JuicyBurger, Samantha says, "So, your sister . . ."

Riley glances at her, prompting her to finish the question.

"You never mentioned her once while telling me your story."

Riley's face is loaded with self-restraint when she says, "Erin is hard to figure out. *We're* hard to figure out."

"In what way?"

"We're different across the board. It can create conflict at times." She keeps her attention aimed out through the windshield but can feel Samantha's questioning look. Riley adds, "Let's just say the relationship got messy after Clarissa died."

"The death of a child can be enough to break up even the strongest of families."

"We're still trying to pick up those broken parts of us and put them back together."

"Any luck?"

"Seems like hit or miss most of the time."

"What does Erin do for a living?"

"She's a lawyer."

"What kind?"

"Defense."

"Ahhh. So she's a tough one, right?"

"Too much for her own good at times."

"What's her last name?"

"McAllister." Riley again takes her focus off the road, looks appraisingly at Samantha. "Why?"

"No reason, really. Just wondered if I'd ever heard of her before. I'd love to meet her sometime."

"Maybe you will," Riley says, then thinks, *That's all I need.*

30

On her way back from another unsuccessful day of job hunting, Riley stops at the grocery store, then Wendy's apartment.

She knocks and waits.

For a long time.

Six more raps and three minutes later, Wendy comes to her door—or it would seem that way, since the peephole is enveloped in darkness.

"Hey," Riley says, holding up a shopping bag. "I grabbed a few items for you at the store. I was going there anyway, figured maybe you could use some supplies."

No response.

"Anyway," Riley resumes, "I'm there a few times a week. Seems I'm always forgetting something and need to go back. So, if you want to, leave a list under your door. It's no problem. I'm happy to grab whatever it is."

Again, nothing.

"Wendy? Still there?"

"Go ahead and leave it on the floor." Wendy's voice is subdued. "I'll get it. Thank you."

"You're welcome." Riley lowers the bag, starts to walk away. She stops, then turns toward the door.

"Wendy?"

"Yeah?"

"The other day, when you asked why I wish people would ignore me? I avoided giving an answer."

"Yes."

Riley looks up at the ugly ceiling. She thinks. Feeling some extra strength after opening up to Samantha about her story, she says, "Something bad happened to me several years ago. After that, people got very mean, and they kept being that way. It's not that I didn't trust you enough to explain. It's because talking about it makes me sad all over again."

"You don't have to talk about it if you don't want to."

"Thanks."

"Because I already know."

Riley gives the peephole a double take. "You do?"

"I may not leave this apartment, but TV is my world. And I never forget a face. I've known all along."

"And you don't—?"

"Nope. Don't give a rat's ass about what they say."

"Why not?"

Wendy falls silent for a few seconds, then, "Because you're kind. I can tell. And because for the first time in a long time, you make me feel like I matter."

Riley's heart fills with joy—something she hasn't felt for a long time.

31

"Hey, what are you doing?" Samantha asks.

"Not much." Riley rests the cell phone between her ear and shoulder while unloading groceries into a cabinet. She closes the door and spots her butcher knife in a half-opened drawer. It hasn't moved today. She's good.

"Riley?"

"Um, yeah. Sorry. I'm back after grocery shopping and looking for a job."

"Any luck this time?"

"Nothing."

"That sucks."

"Tell me about it. Hey, you mentioned maybe being able to help me find something?"

"I'm waiting for a few calls, so try not to stress too much, okay?"

"It's kind of unavoidable when there are bills to be paid."

"Not to worry, friend. I'm on it. In the meantime, if you need some extra cash . . ."

"Samantha . . ."

"I'm not saying—I'm just saying."

"I need to do things for myself."

"Okay, but the offer still stands."

"While we're on the subject of work, you kind of skirted around when I asked what you do for a living."

"Why don't you stop by and see?"

"Right now?"

"Well, you can get your stuff done first. I'll be here for a while."

Riley puts Samantha on speaker so she can add the address into her phone.

The rain has at last taken a hiatus, which is a relief, but . . .

This can't be right.

Riley pulls out her cell to recheck the address. She glances at the building, then again at her phone. Did she accidentally transpose two of the numbers?

This doesn't at all fit Samantha's fairy-tale world. A slick corner office with large windows in the better part of town, yes. But this? It's a dilapidated old redbrick warehouse. Light-gray stains of a nonspecific origin run down the building's front, punctuated by opaque windows, a few of them broken here and there. Off to one side, it looks as though someone used a wall and spray paint to practice their crossword-puzzle skills.

Tires screech. Riley recoils.

What would Samantha have to do with a place like this? She studies the entrance, sees a rather normal-looking guy on the approach. A few moments later, two women come out who also seem okay. Despite the run-down and abandoned appearance, the property seems to be in use, so Riley decides to at least give it a try.

Inside, she takes a freight elevator to the third level. After a jouncy and nerve-racking ride, Riley slides up the grated metal door, then walks out into a desolate hallway, its walls unevenly coated in numerous shades of paint, accented only by nicks and scratches and blemishes. Riley takes tentative steps toward the suite number Samantha gave her; although, *suite* seems like a stretch at best. Closer in, the sound of heavy grinding permeates the hallway, and the smell of hot metal burns through her sinuses.

Okay, this isn't funny at all.

Riley bends her neck around the door frame to see who's inside. Now she knows this can't be the right place, because some guy is at work there. Wearing a jumpsuit and welding helmet, he grinds away at a three-foot-tall hunk of metal, orange-and-blue sparks shooting in all directions.

"Excuse me?" Riley tries to talk above the noise, but the guy doesn't seem to hear her, so she edges closer, rocks back on her heels, shouts louder. "EXCUSE ME. SIR?"

The man turns off the grinder and pivots. He yanks off his helmet, and a long thatch of dark hair tumbles out. Samantha shakes her silky mane, allowing it to cascade past her shoulders.

She smirks.

Riley does her best to curb the expression of shock she knows is playing across her face.

"Well, don't just stand there," Samantha says. "Come on in!"

As Riley moves forward, she catches a strong whiff of melted wax and hot metal that nearly overcomes her.

"So, you wanted to know what I do?" Samantha motions around the room. "Welcome to my world."

"An interesting one, that's for damned sure, and I can't wait to learn about it, but I have to admit, the building threw me off."

"This one is super close to where I live, so here I am. I swear, the place feels more like home than my apartment."

"So . . . you grind things?"

"Well, some people consider it art." Samantha takes Riley past a room divider, and with a flourish waves her hand at a group of bronze statues.

"Holy . . . ," Riley says, walking toward them. "This is . . . amazing."

Samantha points to a pastel-blue sheet draped over a string of wire. "There are others behind this. I'd show you, but it's a huge mess back there right now."

"That's okay," Riley says. She walks closer to the sculptures and narrows her focus. The figures have a Gothic feel to them, winged creatures and hooded humans.

"Sorry for setting you up like this," Samantha says, then through one side of her mouth, "Bad friend alert: my sense of humor can be a little . . . offbeat at times? Not sure if you've picked up on that yet."

"I'm starting to." Riley can't help but notice that even in a filthy jumpsuit, the young woman still looks positively stunning.

Samantha places her helmet on the table.

Riley says, "This stuff is pretty dark."

"It's my therapy," Samantha says, observing her work. "I learned at an early age not to trust anyone except my mother. Then she was gone, and there was nobody else I could talk to. It was safer to express my feelings through art rather than discussing them. Even though these all look dreary, they actually save me every day. They're tangible embodiments of my pain. My sadness and anger."

"What about joy?"

"For a long time, there wasn't any to feel. My art is a reminder of how far I've come."

"Where do you find your ideas?"

Samantha reaches back and pulls her hair into a ponytail. Speaking around the tie in her mouth, she says, "They're not really my ideas. The creations speak to me. It's like they're trying to come out to see the world, and I'm helping them."

Riley walks over to the shapeless form Samantha was just working on and says, "What's going on here?"

Samantha slides her an impish grin and says, "Guess you'll have to wait and see."

"Oh, come on."

"Seriously. I never tell anyone what my projects will be until they're done."

"How come?"

"Mostly because a lot of times, even I don't know yet. I guess I'm not the kind of person who likes to make commitments." Samantha goes to a cabinet several feet away. She opens the door and removes a bottle of red wine. Holding it up, she says, "Quitting time. You in?"

"Let me think about that. Hell yes."

Samantha takes down a pair of wineglasses from a cabinet beside the other. "We can go to my favorite spot."

"How far is it?"

"Very close." Samantha points at the open window.

Riley shakes her head.

Samantha hands her the glasses. With the bottle in one hand, she proceeds toward the window and shoves a foot through the opening.

"Where are you going?"

"Come on," Samantha says before disappearing onto the roof.

By the time Riley makes it there, Samantha is already relaxing in a lounge chair and admiring the brilliant blood-orange sunset. She looks up at Riley and pats the chair beside her.

For a few moments, they sit side by side and absorb the tranquil surroundings. Samantha closes her eyes, draws an indulgent breath, then slowly lets it out through her smile. "This is my healing place. One of them."

"I can certainly understand why."

Samantha unzips the jumpsuit and shrugs it away to reveal the T-shirt and jeans that seem to be her trademark—and Riley understands the full context. Samantha pushes off each sneaker with the other foot and wiggles her toes.

She holds up her glass and says, "Here's to our new friendship in the midst of a mad, mad world."

32

Soothing silence has suffused the past hour.

The sun has fallen beneath the horizon, and a pale-pink moon takes charge. The air is much cooler at this hour, the night sky dark, thick, and boundless.

The two women relax and sip wine. Riley isn't supposed to be drinking while on her meds but figures a glass or two can't hurt.

"This night brings back memories," Riley says, breaking the quiet. "You're too young to know about this, but as a kid I watched one of the earlier space-shuttle *Columbia* liftoffs on TV. The crowd of onlookers, the bustling control room—the whole world—they were all looking on with such anticipation and enthusiasm. Later on, a news station revisited the empty launchpad. I'll never forget that moment. It was evening, and the setting looked much different, everything so positively still. All the excitement I'd seen earlier, all the vibrancy, was gone. I was staring into nothingness, and it kind of frightened me. I remember wishing I could have shot into space with those astronauts."

"What were you wanting to escape?"

"My loneliness. The feeling that there wasn't a place on this earth where I'd ever fit in."

Samantha reflects on the story. She says, "If only life could be that easy."

Riley lets out a mild laugh.

"What is it?"

"Your accent. It's more prominent when you're pensive."

"Hard as I try to rid myself of it . . ."

"Why? It's charming. Where are you from, anyway?"

"Georgia. Athens."

"All those painful emotions you spoke of earlier—did they come from Athens, too?"

Samantha sinks back into the chair and says, "It's an ugly story."

"What happened?"

She tilts her wineglass back and forth, gazing sadly at the red liquid as it splashes against the sides. "I told you my mother killed herself, but I left out the details." She takes a long swallow of wine. "I found her hanging from a rail in her bedroom closet."

Riley pulls her head back to study Samantha.

"She was the only person I ever loved," Samantha continues. "The only person who ever loved me. Then, like that, she was gone. Didn't even leave me a note."

"Do you know why she did it?"

"Hell yeah, I know. It was because of my father."

Riley doesn't ask the next question. She knows there's a lot more of Samantha's grim story to come.

"He was a monster. The worst kind. For years, I watched him abuse my mother both physically and emotionally, but I was too young to stop it. She eventually believed there was only one way out. But for me it ended up being the worst way imaginable. As if the trauma of finding her dead and hanging from that rail wasn't enough, she also left me behind to become his new designated punching bag.

He'd beat the shit out of me." She scoffs. "I used to call them the rainy days."

"Why?"

"Because it always rained after he was done."

"Really?"

"I'd feel the drops on my face, and it seemed so refreshing, cleansing, even, and I'd smile, but when I looked up, there weren't any clouds—there was only the ceiling. I was a little girl when the abuse started, didn't really understand, so I'd wonder where the rain was coming from." Samantha tries to smile now, but it's a sad one. "It took me a while to realize they were my own tears."

"Oh, sweetie," Riley says, feeling her shoulders collapse.

But not a single tear falls from Samantha's eyes. She seems so closed off, so guarded or . . . disconnected? She says, "He told the school I was accident-prone, that I fell against a cabinet, or ran into the kitchen counter, or . . . whatever. I swear, the man knew how to play people like greased keys on a grand piano."

"And they believed him."

With a demoralized expression, Samantha says, "Eventually, he got smarter. He hit me in places that weren't visible. But you know what? During the awful moments when he'd throw me against walls or drive a fist into my gut? It was my mother I hated most. She took the easy way out, even when she knew I'd have to pay the price for it. As far as I'm concerned, she was a coward and as much to blame."

Riley keeps silent. Her agreement is implicit.

"A mother is supposed to protect her child," Samantha says, the words coming out fast as if they can no longer be held inside.

Riley places a hand on Samantha's shoulder and gently rubs in a slow, soothing motion.

"My mom left me so damned hungry for love that, out of desperation, I went to her sister for comfort. You know how kids are. In my sad little girl's mind, I thought maybe she could replace some of the love I'd lost."

"Did she?"

"It was all so completely harmless, but she didn't see it that way. She rejected me—not only that but in the cruelest way possible. Every time I tried to get close to her, she'd shout at me, 'I'm not your mother!' Can you imagine? After what I'd already been through? It hurt so much. The woman ripped a new hole right through my heart."

"That had to be horribly painful."

Through an angry, perhaps even hateful, whisper: "You have no idea." Louder now: "But my father finally got his. A few years later, he died from a massive heart attack. Suddenly, I was an orphan. After that, the pain kept coming. I bounced from foster home to foster home until I was eighteen. All because of my selfish, heartless parents."

"But look at you today. You've really turned everything around."

Samantha snorts. "Thanks to my father's fat life insurance policy. He left it all to me, but not out of love. It was his final shot. The sadist wanted me to feel guilty for hating him. I guess he figured that with every penny I spent, I'd have to think of him. But it didn't work that way. I gladly took every bit of the money. It was a payback well earned."

"You're a strong woman, Samantha Light. I'm glad you survived, and I'm so happy I've gotten to know you."

"It's interesting how we've come to this point. Don't you think?"

"What's that?"

"We've both been trying to heal from mother-daughter relationships that were taken from us, and now we're finally getting the chance."

Riley's lips part ever so slightly.

"Oh hell," Samantha says. "That came out completely wrong. I know I'll never replace Clarissa. Gosh, I wouldn't even think of trying. What I meant was that our commonalities feel sort of healing."

"It's okay. I got what you meant."

"But maybe I could be like a second daughter. You know?"

33

The evening with Samantha, with its intense emotion, has worn Riley out. All she wants now is to be home, crawl under the covers, and grab hold of the rest she craves.

But after pulling into her spot at the apartment building, she notices another plain, dark sedan rolling into the lot—one that looks a lot like the car she spotted that evening after Erin came by. The vehicle makes a slow crawl to another end of the lot and parks facing her. The engine turns off, then the lights, but nobody leaves the car.

My watcher.

An instant warning fires off deep in her bones that the car has followed her here. She remains in place and waits to see whether the driver takes action or stays put.

Another vehicle swerves into the lot, this one a dark SUV. Its headlights flash through Mystery Sedan's windshield, lighting up the interior, and an icy chill shimmies up her spine when she sees two eyes looking directly into hers.

Commotion to the left. Two people leave the SUV and casually walk toward the building.

Just neighbors.

Mystery Sedan's engine turns over, its headlights cutting a swath through darkness, then it takes off for the exit.

They're gone. It's over.

But her trepidation is not. She starts to string together all the unnerving incidents that have occurred outside her apartment ever since she came to Rainbow Valley.

The invisible tracker who followed her home from the store that early morning.

The unidentifiable figure who, just the other evening, like a fleeting shadow, disappeared from her lot and into the darkness. Two visits from Mystery Sedan, and this time, someone inside with those shrouded eyes.

Are they all the same person? A group?

Either way, Riley knows her safety is in question.

34

Several times throughout the night, Riley is awakened by her own panicky screams. Every dream is the same: she sees a faceless person rocking in the chair near her window. Then she jolts into wakefulness and sees the rocker is empty, and a new kind of fear kicks in, one laced with agitated turmoil. The entire process lasts less than a minute, but it goes on in a continual loop until morning.

The sun rises, but it carries the harsh message that rest has become more of a desire than a possibility, so she takes action. She dials the locksmith and can practically hear the guy grinning through the phone when she asks about installing a security bar across the door. Probably because she's making steady contributions to his kid's college fund. It doesn't matter. This is just to keep her safe until she can finish what she needs to do in this town, then leave for someplace better.

After he finishes, she takes a moment to admire the work. Since the bar goes on from the inside, it will protect her only while she's at home, but it's sturdier than the portable door jammer she bought, so at least she'll feel safer during sleep.

She goes to her bedroom and lays out Clarissa's clothes for the day: a violet, sleeveless halter-top dress. She smiles at a memory as she smooths her hand over the dress's soft cotton fabric. Clarissa wore this exact outfit for the father-daughter fund-raiser she organized at school to benefit the local children's hospital. That was Clarissa, always hopeful, always wanting to change the world. Jason was so proud of her as she walked up to the podium and delivered her heart-warming speech for the event. Riley remembers him telling her how he fought back tears of pride.

Now she frowns.

And talks to the clothes.

"You grew up too fast," she says, voice wrecked, while she blinks out a tear.

After a trip to the store, Riley stops at Wendy's place and knocks. A moment later, she hears footsteps, then the peephole goes dark. She holds up a bag of groceries.

"They didn't have the brand of rye bread that you wanted," she says to the door, "so I grabbed another. Hope that'll be okay."

"I'm sure it's fine. Thank you. Go ahead and leave the bag. I'll grab it."

"Why don't you open the door so I can hand it to you?"

"That won't be necessary."

The conversation flatlines.

Riley tries to resuscitate it. "Do you ever get the urge to really do it? To step outside, even if only for a moment?"

No answer, but Riley can tell her neighbor is thinking about it.

"All the time," Wendy softly says.

"What stops you?"

"Lots of things."

"The other day you mentioned fear."

"I also mentioned that I didn't want to talk about it."

"But I'd like to know."

"Why?"

Riley stares at the closed door. "Because of what you said about me. That I care."

More quiet, but this time the air is so thick with unease that Riley can almost reach out and hold it in her hands.

She tries again. "You said I'm the only one who makes you feel like you matter."

"I know."

"So you can trust me."

A long pause.

"You have to know that I only want to help," Riley urges. "Right?"

"I . . . I'm afraid of . . ." Wendy's voice trembles and fails as if she's battling over her next sentence. Then it rapidly spills out. "I'm afraid I'll die out there."

Riley's only response is a weighted breath.

"I bet that sounds kind of weird, huh?" Wendy says.

"No, not at all, actually."

"Really?"

Riley scrubs a hand over her face. "I'm already out here, and sometimes I feel like that's exactly what's happening to me."

35

Smoky gray-blue clouds mottle the skies, their iridescent edges occasionally pulling apart wide enough to let shafts of sunlight through. In those moments, wet leaves and flowers become shimmering diamonds. Puddles dance.

Riley and Samantha stroll around the lake, enjoying fresh air bathed by recent showers.

"Is it always so wet here?" Samantha asks while looking down at a thirsty concrete sidewalk still trying to absorb the moisture.

A nearby bush shakes.

Someone could be hiding behind it, watching me.

Stop it!

"Riley? You okay?

"Yes. Fine. Sorry," she answers, trying to chase away her invasive feelings of vulnerability and danger.

"So, the rain?"

"The rain. Not always, but we do get our share of storms this time of year."

"I'm going to say we've had enough."

"And I'm going to agree with you."

They pass the bush, pass a small pond, then find a dry bench to sit on.

"I was wondering about something," Samantha says, cupping a hand to her forehead and squinting at Riley through a burst of sunlight. "Tell me if I'm being too nosy, but how have you been able to cope with Clarissa's murderer never being found?"

"I suppose the short answer would be that I haven't. After instantly becoming the suspect, I never had a chance. Each day was about surviving until the next one."

"I honestly don't know how you did it."

"I don't, either." Riley observes two yellow Labs off in the distance. Running swiftly side by side, their movements seem so harmoniously choreographed, their happiness so nearly tangible, that it's as though they've been waiting their whole lives to unravel the joy of this moment. "I guess you never know how much strength you have until strength is your only option."

"I like that." Samantha nods. "What a great outlook during the bad times."

"I didn't think it up myself. I saw it on the internet."

The two women laugh.

Samantha says, "And here I thought you were getting all Zen and shit."

"Believe me, if I were that wise, I would have handled life a lot better than I did."

"Considering the circumstances, it sounds to me like you did as well as anyone could have."

"Oh, I don't know, Samantha. I just don't know about anything anymore."

"Have you ever had suspicions about who might have killed Clarissa?"

Riley's intonation becomes somber, her face, too, when she says, "*A suspicion.*"

"Who?"

"Another long story."

Samantha shrugs. "I want to hear all of it."

Riley looks upward to gather her thoughts, to travel through time. Through the heartbreak. The sorrow. The anguish. She can still feel her emotional paralysis, which became all too familiar during that period.

"Before Clarissa died," Riley starts off, "she made friends with a classmate named Rose Hopkins. A very quiet, very introverted kid. She didn't have a whole lot going for herself. You know the type. The social outcast? The loner?"

Samantha nods.

"But my Clarissa had a heart of gold—she was the kid who took in injured birds—so one night she invited Rose over for dinner. It was a colossal mistake, one we'd all regret. Nobody saw it at first, but this was an extremely disturbed child dressed in injured bird's clothing."

Samantha leans in toward Riley and says, "How did you figure it out?"

"Because her innocent desire changed into a full-fledged obsession."

"What was the obsession?"

"Me."

"I'm not following."

"Rose tried desperately to make me her mother."

"*What?* Why?"

"Her real mom was having an affair. One day, she and the guy took off together."

"Poor kid."

"I didn't know her when it happened, but by the time we met, Rose was already adrift in the world. Then she got fixated on me."

"A case of mother envy?"

"Worse than that. Rose wasn't just envious of my and Clarissa's relationship—she wanted it for herself, but by the time I figured that out, it was too late."

"How did you miss it?"

"Everything started out so innocently. This child's pain was palpable. She was sad and aching for love. Growing up, I was also a loner, so I felt sorry for her and made a few small attempts to smooth over the rough patch she'd fallen into."

"She got too attached," Samantha says.

"That would be putting it mildly. Clingy and disruptive is more like it. Then the accident with my husband happened, which took her to a new level."

"What happened?"

"I told you he died, but I never gave the whole story."

She tells Samantha about the camping trip and the accident that ended Jason's life.

"The moment he went off the edge, it was like Rose's mind did the same. It was the breaking point, when her reality started to bend and buckle. The situation got out of control in a hurry."

"How?"

"With Jason gone, Rose decided I needed her more than ever and that she was the only one who could help me heal from my loss. She no longer just thought of me as her mother—she began to *believe* I was. This child invented a brand-new truth for herself, wouldn't let go of it, and in the process turned our lives upside down."

"You couldn't stop her?"

"I couldn't *escape* her. Not with Rose and Clarissa going to the same school where I taught. Between classes, she'd come running up to me in the hallway with this exuberant smile, calling me Mommy. On one side, it was unnerving, but as a teacher who, for years, saw so many broken children, it was hard to watch this little girl bleed out emotionally right in front of me."

"While dealing with the loss of your husband at the same time, no less."

"But that was only the beginning."

"It got worse?"

"Much worse. She began sneaking into our house. We'd come home and find her sprawled out on the living room floor, doing her homework. Then she started competing with my daughter for attention. One time, Clarissa got a bit mouthy with me. Rose stepped in and scolded her, saying, 'Don't you dare talk to Mother that way!' She actually thought they were sisters. She went from needy to downright frightening. Her weird behavior escalated so fast that it made my head spin. It was like the kid could walk through walls, which made it even harder to keep tabs on her. Soon, personal items started to go missing. My jewelry, clothing, even my lipstick. I almost flipped one day when she walked through the door wearing it."

Samantha quivers at the image.

"I know," Riley says. "It was all so alarming. Rose was stealing mementos so she could feel even closer to me while we were apart. A fifteen-year-old girl was stalking me like an adult."

"Did you call the police?"

"I was hesitant to bring them into it. I mean, she was just a kid, and I'd hoped to resolve this by talking to her father."

"What did he say?"

"I tried several times to reach him, but there was no answer. He didn't even return my calls. Finally, I had to stop by their house. He was shocked, said he had no idea she'd been doing all this, which actually shocked me, too. How can you have such a troubled kid and not notice?"

"You do. You have to, right?"

Riley blows out a weary breath and shakes her head. "That's what I thought, which left me wondering, had she fooled even him, or was he trying to hide what he already knew about her?"

Goose bumps spring up along Samantha's arms. She tries to rub them away with a hand. "This is such a strange and frightening story."

"Here's where it gets *really* disturbing." Just thinking about what she's going to say makes an eerie sensation wriggle down Riley's back. "After I spoke to Rose's dad, he decided to ground her. That night, I woke up to a strange noise, and it took a second or two to find my bearings and realize where the sound was coming from. I felt a warm and wet sensation on my body. I looked down and screamed. Rose was in bed with me, curled against my chest and—"

"No. Oh hell no!" Samantha says, raising both hands in the air, shaking her head back and forth.

"—trying to breastfeed, but even creepier was the way she looked up at me." Riley shudders. "Like a helpless baby. It made my bones freeze."

Samantha moves away from Riley as if the distance might help ease her rattled nerves. "What on earth did you do?"

"I jumped out of bed, yelled at her, and said that if she ever showed up in our home again—or anywhere near it—I'd call the police and have her taken away. But as I spoke, I saw a cloud move through that child's eyes. It wasn't anger. It was something else. Like I'd snipped a hazardous hot wire. Right then, I knew Rose had moved to a new level, that she'd become even more dangerous. The next night, I pulled away my sheets. Across my pillow, with the lipstick she'd stolen, she'd written the question, 'Why Mommy? Why?'"

"Holy shit . . ."

"Got that right. For the next several weeks, I was worried Rose would come back and try to do us harm, but she never showed up again. In a way, that was scarier because I couldn't shake the feeling she was still out there, still watching me. Then Clarissa was murdered. Not long after, I found out Rose and her father had moved away."

"You think he knew?"

"I never understood what the hell he knew, but I'll tell you what. It was nothing good."

Like a dying bloom, the skies shrink and close, and darkness returns, and the air turns cold.

Like the start to a finish.

36

Both women are quiet on the way back to their cars.

There is no break in the clouds, no sunshine, just shades of gray overcast chased by an oncoming dusk.

At their cars, Samantha asks, "Did you tell anyone about your suspicion that Rose killed Clarissa?"

"I did. When I first told Erin that one of Clarissa's friends had been acting obsessive, she went down to the school to check out the situation but didn't get far. Sure, a couple of teachers agreed that once or twice Rose had called me Mommy, but they said it didn't raise any flags for them, that it seemed pretty innocent, and they thought I might have been overreacting."

"Erin didn't believe you?"

"It was more like she couldn't find enough convincing evidence."

"But you told her about the really crazy stuff, right?"

"Erin was on vacation in Ireland when that part started. By the time she came back two weeks later, it was all over. I told her what had happened, but since there wasn't much else to do, we let it go. Then after my daughter was murdered, I explained my suspicion about

Rose, but Erin's a lawyer. She said all I had was a suspicion but no solid evidence."

"What about all the horrible things Rose did to you? Wasn't that enough proof?"

"The only person who could corroborate the story was Clarissa, and she was gone. With Erin's visit to the school not panning out—and my deteriorating mental state—she was getting skeptical."

"But the message Rose wrote on your pillow. That was solid evidence, right?"

"I showed it to Erin, and that convinced her to give this one last try, but it ended up being the deal breaker. We went to Rose's house, and that was when I found out they'd moved."

"Couldn't Erin go to the police and have them track Rose down?"

"She had no interest. Seeing the empty house only raised her doubt. It didn't matter what I said after that."

"But she's your sister. How could she not believe you?"

"That's a more involved, historical discussion. Anyway, with the head injury, the memory issues, and my mind going downhill, my information seemed unreliable."

"Couldn't you have brought that pillowcase to the police?"

"What was the point? All it said was, 'Why Mommy? Why?' which proved absolutely nothing. I did try to tell Sloan about Rose, but by then she was already convinced I'd killed my daughter. I'm sure she thought I was cooking up evidence to take the suspicion off myself. And pointing my finger at a child? That not only further chipped away at my credibility—it also painted me as a bigger villain."

"So she ignored a lead from the victim's mother?"

"The cops went through the motions and looked into it but said they found nothing to support my theory. That didn't come as much of a surprise. I'm sure they didn't look too hard, and like I said, this kid never left tracks."

"I'm sorry," Samantha says, obstinately shaking her head, "but I would have gone right back to the police, and I wouldn't have stopped until they listened."

"Oh, I did, but by then I'd already started losing my mind, and anything I said just made me look crazier. I kept walking into the station, and the cops kept kicking me to the curb."

Samantha lifts her hair with both hands and lets it drop past her shoulders. "You slipped through the cracks. You were completely railroaded. You know that, right?"

"I do."

"But it's never too late to find justice."

"Justice was all I ever wanted."

"This is total bullshit!" Samantha lets out a heavy breath, purses her lips, then says, "We could nail her for the murder once and for all. I can help find her. Do you have anything else? Like where Rose might be living these days?"

"I've got nothing. And at this point, I wonder if it would even matter. Nobody bought my story the first time."

"Let's start looking. Seriously, we could do this."

Riley tries to give it some thought, but her mind is worn down by the surge of memories she's shared. "I don't know what to think anymore, Samantha. It would help if Erin believed me, but that ship sailed long ago."

"For Chrissakes! I understand why you think she didn't believe you—although I don't agree with it—but the other part, the one you said is complicated?"

"My mental disorder was like feeding a monster, and now it's bigger than us both. The relationship has suffered so much damage that I'm afraid we may not stand a good chance of repairing it."

"This is so heartbreaking." Samantha thinks about that. "And I can understand your pain. Not the same way, but I understand it.

I know what it's like having to fight through a world where there's nobody to stand beside you."

Riley considers her for a moment, then swiftly looks toward the lake. She rubs a palm up and down the center of her chest as if by doing so she might, for once, be able to mend deep emotional wounds left by years of trauma, by two sisters who once cared so very much for each other.

"What is it?" Samantha asks.

Riley is still looking at the lake. She shakes her head.

"Riley."

No answer.

"Riley," Samantha again says. "You can tell me."

"It's just that . . . I feel so untethered, so completely . . ."

"Lost? Alone."

She at last looks at Samantha and nods.

Samantha says, "Maybe we can find our way back together."

37

Riley and Samantha have been nearly inseparable for the past few weeks. When they aren't together, they're chatting by phone like girlfriends who have known each other all their lives.

Riley rests in a brown beanbag chair at the studio, sipping wine while Samantha works on one of her creations: a woman spreading her wings.

"So, tell me," Riley says, "what do you love most about doing this?"

"Gosh, there are so many parts. I feel like I could list them all day long." Samantha steps back to inspect her work. "It's the smell of melting wax and hot metals. Feeling the warm, wet clay in my hands. Running my palms over the finished surface. But most of all, it's the excitement of watching essentially nothing turn into something that deeply moves me."

"Sounds like quite an experience."

"It's indescribable, a mind-body-and-soul kind of thing. It's my true north."

"True north?"

"It's like we come into this world with no direction and spend the rest of our lives trying to find one. If we're lucky—and few of us are—we stumble across the path that leads us right to it." Samantha goes back to her work.

Riley asks, "What's that you're doing?"

"I'm applying acid and heat to give the bronze a patina effect."

"What happened before now?"

"A lot. First, I had to sculpt a clay model, then I covered that in silicone rubber, followed by plaster, which formed a mold, preserving all the details of the original. Then, when I removed the plaster and rubber mold, I had an exact negative of the original. There are a few more steps using molten wax and other materials before the bronze is poured, but I won't bore you with those. You get the idea."

"Who do you sell these to once they're finished?"

"Private buyers, a lot of them through my website and other channels, but my goal is to eventually open my own gallery."

"Wow. I guess I had no idea so much work was involved in all this."

Samantha kneels and continues applying the acid. "It probably seems that way, but when you're passionate about something, it never feels like work. I kind of separate from myself in the process. It's a glorious feeling."

"How so? How's that glorious?"

Samantha looks at her for a moment as if she's thinking about an answer. "Detaching can be an escape. Sometimes it just seems safer on the outside than inside my head."

Riley lowers a brow, then finds distraction by checking out the mystery statue, no longer a solitary block with what appears to be the start of a head resting at its base. Just a head.

Samantha sees Riley's interest but doesn't respond to it.

Riley says, "I'm assuming there will eventually be a body to go with that head."

"Yes." Samantha laughs. "There will."

"Still won't tell me what it's going to be?"

"Still going to keep asking?"

"Probably."

Samantha picks up her wine and sips, then says, "I've got works in progress all over this room. Why so much interest in that one?"

"I don't know. Maybe because I saw it from the start? Seems more mysterious that way."

Samantha bobs her head from side to side. "I guess I can see that."

"So, does my very astute artistic interpretation merit an answer now?"

"Nope."

"How come?"

"It doesn't work that way," she playfully says. "You know the rule of the land here."

"'I never tell anyone what my projects will be until they're done,'" Riley mocks.

"You got it."

Samantha puts down the brush and container, takes off her glasses, and places them nearby. She walks up to Riley and stares at her for a long moment.

"What's wrong?"

Samantha lifts a tuft of hair on each side of Riley's head, lets them fall, then examines her face.

"*What?*" Riley again asks.

"So, don't take this wrong, but I would love to help get you a makeover."

"What exactly are you telling me here? How awful I look?"

"Oh, like I'd really say that!" Samantha laughs. "No, you nut! You're a very attractive woman."

"For my age . . ."

"It's not that at all. But I feel like you're hiding what works for you. Look, after hearing about your past, I've realized how much you've been through these last several years. I was just thinking maybe some new clothes and a fresh cut and color might lift your spirits."

Samantha's intent seems innocent enough. Riley looks down at the worn and nicked heels on her shoes. "I actually have been thinking lately that maybe it's time for a new look. And you clearly know a lot about style and fashion. I could probably use your advice."

"I do love me a project," Samantha says. "Let's do this! I've got a girl. She's new to the salon and doesn't have a big client list yet. I could call and see if she's got anything open in the next few days."

"Gosh, Samantha. I don't know if I can afford—"

"Don't worry about the money. It's my treat."

"No. Absolutely not. I won't let you."

"Nonsense. This was my idea. Besides, what's the purpose of having all that bastard's money if I can't use it to help out a friend?"

"But hair and clothes? It's too expensive."

"Riley, when's the last time you did something nice for yourself?"

"I don't remember."

"My point exactly. You totally deserve this."

Riley's eyes scan Samantha's, searching for the assurance she needs to say yes. She thinks on it, then, more definitively, maybe even a little excitedly, says, "Okay, but only if you let me pay you back."

"Not necessary."

"I mean it!"

"Okay! Whatever. You can pay me back someday."

Samantha's phone goes off. She lifts it from a table and slants her head sideways to check the screen, grimaces, and says, "Ugh. A business call. Can you give me a minute while I take it?" She carries her phone into the hallway and starts talking.

Riley looks at Samantha's eyeglasses while she waits, then lifts them. So classy. So smart-looking. She tries them on.

So . . . fake?

38

Samantha locks up her studio, and they stop at a French restaurant for lunch—a very expensive French restaurant. As always, money is no issue, so when the check arrives, Samantha takes out the plastic and, like that, makes it go away.

Riley can't stop looking at her glasses.

On their way back, Samantha invites Riley to see her place. After previewing that fancy lobby, Riley is dying to see what the apartment looks like.

"It's a little messy right now," Samantha says as they walk along the mezzanine that leads to her apartment. "The cleaning girl doesn't come until tomorrow."

Riley nods. Of course Samantha has a cleaning girl. Samantha has everything.

At the door, Riley looks on while Samantha punches in numbers on the keypad.

0808

A rather simple code for such high-security digs, Riley thinks. *Much simpler than that gate code I made off with.*

As she expected, the place is expansive and gorgeous. The living room floor is covered with dark wood that does not look like laminate. Even the lighting is top-notch and stylish. Black domed lamps hover at varying heights like flying saucers coming in for a landing.

She won't be seeing my place, that's for sure, she decides, then wonders what Samantha would say if she knew Riley's dump was right next to this building.

And that sofa set . . . soft, supple leather! Her favorite. The mark of extravagance. Riley walks up to it, breathes in its glorious smell, and runs her hand across one of the pillows, admiring the look and feel of it, the quiet, rugged beauty, sexy and sumptuous and classy all at the same time. Temptation takes hold, and all she can think about is falling into the plush leather cushions, then leaning back and drowning herself in the pleasure.

She goes for it.

"That was the first piece of furniture I bought for this apartment," Samantha yells from the kitchen. "I absolutely love leather. So strong and soft at the same time. Don't you think?"

"Uh-*huh*," Riley quickly responds with enthusiasm she can't contain.

She leaves the couch to join Samantha in the kitchen. There, it's all about the built-in stainless steel appliances, accentuated by red-and-black-spattered granite countertops.

"Samantha," Riley says, "your place is great."

"Oh, you're so sweet to say that," Samantha replies with her silver-tongued southern twang. She grabs the handle on her refrigerator door, then adds, "I really do like it here."

What's not to like?

When Samantha opens her fridge, there isn't much food to speak of inside, but she definitely likes her vitamin waters and cold-pressed juices, which stand tall and in great numbers, filling every shelf, including the ones on the side. Even her vegetable bins are crammed with drinks.

Samantha notices Riley noticing the lack of food. With a bashful smile and shrug, she says, "I do a lot of takeout. It's easier."

Riley acknowledges the comment with a single downward bob of her head, and Samantha asks her which drink she'd like. Riley opts for the blue vitamin water. Even though she has no idea what blue is supposed to taste like, the idea intrigues her.

"Let's show you around," Samantha cheerily says after grabbing herself a bottle filled with a liquid that looks like green, sludgy plant matter.

Samantha's sleeping quarters are almost as big as Riley's entire apartment. A California king bed, indeed fit for a king, rests in the room's center and faces a series of floor-to-ceiling windows, which boast a much more flattering view than Riley's place ever could. Stylish furniture pieces made of sleek ebony rest beneath recessed ceiling lights that fill in all the right spaces, showering them with soft, pale-blue illumination.

Riley absorbs downtown's dramatic skyline and nearly has to catch her breath. Never before in her life has she seen anything like this. Never before has she experienced on such an intimate level how remarkable a privileged life can feel. The kind of life she and Jason would sometimes dream about. But deep down, they always knew that as long as they had each other, it would be enough.

Samantha appraises the view as if it were her kingdom, then through a long sigh says, "My Lord, I wonder what all the poor people are doing today."

Riley flinches.

Samantha says, "I'm totally kidding!" She gives Riley a playful shove.

Riley's smile feels tiny.

"Sorry," Samantha says, looking down and placing a finger against her lips to suppress the grin. "Everyone tells me I've got a weird sense of humor."

Riley cuts herself loose from the conversation by finding distraction in the bigger-than-big-screen TV mounted to a wall. She examines the bed's positioning and asks, "How in the world can you watch television without getting a crick in your neck?"

"Jump on and see!"

Riley does.

"Go ahead," Samantha urges her. "Make yourself comfortable."

Riley does that, too. She sinks into the silky down pillows, then lets out a screech of surprise when the bed vibrates and rotates toward the big screen. She looks at Samantha, standing a few feet away, aiming a remote at her and giggling.

"Oh. That's how," Riley says, trying for carefree.

"Pretty cool, right?"

"Pretty damned amazing is more like it."

Samantha waves off the comment. "It's just stuff."

Riley sits up to visually assess Samantha, who responds by angling her head.

"Where does all your complexity come from?" Riley asks.

"The School of Hard Knocks?"

"One thing we've got in common."

"We have plenty in common," Samantha says. "More than we probably realize, I'll bet."

39

"Oh my Lord," Samantha breathlessly says, clutching Riley by the shoulder with one hand and pointing with the other. "Would you look at those shoes? They're gorgeous!"

"Four-and-a-half-inch red pumps aren't exactly my style, but you'd look amazing in them."

Samantha lifts one to examine it, and her face lights up like a pinball machine. "My size, too. Seems like they're meant to be." She puts them back and moves on.

"Aren't you going to buy them?"

"I don't know." Samantha shrugs. "Maybe I'll grab them later. Let's take care of you first—that's what we came here for."

About fifteen minutes later, Riley steps out of the dressing room to model a pair of blue jeans and a white top beneath a red leather jacket. She readjusts the waist, then self-consciously tugs the jacket lower.

"Quit fussing." Samantha rises from the waiting chair and walks up to Riley. She repositions the collar and says, "Perfect. You look awesome in this."

"I look like a wilting American flag."

"Now stop that. You do not."

"It's awful contemporary for this body. Feels like I'm trying too hard."

"Are you kidding? You can totally pull it off. Trust me, that looks amazing. We're grabbing the whole outfit for sure. Now go try on the others." Samantha retreats to her chair.

Slap, slap, slap.

Riley's eyes whisk toward the source.

With one leg crossed over the other, Samantha flexes her foot, forcing the heel on her shoe to snap on and off. She notices Riley's startled expression, cringes, and stops. "Sorry . . . it's one of those annoying habits I've never been able to shake. Like cracking your knuckles. I swear, half the time I don't even realize I'm doing it."

Riley relaxes. It's just a coincidence, a common behavior lots of women have. This has nothing to do with Patricia. Through a conciliatory laugh, she says, "Don't even worry about it. We all have our hang-ups."

"Hell, I've got so many I'd lose count trying to tally them all up. Oh, hey, I want you to try on another top I love." Samantha snaps her fingers at a teenage salesgirl and says, "Yoo-hoo. You! Go and fetch me that emerald top I saw earlier."

Teen Clerk shakes her head.

"For heaven's sake, you saw me looking right at it. Don't you remember?"

The girl appears to be putting her mind into rewind. She shakes her head again.

Samantha's laugh shows shades of irritation. "Never mind. I'll find it." She rolls her eyes at Riley, then walks out onto the floor.

Teen Clerk looks apologetic. Riley offers her a peacemaking expression and says, "She's just feeling a little rushed today."

The girl tries to shrug it off, and Riley goes into her dressing room to try on a few more items.

Minutes later, Samantha knocks on the door. Riley opens it and peers through the gap to find her holding up the blouse.

"Right?" Samantha says, baby blues dancing with zeal. "What did I tell you? Absolutely beautiful, yes?"

Riley takes it and closes the door. When she emerges wearing the top, Samantha says, "I adore this. It's gorgeous. We're buying that one, too."

"We've already done a lot of damage. There's got to be over a thousand dollars' worth of clothing in those shopping bags. I think maybe we should call this a day."

"Please, this is nothing. You should see me when *I'm* out doing retail therapy. What you have here is a mere fraction of what I can run up. I'm constantly finding clothes in my closet I don't even remember buying. It's like a sickness."

"But in those cases, you're spending the money on yourself, not me."

"Riley, please. Let's not do this again. You're my friend. You've been through a rough period. I'm helping you out a little. Besides, I get something out of this, too."

"Yeah, the bill."

"No, not *the bill*." Samantha gives Riley another of her playful shoves. "For real, I can afford this. I love to buy people things. That's how I am. It makes me feel better about myself."

Riley blinks at her.

Before Samantha can respond, a commotion starts up across the room. An older clerk is questioning the teenage salesgirl, but from this far away it's difficult to hear the conversation.

Teen Clerk presses both hands against her cheeks and shakes her head. Lady Clerk walks away, shaking hers.

"I'm sorry!" the girl says to the woman loud enough that Riley and Samantha can hear her.

"I wonder what that was all about," Riley remarks.

"I'd say the kid didn't do what she was supposed to, and someone opened a can of whoop-ass on her." Samantha glances down at her watch and says, "Hey, we need to pay for this stuff and jam. You've got a hair appointment in a few minutes."

40

Zoey, Samantha's new stylist, is probably not much older than Samantha. A rocker, for sure, as illustrated by the black and faded Foo Fighters concert tee, but girlfriend's got a lot more than that going on. She wears the obligatory wire nose ring, and her hair is quite interesting. The base color is blonde: blonde as blonde can be, almost white, accented by tendrils of many colors, which look like they shot out from a Play-Doh can. Some green here, blue there, and pink in other places.

Despite Zoey's rock-and-roll fantasy, the salon is well-appointed, the theme a brand of industrial chic. Metal pipes painted black crisscross high ceilings that meet redbrick walls, the room fronted by windows made entirely of refurbished factory-paned glass. The appointment won't be cheap. Not that it matters. Samantha is footing this one, too.

Riley sits in the hairstylist's chair and thumbs through a cut-and-color book she's been considering for the last five minutes or so. Samantha looks on, sipping her fourth glass of wine, which comes courtesy of the salon.

"I like this one." Riley points to one of the pages.

Samantha drinks some wine and considers it. She swallows fast, shakes her head, and says, "I don't think that will work for you, sweetie. Her hair is longer, and the style doesn't fit the shape of your face."

Riley flips through more pages, then stops and says, "Ooh, I love this!"

Samantha again shakes her head. "The color's all wrong. Too light. It doesn't match your skin tone." She considers Zoey for support.

"Oh, I don't know . . . ," Zoey says. "We might be able to make it work with the right highlights."

"I'm thinking you'll need to go much darker," Samantha insists. She steps in closer, almost loses her footing, then saves herself, but not before nearly spilling wine onto Riley's shoulder.

"Floor's a little uneven in that one spot right there," she burbles under her breath, then clumsily sets her glass on the console. She takes the book from Riley and says, "I'll find you something."

Riley waits and observes Zoey, who makes a valiant effort to hide her growing impatience—an attempt foiled by the periodic checking of her watch. But oddly, she doesn't seem the least bit concerned about Samantha's drinking, which makes Riley think this is not an unusual situation.

Samantha's face brightens. She turns the book around and says, "This."

"That?"

"Yes. It would be perfect on you."

It looks exactly like Samantha's—same dark shade, same cut. Riley stares at the page, unsure what to say or even how to say it.

"Well?" she prompts. "What do you think?"

"Samantha, this is the same as yours."

"No, it's not."

"Yes, it is."

With unsteady hands, Samantha holds the book farther away, studies it, and says, "Okay, maybe it's kind of similar."

Riley examines the page again. Are they looking at two different pictures? She points to the photo and says, "That one, right?"

Samantha gives her a quick nod and grin.

Riley labors to sound self-reliant when she says, "I just don't want to have hair like yours. I want my own."

Zoey has taken to organizing hair products on a shelf, clearly pretending she can't hear a conversation on the verge of boiling over.

"I really don't see what the problem is," Samantha says through mild laughter that sounds a tad more critical than reassuring. "You have to trust me here. I really know what I'm talking about when it comes to this stuff. Just do it. You'll love it once it's done. Zoey? Come here and see—"

"No!" Riley explodes, feeling cornered and bullied. "I said no!"

Samantha takes a step back and shoots her a wide-eyed stare.

"I'm sorry," Riley says, trying to speak calmer, "but you weren't listening to me. I don't want your hair."

Samantha nods toward the top of Riley's head and says, "You think *that* looks any better?"

"Okay, now you're just being cruel. I didn't come here to be insulted."

"Oh, come on . . ." Samantha's expression softens. Her tone is placating. "You know I didn't mean it that way."

"I really don't see how it could mean anything else."

"I just can't win here." Samantha throws up her hands in frustration. "I won't say another word."

The only sounds at the moment are loud, staccato ticks from Samantha's shoes as they march across the tiled floor toward the waiting area. She takes her seat.

Riley leaves her chair and follows. Standing before Samantha, she asks, "What's gotten into you today?"

"What do you mean? You asked for my opinion, and I gave it."

"Then you insulted me when I didn't agree with it?"

Samantha picks up the glass, tosses back her last bit of wine, and says, "Look, pick whatever style you want. I'm done here."

"You know what? So am I," Riley says. Then to Zoey, "I'm really sorry about this, but I think I'll wait on the hair."

41

Things are uncomfortable on their way out.

And extremely quiet.

It seems as though Samantha has managed to shed some of her irritation, but she still looks bruised, and Riley is still put off by Samantha's behavior inside the salon.

"Samantha," Riley starts when they're at the parking lot, "we should talk about this."

"What's there to talk about?" Samantha says, moving too quickly with a slight stumble in her gait. "You didn't like the hair I suggested. I get it."

"We've been through this, and I explained myself. Would you just listen to me? The whole purpose of this trip was to discover a new identity. My own identity. Changing hairstyles—especially the color—is a big deal for me. I've been away from society and want to fit in again, but how you acted in there wasn't the way to help me do it."

"*Me?* What did *I* do wrong? You were the one who blew up."

"I told you I was sorry, but you made me feel pushed back, then you tried to punish me for it. You were being so aggressive that I could barely defend myself."

"Honestly, Riley, it's just hair. You can always change it."

"Samantha, that's not the poi—"

"And did you ever consider that maybe—just maybe—the hair suggestion wasn't about looking like me? Did you even consider that my intentions could have been purely innocent? That I was actually trying to help you find the fresh new start you want? Going from light to dark is a fresh new start. And you could have easily gotten a different cut to make it more you." Samantha holds a gaze on Riley, one that demands a reply.

Riley wavers for a moment and reconsiders the conversation. Was she the one who overreacted? *No, wait,* she thinks, then says, "But you never explained that in the salon. And . . . and you were making me nervous with all the wine."

"Oh, great. So now I get to hear a lecture about my drinking habits."

"I was not lectur—"

"I swear." Samantha grabs her hair in clumps and looks upward. "You'd think I was trying to sabotage your life. Why can't you trust me?"

"I do trust you."

"Then maybe you should act like it. Why not give the hair a try? I'll be fine if you don't like it. I'll even pay for a new style."

"Money isn't the point here, and I wish you'd stop trying to—"

"What, to pay for everything? Believe me, I know. You remind me every damned time I try. It's insulting."

"That's not fair."

"You know what's not fair? What's not fair is how you overreacted in there. You were unkind when I was trying to help. You completely twisted my good intentions. You yelled at me, right in front of Zoey, then marched out of the salon. For crying out loud, I brought you to her. It was embarrassing!"

"I—I didn't mean to—"

"Now I'll never be able to show my face in there again!"

Riley starts to speak, fumbles over the first word, then says, "I—I think it would be good if we talk about this when you're feeling better."

"Really? Again with the alcohol? This is such bullsh—"

"I didn't mean it like that! I meant because you're so angry. Samantha! You're acting like a child!"

"Me? *I'm* acting like a child? Why are you being so mean? Why are you—"

"SAMANTHA, SHUT UP! JUST SHUT THE FUCK UP!"

There's nothing but deafening silence between them.

Looking into Samantha's tearful eyes, Riley sees concussive rage about to go off and knows this has gone too far.

Way too far.

42

Riley rises from the chair situated opposite Patricia's. She straggles to the bookcase, takes down a hardback from the shelf: *The Psychology of Body Language and Micro Expressions.*

She flips through it. Patricia watches.

Riley puts the book back in its place, then chooses a different chair—obviously the wrong one, because no matter how much she moves around in it, comfort seems elusive. She springs up, chooses another chair. But not the original one.

"Riley," Patricia says, "is something wrong?"

"What gives you that idea?"

Patricia lets her question stand.

Riley says, "Look, I've seen enough therapists in the last few years to know how it works here. I ask a question, then you answer my question with another question. And somehow through this crazy dance, I'm supposed to self-actualize so I can better fit into a society where everyone else is screwed up, too. Isn't that how it goes?"

Squaring her sight on Riley, Patricia says, "Would you like to talk about what's bothering you?"

"See? A question with a question."

Patricia waits.

Riley stretches out her legs and crosses one over the other: she deliberates. It's hard opening up to the person whose job is to examine and judge Riley's mental competency. Not exactly fertile ground for trust building. But since she and Erin no longer talk feelings, her options seem scant.

Patricia seems like a lot less work. She might even have helpful advice about how to fix this mess with Samantha. Riley gives it a shot. She draws a breath and holds it. She lets the breath out, then says, "So, I made a new friend, and we were getting along fine, and then we got into this big fight."

"About what?"

As Riley tells the story, a conflicted expression gradually builds across Patricia's face.

"You have a look," Riley tells her.

"Which look is that?"

"Not the Therapist Stare—the other one—like you're getting ready to take me to task."

Patricia pauses as if carefully weighing her words before speaking.

Slap, slap, slap.

Riley's lips twitch.

Patricia says, "I understand your frustration with Samantha. What I'm wondering about are the finer details. The interaction."

"Not sure what you mean."

"Well . . ." Patricia looks into her lap, then up at Riley. "You do have a choice in situations like this."

"Yeah, I know. Not to get the hair she wanted me to."

"True, but this isn't just about the hair. I'm talking about how you responded to her."

"She provoked me and forced me to act that way."

"Did she?" Patricia's knowing grin challenges Riley. "Or did *you* force you to act that way?"

"She was drinking. She insulted me."

"I'm not saying Samantha did everything right."

"But?"

"What I'm saying is that you had a choice about how to respond. Just like she had a choice how to give you the information about a new hairstyle."

"You mean I overreacted?"

"I'm not here to judge you, and I only have what you've explained to me. So maybe you can look back at what happened and ask yourself that question."

Riley concentrates on Patricia for several seconds, again questioning her own perceptions, then drops her gaze and fusses with her hands.

Once more, Patricia waits.

Riley says, "I probably overreacted."

"Probably?"

"No, I did. But I felt like she baited me."

"And you took it."

Riley lets out a long sigh and says, "Okay. You're right. I could have handled the situation better."

"But do you get what I'm trying to do here?"

"Make me see the disagreement more clearly."

"Well, that, but I'm also trying to help you recognize you can become empowered in situations where you feel powerless."

"I guess I never thought about it that way. But do you think Samantha was telling the truth? About her good intentions?"

"I wasn't there," Patricia reminds her with a smile. "So again, that's for you to decide, but let me ask something: How long have you known her?"

"We met a few weeks ago."

"That's really not a lot of time to know someone well."

"It's . . ." Riley again becomes restless in her chair. "It's hard to explain. We have things in common. Our histories have brought us closer together."

"Sounds kind of mystical, don't you think?"

"Not to me."

The Therapist Stare. "And how old is Samantha?"

"Early twenties."

Patricia's head pulls away, and her shoulders jut forward.

Riley's eyes get tight and narrow. "Do you see a problem with that?"

"I just didn't realize she's half your age."

"I didn't think it mattered."

"Okay . . ." Patricia backs off. "Another question: Have you had a chance to observe how she interacts with others?"

"Why?"

"You asked about her intentions at the salon. Interactions can be a good way to view people as they really are instead of how they want you to think they are."

"Meaning?"

"As Dave Barry says, if someone is nice to you but rude to the waiter, they are not a nice person."

Riley revisits the way Samantha treated the salesgirl after becoming irritated with her and says, "Is that Samantha?"

Patricia shakes her head. "I don't know. I'm just helping you navigate through the disagreement and see all sides. You were both angry and unreasonable, so one argument probably isn't an accurate gauge to judge her by, just like it isn't for you."

Riley nods, awareness taking shape.

"What I'd suggest is that maybe it would be a good idea to know her better before making definitive decisions about her character."

43

Riley is about to make breakfast when she hears knocking on her door. She's not expecting anyone. And with the way life has gone lately, she's not too keen on finding out who may be on the other side.

She creeps toward the peephole, peers through it, then lurches away from the giant, shifting eyeball that looks as if it's trying to snoop inside her apartment. She steps to one side of the door and out of view.

Two knocks, harder, then, "Riley? You in there?"

Samantha? What is she doing here?

Riley tries to recapture oxygen amid her rapid-fire heartbeats. After their disagreement, a visit from Samantha is not only unexpected—it's enough to cause a damned stroke. And not only that. She's taken great pains to keep Samantha from seeing this place. Now, here she is.

Riley unlocks and removes the security bar, gives the dead bolt a twist, then opens the door.

Samantha stands in the hallway, holding a large gift basket. On her face, she wears a remorseful expression. She raises the basket higher and says, "I come bearing caffeine. And to apologize."

Riley considers the basket, overflowing with what looks to be an expensive assortment of coffees and dark chocolates.

"This is getting kind of heavy," Samantha says. "Would it be okay if I bring it in?"

Riley opens the door wider, then steps aside to let her in.

After gingerly placing the basket on the dining room table, Samantha says, "I know this is ridiculously bad timing, but would it be okay if I use the little girls' room right quick?" A self-effacing smile. "I shouldn't have downed that giant coffee so fast before coming here. Am I ever paying a price for it."

Riley points to the bathroom. As soon as Samantha is inside, Riley rushes to the window, hides the binoculars, then pushes the chair away.

Several minutes pass, but Samantha still hasn't come out. Knocking on the door, Riley asks, "Is everything okay in there?"

The toilet flushes. The door opens. And Samantha comes out, letting her demure expression apologize for taking so long. She passes Riley, then proceeds to the living room and sits.

Riley follows and does the same.

Awkward silence for a moment.

Then Samantha says, "I feel really bad about what happened."

"Me too," Riley quickly replies. "I thought it over and realized I didn't handle myself as well as I could have."

"It was just a misunderstanding. That's all."

"Right." Riley smiles, but the smile loses steam when she sees the woman's five bandaged fingers. "Samantha! What on earth happened?"

"Oh, it was nothing." She raises her hand, looks at her fingers. "It was so stupid. I wasn't paying attention while I was cooking dinner, had an accident, and burned them.

"You burned *all* of your fingers?"

"Yeah. I reached for the pot handle, but it was super hot, and my hand slipped." A sad, bashful grin. "Guess I was more upset about this than I'd thought."

Samantha? Cooking? Riley has seen the inside of her fridge. All those drinks and not a speck of food in sight.

I do a lot of takeout. It's easier.

"This is why I don't cook much," Samantha says as if reading Riley's thoughts. "I'll be paying better attention next time I try—that's for sure. Anyway, you were right. I had too much to drink, and I didn't mean to insult your hair. What I was trying to ask was why you were so attached to the old style. It seemed to make sense in my head at the time." She scrunches her nose. "Not so much now."

"Really, it's okay."

"No, it's really not. Drinking can make me act a little badly sometimes. Like, oversensitive? I guess the hair salon felt like a big letdown because I was having so much fun before that."

"*You* were."

"No, no . . . I meant us. *We* were. Shit, I'm so nervous that I can't even say things right. Anyway, ever since we met, I've felt so much hopelessness in you. Defeat, even. And it broke my heart. It really did. But the second we walked into the salon, all that changed. Your face lit up, and it was so great to see. Then you got frustrated, and before either of us knew it, everything went sideways. By then, it was all such a mess that I didn't know how to get us out of it. You know?"

"I think we both felt that way."

"But honestly, I want you to understand that my frustration came from a good place. I just didn't express it very well. I guess I'm a lot more like my creations than I'd realized."

"How's that?"

"A work in progress. Look, I know I'm not perfect, but I don't want to lose this friendship. I really don't. So what do you think? Bygones and all that?"

"Absolutely."

"And I want to make it up to you. We can go back to the mall and buy something nice for your job interview."

"I've already got plenty, thanks to you. Maybe we should wait and see if I actually get an interview?"

"Maybe you already do," Samantha says through a mischievous grin. "A friend of mine has an opening, so I put in a good word for you."

"Samantha . . . Wow, I—are you serious?"

"As a heart attack."

"When?"

Samantha produces a slip of paper, hands it over, and says, "Be there tomorrow at ten a.m."

There's only a name and address, so Riley asks, "What's the job?"

"Oh. Sorry. It's for a waitress. I know that's not the most glamorous job, but at least it'll give you some cash to get on your feet."

"Believe me, it's fine. You have no idea how much this means. Seriously, it couldn't have come at a better time. Thank you so much."

"I'm just happy to help."

"What kind of restaurant is it?"

Samantha is about to answer when a loud *bang* goes off near the door, scaring the bejesus out of them both. When they investigate, they find Riley's security bar lying across the floor.

"Oh my Lord!" Samantha says, fanning herself. She clears her throat and asks, "So what's up with Mr. Heavy Metal here?"

"You know . . . the neighborhood," Riley explains, simplifying a conversation much too involved to finish.

"About that . . . ," Samantha says. "How come you never told me we were neighbors?"

Riley feels her posture crumple a little. "I was embarrassed."

"Heck, I don't care about that. I like you for you, not where you live."

"Right," Riley says, relief in her tone. Then she asks, "How did you know where I live, anyway?"

Samantha quirks a brow. "You can learn pretty much anything about a person on the internet."

44

The interview isn't for another hour, and Riley decides to leave early so she's not late. But when she opens the door, an ugly surprise greets her.

BITCH!

Written in red spray paint across the door. Red: the color of fury.

She staggers into reverse. Whoever did this could be the same person who wrote on her car door, maybe her headboard, too.

But when did this happen?

The writing wasn't there when Samantha left last evening. She touches a finger to one of the letters—it's dry. The message has been here for a while. She considers another possibility. Could Samantha have returned yesterday to do it?

That doesn't make much sense.

Samantha didn't come over to cause trouble—she came to make peace, to smooth the relationship over. And there's certainly no shortage of other possible suspects. The public hates Riley, and the watcher isn't likely in love with her, either.

Or should that be watchers?

Aileen was hesitant to let Riley live here because of potential security issues, and Riley did her best to handle the breaches herself to ease those fears, but she can no longer afford to keep quiet. With each passing day, her security is more at risk. She needs to alert her. Start being proactive instead of reactive. Besides, Riley has kept a low profile in this building. Aileen hasn't even met her yet.

On her way downstairs, she decides she should first talk to Wendy. After three hard and fast knocks, she waits for the peephole to darken.

It does not, and she feels her patience unravel. She knocks harder this time and yells, "Wendy, please answer! This is very important! I need your help!"

She hears footsteps, then light evaporates from the peephole.

"I need to know if you saw anyone suspicious coming or going from my apartment during the last twenty-four hours. Anyone at all."

"No, but it's not like I stand here looking out my peephole all day long."

"I know you don't. Just thought I'd check. Can you do me a favor, though? If you notice anyone else coming or going from my apartment, will you let me know?"

"What's going on? Do I need to be worried?"

"No. You don't. But I do." Riley takes in a shaky breath, releases it. "This is about my safety. So can you do that for me?"

"I can't leave my place," Wendy reminds her.

"I'm not asking you to, but if you hear anyone coming down the hall, look out through your peephole to see who it is. And keep track of the time when it happens."

Riley writes down her cell number on a slip of paper, then slides it under the door. "And if you see someone trying to break into my apartment, dial 911, then me."

"I'd have to open my door and look out. They could see me, then *I'll* be in danger."

"Wendy. I risked my life to help you during the fire. I've made a commitment to take care of you. Do you think we can do that for each other?"

Wendy's silence indicates she's wavering.

"Besides," Riley pushes harder, "do you really want someone dangerous on our floor?"

"Fine. Okay. I'll do it."

A few seconds later, light flickers through the peephole, then a slip of paper slides out from under the door.

It's Wendy's grocery list.

Riley takes it. She's about to proceed to Aileen's office but, after glancing back at her apartment, notices her door is cracked open a few inches.

She didn't leave it like that.

There's no way I would, not after what just happened . . . Or did I?

She considers the second stairwell at the other end of the hallway. If someone slipped in and sneaked away from that side, would she have noticed?

She hurries back to her place, pushes the door open wider, and her fingertips feel a little cold, a little numb.

This doesn't look right.

Using caution, she treads inside, scans the apartment, and stops in place. It's not just her fingertips feeling the chill anymore—prickly goose bumps run up and down her arms.

The doll has vanished from her side table. She thinks about its repositioning last week. This is no lapse in recall, no slip of the mind, and certainly no overreaction. With one part hesitation, one part fear, her vision drifts toward the foot of her curtains, afraid of what she may find.

No Mary Janes stick out from beneath them. She finds a small dose of relief, but it fizzles fast when she looks off to one side. The doll is on the floor.

Several feet away from the table.

Facedown, limbs splayed.

As if someone gave it an angry shove.

She has to take action. She hurries downstairs to Aileen's office and explains about the door graffiti and other frightening incidents.

"Did you call the police?" Aileen asks.

"This last thing just happened."

"And the other times?"

Riley hesitates for a beat, then lies. "All they did was take a report."

Aileen's lips collapse into a hard magenta line.

Riley says, "If you don't believe me, check it out for yourself." She glimpses her watch. "Look, I'm going to be late for an interview. You've got a security issue and property damage upstairs, and something needs to be done about it. I'd like to have my lock changed after your people remove the graffiti."

Aileen lets out a dramatic sigh as if having to take care of the matter, and do a little extra work, might kill her. "Fine," she grudgingly yields. "I'll have someone go up and have a look."

Riley takes off, hoping she can still make it on time for her interview.

45

The job opening is for a waitress, all right.

A waitress at Francine's Pancake House. As in everything covered in sticky syrup. As in the place is dark, dingy, and outdated. Orange vinyl clings to booths fronted by faux wood tables of a peculiar color that doesn't grow on trees. Even within the closed doors of this rear office, the odor of burned pancake grease and stale syrup hangs heavy on the air.

But it doesn't appear as though Francine enjoys her own pancakes. The woman is rail thin, so much that the flesh hangs off her arms like sleeves on a distressed leather bomber jacket. Wiry hair the color of an old gray T-shirt washed too many times and no particular style. Beady eyes, round and gleaming. If there's any joy to be found, it's trapped beneath the skin on her weather-beaten body.

Riley stretches an arm across the desk to shake Francine's hand, which feels much like grasping a twig. So far, Francine doesn't seem to recognize Riley. Not many have lately, which gives her hope that the media coverage may indeed be falling away.

"A friend mentioned you're looking to hire," Riley starts off.

"And your friend would be?"

"Samantha Light."

Francine's beady eyes get squinty. "I don't know who that is."

"She told me you were friends."

"I don't know who that is," Francine again says, this time like she's correcting an obstinate child.

Good Lord.

"In any event," Francine goes on, "the job is minimum thirty hours per week, but you can fit in forty if you'd like."

How about zero?

"Do you have experience waiting tables?"

"Yes. I did it all through college."

"When can you start?"

She'd rather not start at all. This place is the worst. But at the moment, being picky is not an option. The bills are piling up, and next month's rent will be due soon. So Riley tells her she's available to start right away.

"Very well, then," Francine says, her smile unpleasant, as if the only thing holding it open is a sour lemon wedge. She stretches her arm to a metal cabinet a few feet away from her desk. She takes out an orange polyester uniform with a brown zipper running down the front and the most hideous floral collar Riley has ever seen. Francine says, "Your shift starts at noon."

"You mean today?"

"Did I say *tomorrow*?"

"No, of course not . . . I was just making su—"

"Do you want the job or not?"

"Yes. Absolutely."

Francine shoves the uniform at her.

Riley accepts it. She walks toward the door.

"One more thing."

She turns back.

Francine nods at Riley's purse. "We have no lockers here for belongings. Unless you want them to get ripped off, I'd recommend bringing only your ID and keys onto the premises. You can keep them in a pocket during your shift."

Great. All this wonderment and a band of thieves working beside me.

46

Francine's Pancake House is very noisy, very chaotic, and, of course, very sticky.

And Riley's stomach feels achy, probably no coincidence.

Only hours into her first shift and she knows that she's living a new nightmare. Nobody seems to recognize her, so there's that, but it still doesn't diminish how disgusting the place is.

"Excuse me!" a woman sitting with her family shouts, hands flailing. "We've been here for twenty minutes! What do we have to do to get some service?"

Riley knows for a fact that they walked in five minutes ago. Still she nods and hurries toward them. The couple's children are playing under the table, ramming their bodies into the legs and giggling and screeching. Silverware rattles. Syrup dispensers shuffle and knock together. The parents ignore the unruly behavior, even as a spoon shoots out from under the table, then a fork with a wodge of bright-purple chewing gum stuck to it. Next comes another round of tiny giggles.

Riley draws a breath. She puts a pen to her pad, waits for the adults to order, but has serious doubts whether she'll be able to hear anything over the racket those kids are making. Not a problem. The woman is—without any effort at all—fully capable of shouting over her children's commotion. The ones she's still ignoring. Between the banging, and the mother's loud mouth, Riley's ears start to ring. Two orders of pancakes and two of the Captain Flapjack Meals later, she can't walk away from that table fast enough.

"Hey, lady!" a guy yells from the corner table.

Riley bustles over.

The man points to his young boy. The child is in tears, practically hyperventilating while simultaneously blowing snot bubbles through his nose. Brown syrup oozes from both corners of his mouth like viscous motor oil. His fingers are glued to the table by a gooey mess.

"You see him?"

She'd have to be blind not to. She nods.

"My kid's upset!"

Hard to miss that, too.

Dad shoves three empty syrup dispensers across the table at Riley. "There's no mango, rhubarb, *or* banana left."

Mucus Monster has stopped his hysterics, now pacifying himself by sucking on three fingers from each hand while a string of drool slides down one wrist and lands on the table. It makes Riley queasy. She takes the dispensers, tells the man she'll be right back with refills.

And immediately hears someone holler her name. She whirls around and loses her grip on one of the empty syrup jars. It hits the ground running, rolls along the carpet, and finds a new home under another table. The two women sitting there look at the jar, look derisively at her, then go back to their meals.

"Riley!" she hears again. It's Francine, the Pancake Queen, who has obviously witnessed the Lone Syrup Jar Carpet Race, as evidenced by her pinched lips and reprimanding scowl. Pointing her twiggish finger at the table beside her, she says, "The busboys are busy at other stations. I need you to wipe this down. Right away."

"In a moment," Riley says. "I have to find more syrup for—"

"*Now*," Francine barks.

Riley considers the man and boy still impatiently waiting for their syrup. She raises an index finger and mouths, *I'll be right back*, then rushes toward the table in need of cleaning.

It's a mess. Not only has someone spilled an open jar of syrup onto the table, but the stuff has also managed to hit the chair and gunky carpet on its descent. Riley throws down the only rag she's got, then hustles toward the kitchen to grab another. On her way there, two tables filled with customers try to flag her down. Unable to tolerate this pancake pandemonium any longer, she ignores them and keeps moving.

Instead of the kitchen, Riley speeds into the employee bathroom, closes the door, and tries to recapture some stability.

This special place in hell is beyond tolerable. She feels as if she'll die if she has to suck in another breath of the sugary, grease-spattered air. But she can't afford to quit. Not yet, anyway. Not unless she finds something better. Until then, she's stuck in this ptomaine tavern.

"Where are you? There are customers waiting!" Francine demands from outside the door.

Riley has never heard of anyone being fired for using the bathroom. It falls somewhere under the header of human rights.

Hopefully, this place at least adheres to those guidelines.

47

By early evening, Riley's feet are numb. A blister is emerging behind one ankle.

And she smells like a pancake.

Arriving at her apartment, she's relieved to find the graffiti has been removed. The locks have not been changed, but at least Aileen has stepped up to take some action. Since the office is already closed, she'll need to follow up on the new locks tomorrow. In the meantime, she's safe for the night, thanks to her security bar.

As soon as she's inside, she checks the side table. The doll is where she left it, but that still doesn't explain what happened earlier today.

Out of fear or paranoia or . . . she doesn't even know anymore, she goes to her window, grabs her binoculars off the chair, and tries to see if anyone suspicious is lurking around her building. Nothing out of the ordinary.

She lowers the binoculars, then lurches backward.

It's the apartment across the way, the one where the curtain snatcher lives, that has caught her attention. She loses her grip on the binoculars, dropping them onto the floor.

Is that someone standing and looking at me?

She doesn't know, can't be sure. The sun is setting, and its reflection forbids a clear shot, revealing only shadows behind the glass.

The figure moves closer to the window, and Riley barely makes out an outline of someone, possibly male.

Wait . . . What's on his head?

For no apparent reason, the watcher nods.

And ice water spills down Riley's spine.

The person changes stance, and something a lot like hot, tempered steel, something that could slice to the bone, cuts through her. The watcher's head position, the overall body language—a hand planted firmly on each hip—leave her with an unsettling sense the guy is looking boldly, defiantly, right at her.

Then he leans in and, with a fell swoop, closes the drapes.

That apartment is on the second floor and the opposite side of the building from Samantha's. So whose is it?

She needs to find out.

She runs out her door, locks it up, and flies down the hallway.

Outside, Samantha's car sits in its spot, which will make this mission more difficult. She'll need to work quickly, invisibly, to avoid running into her. She looks up at the mysterious apartment, sees light behind the closed drapes, and her heart pumps out a driving beat.

After punching in the security code, she enters the building. In the lobby, she makes a quick visual sweep to be sure Samantha isn't anywhere around. At the elevators, she runs into a maintenance guy—or, rather, the maintenance guy's butt crack. He's trying to fix a light socket on the wall. She observes the leather tool belt lying near his feet. She sidles closer, makes sure nobody's watching, slips a screwdriver out from the belt, and sidles away some. She shoves the tool into an inside pocket of her jacket as Maintenance Guy turns his head to look at her. She gives him a disarming expression, then enters the elevator.

She walks out onto the second floor, then cautiously advances toward the apartment in question. She grips the screwdriver under her jacket; whoever's in there could be extremely dangerous.

At the doorway, she notices a flicker of light from the bottom, then the peephole turns dark, and the hairs on her scalp rise. A pervading sense of fright follows. With mere inches between them, her watcher stands on the other side, observing her.

A blast of warm air grazes the back of her neck. She gulps and whirls around in time to see a man advancing past her. He smiles a hello. She acts as if she belongs there, purses her lips, and scrutinizes him with mistrust.

The man throws her a befuddled look, and she watches him disappear around the next corner.

She returns to the darkened peephole and finds her attitude has shifted. No longer is she frightened—she's indignant. The watcher is a problem, and she has to take care of this.

"I KNOW YOU'RE IN THERE!" she shouts, pounding on the door. "COME OUT AND SHOW YOUR COWARDLY FACE!"

No response, so she pounds harder, yells louder, but still nothing.

She considers the opening beneath the door. She crouches down to peek under it and finds what looks like a pair of black work boots aimed directly at her. Her lungs go airless. She stands in time to see a security guard exit the elevator and head in her direction.

Time to go.

The guard notices her as he comes down the hallway.

She speed-walks away.

48

Another restless night.

Riley's stomach hurts again, sleep deprivation is becoming a way of life, and stress is taking a toll on her body.

Pull it together.

She has to get a grip on herself.

Get out. Stay strong. Trust your truth.

Take action.

She hops out of bed, tries to tame her hair, then throws on some clothes.

Downstairs, she makes a crosscut toward Aileen's office. The door is open, so she enters.

Aileen sits behind an old industrial tanker desk, bulky and gray. She rapidly keys in numbers on an office calculator that spits out paper just as fast. While it seems that Aileen is aware of Riley's presence, the woman doesn't seem particularly interested by it.

Riley makes noise with her feet.

Aileen stops, raises her gaze, and says, "Ms. Harper. How can I help you?"

"I want to thank you for taking care of my door so quickly. I really appreciate it."

Aileen doesn't answer that one. She only looks confused.

"For removing the graffiti?" Riley reminds her.

"Oh." Aileen places one hand over the other and rests them on her desk. "I did send the janitor up to take care of it, but he said there was nothing there."

"Of course there was." Riley lets out a nervous, irritated laugh. "It was written across the door in blazing red. I can't see how anyone could have missed that."

Aileen steeples her penciled-in brows, shakes her head.

"Well, someone removed it," Riley says, "and I doubt it was one of the neighbors."

Aileen gives her a condescending look, and Riley suppresses the urge to lash out.

"I know what I saw. I'm not making it up," she insists, realizing that, in retrospect, she should have taken a picture of the damned door, but she was too worked up at the time to think about it.

"Well, whatever did or didn't happen," Aileen says, "it no longer seems to be a problem, so I guess we're all good, right?"

"No, we're not *all good*. I requested a lock change. Someone's been breaking into my apartment."

"And I'm going to deny that request."

"What? Why?"

Aileen tosses up her hands. "Because there's nothing to prove a break-in has occurred. That's why. Besides, you've already changed the lock on your own. Without prior approval. Incidentally, I'll need a copy of the new key immediately."

"But that lock isn't doing any good. I changed it before this latest incident."

Aileen rotates her head almost completely sideways. "You mean the graffiti that appears to have never happened, that nobody else witnessed?"

"I saw it. Isn't that enough?"

Aileen's cynical expression asks Riley if she really wants an answer to that question.

"I can't believe this! If you refuse to change the lock, I'll have no other choice but to do it again myself."

"You most certainly will not," Aileen says so sharply that her lipstick-stained dentures clack. "And any further unauthorized alterations to the apartment will result in a citation."

"Then what am I supposed to do? Wait until someone breaks in and actually hurts me this time?"

"If you can document that a break-in has occurred, I'll be happy to reexamine the situation." She looks at the door, looks at Riley. "Is there anything else I can help you with today?"

Riley's only response is a scowl.

On her way back toward the stairs, she angrily mutters, "My living conditions are shitty. My job is shitty. And my life? *That's* a complete mess."

A passing neighbor observes Riley's external self-debate and slips her an uneasy glance.

She pays him no mind. She wants to scream. Cry, even.

But instead she decides that it's time to take a leap, make some changes.

I'm also trying to help you recognize you can become empowered in situations where you feel powerless.

Patricia said it. Now Riley's putting it into action.

49

Riley sits in Zoey's chair and stares at her reflection in the mirror. Scissors flutter and snap while clumps of hair drop to the floor all around her—hair that's no longer familiar, hair with a completely new color.

Samantha's color.

Though she at first resisted the idea of having the same style, recent circumstances and events have changed her thinking. At the time, she wasn't able to consider anything other than defending herself. But now she realizes that Samantha actually made a few good points. It was her delivery that stank.

There's no question that Samantha is beautiful. There's also no question that she has great taste and style. Riley wants to feel the way Samantha does, feel that air of confidence. No, she doesn't just want it; she craves it. If this new style makes her feel even a fraction better about herself, then why not give it a try? Samantha told Riley she needs a fresh new start, and these last few days have been lousy enough to prove the point. A drastic hair departure could feel like hitting the reset button.

The clipping stops.

"So?" Zoey says, looking into the mirror at Riley's reflection. "What do you think?"

Riley primps her new hair and smiles. "I think I love it!"

Already she feels better. Prettier, too.

She walks out of the salon feeling like a new woman, a better woman, her battery charged, ready to take on new challenges.

And ready for some exploration.

On her way up in the elevator to Samantha's, Riley turns a wary eye toward the curtain snatcher's second-floor apartment.

That place is evil.

She shouldn't be doing this. But she can't help it. Samantha is still at work, and with Riley's spirit lifted, her clandestine visit feels exhilarating in a naughty way.

On Samantha's floor, she looks up and down the hallway to be sure nobody's watching. She punches in the simple code, opens the door.

She's in.

She flips on the lights and steps into the life she's always wanted but knows she can never have. A life so much better than hers. She heads straight for the couch with its soft, supple leather.

She smiles.

She falls into the downy, sexy cushions, indulging herself in the experience, breathing in the leather smell that rushes over her, and trying to imagine life through Samantha's eyes.

Pretty cool.

No, it's astounding. She's in heaven.

But hungry. She hasn't eaten anything all day.

In the kitchen, she reweighs her previous thoughts about those burns on Samantha's fingers. There's still no food in the freezer or fridge.

Except . . . she discovers a bakery bag filled with fresh double chocolate chip cookies on the top shelf. And six containers of cherry yogurt.

Samantha can't cook those.

The cookies look delicious. She wants some, can't resist the urge to sample them. So she takes two. She's about to close the door but contemplates a container of cherry yogurt. She snags it.

The cookies are amazing—they make her feel rich and confident. After satisfying her hunger, she moves on to Samantha's bedroom. She sinks into the mattress, firm but not too much, soft but just right. Quite a change from the hand-me-down, hard-as-welded-steel mattress that Erin gave her.

She leans into the pillows and enjoys the breathtaking view of downtown. She loves it here, loves to drink in the luxury of a life that, before now, she could only imagine or, at best, see through television shows and movies.

She spots a remote resting a few inches away on the mattress. She grabs it, pushes a button, and a gentle, mechanical noise sounds off while the bed rotates toward the window. She pushes another button, and the bed answers with a smooth, upward movement, which enables her to better enjoy the view.

After a few minutes of R & R, she decides to check out Samantha's closet. It's larger than Riley's bathroom and filled with pretty clothes. She sorts through several hanging blouses and plucks one out that's purple and green. She pulls off her top and puts this one on. *Gorgeous,* she thinks, spinning around to enjoy her new Samantha hair and new Samantha blouse reflected in the tall mirror. For a brief moment, she sees Samantha smiling back at her. She marvels at the woman, and in a thick southern accent whispers, "You're so pretty."

She takes off the Samantha blouse, returns it to the rack, then puts on her own again. Then she does a double take at a pair of red pumps resting on a shelf—the same shoes Samantha was ogling that day at the mall.

Maybe I'll grab them later.

She grabbed them, all right, but did she steal the shoes or come back to buy them? It doesn't make sense. Why would Samantha shoplift something she could have easily bought without blinking? But Riley's thoughts change direction when she reflects on all that commotion at the front of the store. Was it because the shoes disappeared? If that's the case, was it in retaliation against the salesgirl who made her angry? She looks at the size; it's the same as Riley's.

Bet she won't even notice.

Samantha has so many pairs of shoes—rows and rows of them—that it would be hard to keep track of them all. She even said she finds things in the closet she has no memory of buying. So Riley stuffs one shoe into each jacket pocket as souvenirs from her visit, then rearranges the others to create an effect of fullness.

Now she's even more intent on finding out about Samantha's life.

She goes to the office. The desktop is as neat as can be: only a lamp, a stapler, and a container holding three pens and one freshly sharpened pencil. She opens the bottom file drawer and digs through folders. The effort proves boring—until she comes across some financial statements. Samantha wasn't presenting the entire picture while discussing Daddy's finances. The insurance policy she mentioned pales in comparison to the financial portfolio Riley finds. Under the name of Capital Ridge Family Trust, it would seem he left her with about as many zeros as a mission to Mars has miles.

The sadist wanted me to feel guilty for hating him. I guess he figured that with every penny I spent, I'd have to think of him.

That's a lot of guilt.

Besides being so fucking lovely, this apartment is a gold mine of information, but time is running out. A check of her watch confirms it: she needs to leave before Samantha comes home from work. After fixing the bed, refluffing the couch's heavenly brown leather pillows, and looking the place over for other signs of disturbances, she's gone.

50

In the hallway outside Samantha's apartment, Riley's cell goes off, and sparks explode inside her chest. She catches her breath, looks at her phone, and nearly loses her marbles.

"Hey, beautiful!" Samantha says before Riley can speak. "I was heading up to my apartment and thinking about you."

Unholy hell!

Samantha is in the building. Even worse, she's on her way to this floor. Riley's feet break into a hotfooted walk toward the elevator.

Wait! No! What am I doing?

She reverses directions, mouth so dry her tongue feels coated in wax, tightness in her gut she's never before experienced. But this open floor plan offers no place to hide, and Samantha could easily see Riley on her way up in the elevator.

"Still there?" Samantha asks.

"Yeah, still here," Riley says, walking faster, swiping her vision in every direction, and trying not to sound as if she's about to vomit up all the tension in her belly. She sees a maintenance closet, prays it's not locked. The handle spins free of any resistance, and Riley jumps inside. She closes the door, collapses onto a mop, and tries to inhale a sustaining breath but instead ingests the toxic odor of ammonia and Lord only knows what else.

"What are you up to?" Samantha asks.

Hanging out in a broom closet.

"Oh, nothing," Riley lies while she struggles to find her bearings. "Just got in from the store." An aluminum pail beside her falls to the floor with a resounding crash. Riley nearly jumps out of her skin.

Samantha asks, "What was that?"

"Sorry. That was me. I knocked something over."

"Oh. So what did you go out and get yourself? Anything exciting?"

You have no idea.

"Hardly." Riley wrestles out an awkward laugh, then adds, "Not unless the grocery store has come out with a new line of excitement. But no, I just picked up a few items."

"You sure go there a lot. To the grocery store."

Riley stops the bead of sweat rolling from forehead to cheek with a hand and unthinkingly blurts, "Well, this time I had to go for Wendy."

"Wendy?" Samantha sounds surprised. "Who's Wendy?

Why did I just tell her that?

"It's a friend who lives on my floor."

"You never told me about her."

Another compulsory laugh. "Well, I'm telling you now."

"You probably just forgot," Samantha says in a tone that sounds self-pacifying. "But can't she pick up stuff for herself? Is she disabled or something like that?"

"Something like that, yes."

Silence. Then Samantha's voice brightens. "I have exciting news! I was actually calling to offer you an invitation!"

Riley sticks her head out from the broom closet and looks in both directions. While she's racing toward the elevator, one of Samantha's shoes falls from her pocket to the floor. She scoops it up, keeps moving, and says, "An invitation? To where?"

"I've got a showing tomorrow night. The Rocky Oaks Gallery has some of my pieces. Nothing terribly fancy, just a few people, but since I'm new in town, it's an opportunity for them to get acquainted with my work. It ends up being more like a social gathering than anything else. Kind of fun, really. You know, drink a little wine, grab a bite or two. Mingle and all that. I realized today that it might be a good chance for you to meet some people, too, maybe show off one of those banging new dresses I got you."

Riley blows through the building's front door and thinks, *An opportunity to crawl deeper into Samantha's life? To rub shoulders with others who interact with her?* She'll take it.

"I'm in," Riley tells her.

51

As soon as Riley opens her door, Samantha cries with exuberant delight, "Oh my God! You went back and got the hair I wanted!"

Riley tugs at a lock. "Do you like it?"

"Are you kidding me? I love it. Now we look like mother and daughter."

Riley stiffens.

Samantha frowns at Riley's hair.

"What is it?" Riley checks herself in the living room mirror. "What's wrong?"

"It's . . ." A self-deprecating shake of the head. "It's nothing."

"Samantha . . ."

"No. I'm going to sound petty."

"Tell me."

"It's just . . . I wish I could have gone with you. It would have been a special moment for us."

"But I wanted to surprise you. I thought you'd be excited about it."

"Now stop that. You know I am."

"Except?"

"Nothing." Samantha raises both hands and shakes her head. "I'm being silly. I'm so happy you decided I was right, after all."

Riley opens her mouth to speak, but Samantha interrupts with, "Did you have the new hair for your interview?"

"No, I had it done after."

"Oh. Well? How did it go?"

"I got the job."

"That's great! When do you start?"

"I actually already did. Two days ago."

Samantha looks as if someone took a cleaning rag and wiped the reaction from her face. "And you didn't tell me?"

"I *am* telling you."

"After you already started."

"It all happened very fast. I had the interview, and they wanted me to start that afternoon. We only spoke briefly by phone yesterday, and so much was happening."

You know, like breaking into your apartment, then spending some extra time asphyxiating inside the Toxic Cleaning Closet.

Samantha's features relax—or seem to. "You're right," she says. "I'm being childish. It just makes me sad that we missed another special moment."

"But we're having it now."

"Right. Of course. I guess . . . ," Samantha says, squinting over a hard smile. "I'm just acting nervous about the showing."

"Of course you are. But speaking of the job . . . It was the strangest thing." Riley chuckles in an attempt to sound diplomatic and avoid further destabilizing Samantha. "You said a friend of yours was hiring, but when I mentioned your name, she didn't seem to know you."

"I think you heard me wrong. I didn't say I know the person hiring. I said a *friend of mine* does."

"You did? You sure?"

"Yeah. I remember exactly."

Riley doesn't.

Was it my mistake? Did I hear her wrong?

It's possible, so she nods as if gaining clearer understanding on the matter.

Samantha pushes past Riley. About halfway through the living room, she says, "My word! What smells so delicious? Did you go ahead and fix us some plates before the showing?"

"It's for Wendy. I decided to drop off a dinner before we leave."

Samantha keeps walking and says, "Well. Let's see if we can't try to make you look pretty."

"Seriously, girl, you can only do so much primping."

"I prefer to call it damage control," Riley says. She checks her shoes in the mirror, and her mind momentarily flips back to the ones she sacked from Samantha's closet. She chases the thought away, then adds, "I look old and frumpy compared to your amazing body."

Samantha takes a fast sip of her third glass of wine from a bottle she brought in her purse. "Yeah, amazing by the grace of a good plastic surgeon."

"Really?"

"I bought the boobs a few years ago."

"Why?"

"Because I could?" Samantha laughs. "And because I've always hated my body."

"Did it make you feel better?"

"Not completely, but I can at least stand to look at myself in the mirror sometimes."

Riley reconsiders her own reflection, lets out a defeated sigh, then notices Samantha is inspecting her.

"What now?"

Samantha quirks her mouth to one side. She digs through her purse, pulls out a makeup tube, and says, "Let me show you a little trick."

She applies a pink, satiny liquid to Riley's cheekbones above the blush line. When she finishes, Samantha places both hands on Riley's shoulders, spins her toward the mirror, and enjoys looking at the reflection with her.

Riley moves in closer. She touches her face and sees her expression animate.

"Right?" Samantha says, beaming at her. "Sometimes it's those small touches that make the biggest difference."

"Wow . . . what *is* that stuff?"

"Liquid spot highlighter." Samantha closes the cap. "I swear by the stuff. "

"I've got to have some of that. Where can I find it?"

"Here." Samantha aims the tube at Riley. "Take it. I've got another one at home."

"Thanks so much." Riley looks into the mirror again and moves her head, allowing the light to play across her face.

"See? You need to listen to me more." Before Riley can respond, Samantha looks at her watch and says, "Oh wow. I didn't realize how late it is. We should get going."

But about halfway down the hall, Riley's feet come to a stop. "I can't believe this. I forgot the dinner for Wendy." She starts digging through her purse for the apartment key. "I'm so sorry, but I have to go back."

"Riley . . . ," Samantha says, tension riding through her voice, "we don't have time. I'm supposed to be at the gallery."

"I promise, it'll only take a minute."

She lets out a miffed sigh. "Well, go get it. You could have already been done by now."

A few moments later, Riley is knocking on Wendy's door.

"Wendy!" she yells, splitting her attention between Samantha's rising impatience and the door. "I have your dinner, but I'm in a hurry. Can you come out?"

No response.

"Seriously, Riley, I have to get to the showing. Can't you just leave it out here for her?"

Riley knocks faster, louder.

The door opens a crack. Wendy says, "It's about tim—" then flinches at Riley's new hair, then locks her gaze onto Samantha.

Samantha cringes and steps into reverse.

Wendy doesn't seem to be doing so well herself; she's motionless, except for her hand, quivering and clamped on to the door.

Riley messed up. She shouldn't have brought a stranger by, but with all the nonsense between her and Samantha, she wasn't thinking clearly. Now she's managed to upset both of her friends. She offers Wendy a skittish smile and hands over the plate. Wendy flicks a cagey glance at Samantha, then slams the door shut.

They proceed down the hallway, both women quiet, but Riley suspects that each has a different reason for it.

"Okay," Samantha says, breaking the loaded silence. "So, I'm afraid to ask, but I have to. What's up with that woman?"

Riley makes her expression unreadable and says, "Wendy has a few problems."

"That seems like an understatement. Seriously, I wouldn't even know where to start."

"She's not that bad once you know her."

"But why would you want to?"

Riley provides no answer. She has a bad taste in her mouth, and all at once she's feeling more nervous than excited about how this evening will go.

52

The gallery is packed.

If Samantha thought this was just a few people, then Riley wonders what her idea of a big crowd is.

A woman wearing a long white gown sits before a golden double-strung harp, her baroque music effortlessly carrying over the crowd. Samantha's dramatic sculptures rest on black lacquered pedestals beneath strategically placed spotlights, creating a beautiful and electrifying effect. Samantha is busy talking, laughing, and working the crowd with her charm and beauty.

Riley is no expert on art showings, but she has a feeling this isn't the norm. Samantha probably poured big bucks into the event and went way overboard, as only Samantha can do.

A white-shirted, bow-tied waiter drifts up to her, his tray filled with unidentifiable yet extravagant-looking hors d'oeuvres. Riley accepts two—anything to keep her hands busy. She puts her head down while nibbling, then gawks at her shoes. Under the bright lights, she can see they're all wrong for this dress: worn, nicked, and about a shade or two shy of clashing, they create an impressively unappealing example of what happens when old and new collide, negating everything she loved about this dress when Samantha bought it for her.

She looks across the room to again check on Samantha, still mingling, still charming the pants off people.

Now she feels more uncomfortable.

In a concentrated effort to attain some social lubricant, she drifts toward the bar. She again considers the warning about drinking with her meds, then dismisses it. She's already violated that rule several times without any negative consequences since meeting Samantha and figures there's no harm in furthering the trend. She orders a glass of wine and finds a spot near the wall where she can continue perusing the room.

"Hey, you!"

Here comes Samantha, her eyes wide, her smile high-voltage.

"Isn't this so cool? I had no idea so many people would show up."

Noted. Agreed.

Samantha's smile loses a few amps when she says, "What's wrong? Aren't you having a good time?"

"Of course. This is wonderful!"

Liar.

The smile recharges. Samantha throws both arms around her and squeezes a bit too hard. She pulls away, takes a firm grasp of Riley's shoulders, and says, "I'm so happy you're here. I wanted to make you proud of me."

"I'm very proud of you, sweetheart."

Samantha radiates with surprised excitement.

"What?" Riley asks.

"You called me *sweetheart*! You've never done that."

Riley feels her teeth grinding and forces her jaw to relax. She peruses the room again and sees—

"What's wrong?"

"I think that harpist over there is staring at me," Riley says, scrutinizing the woman.

Samantha takes a look, then shakes her head and says, "I don't think so. I think she's just looking in this direction."

The harpist closes her eyes and moves to the music.

Not everyone is watching you.

But some people have been lately. Like the man several feet ahead—a very attractive man, about Riley's age, who is looking her way. Her programmed response is to glance over her shoulder and see if he's checking out someone else, but all she finds is the empty wall. When she looks back, the man is grinning.

"Hey," Samantha says under her breath, "that cute guy over there is totally checking you out."

Riley quickly downs the rest of her wine.

"Go on!" Samantha shoos her away with both hands. "Walk over and talk to him!"

"I don't know . . . I'm not sure I'm ready for this."

"Oh, nonsense. You're more than ready, and you look great tonight. This is exactly what you need, so go flirt with the sexy hunk."

Samantha waltzes off and goes back to her mingling. Riley bashfully—and maybe too stiffly—gives the man a smile while at the same time realizing how out of practice she's become at dealing with men. But he takes the cue and immediately begins walking toward her.

Oh no. What should I do now?

A wave of heat sweeps up her neck. In an attempt to collect her nerves, she busies herself by looking down at her watch.

"Gotta leave soon?"

She looks up. The man stands before her with a smile—a rather cute and dimply one—and at this close range she also can't help but notice his sparkling green eyes.

"Well?" he asks, seemingly unable to take those beautiful liquid eyes of green away from her. "Do you?"

"Do I what?"

He nods toward her watch. "Have to go?"

"Not really . . ." Her mind fumbles. "I mean, no! I don't."

He extends a hand and says, "I'm Randall."

"I'm Ready . . . I meant—oh God—I'm Riley." She buries her face in her hands, speaks between her fingers. "I can't believe I said that."

Randall doesn't seem the least bit put off by the comment; in fact, he laughs with good-natured amusement. He flashes the dimply grin again. "Don't come to these showings much?"

"Don't come to them at all," she says, still trying to recover from her faux pas. "Hard to believe it, right?"

"I completely understand." Randall puts a comforting hand on her shoulder, the heat from it sending her heart into a fast, irregular flutter. He observes the crowd. "These people can be kind of stuffy. The secret is to find the right ones to hang out with." He winks. Now, Randall isn't just smiling; he's sporting a hearty grin.

Beautiful teeth, too, she notices, nearly as white as the crisp oxford he wears beneath his navy blazer.

"But I'll share a secret with you." Randall leans in toward her, speaks with exaggerated confidentiality. "To be perfectly honest, I like my dog more than half the people in this room. Too affected. Know what I mean?"

A loud and unexpected giggle escapes her. Embarrassed, she looks down at her ugly shoes. In an effort to keep Randall's attention away from them, she sends her gaze across the gallery and inadvertently locks eyes with Samantha. Though there's nothing to prove it, she has the strangest feeling Samantha's been monitoring the situation with her and Randall the whole time. Samantha's expression is at first dull, then it pops with zest, and she gives Riley the thumbs-up.

"So?" Randall says.

She flips back to him.

"Want to escape all this stuffiness? We could go to the patio. I hear they have more air out there."

"Yes," she tells him, "that sounds great."

They're about to walk through the exit when a heavy hand comes down on Riley's shoulder. She startles, looks, and finds Samantha standing there.

"Hi," Samantha says to Randall with a grin so ambitious it seems as if it's about to break open. Then to Riley, "Aren't you going to introduce me to your new friend?"

"Um . . . yes. Randall, this is Samantha Light."

"Riley's friend!" she adds.

Riley catches a weighty shot of alcohol breath, and Samantha reaches out to shake Randall's hand. "Thanks so much for coming this evening."

"It's a pleasure to meet you," Randall replies. "I'm really enjoying your work."

"And I really appreciate the compliment," Samantha says, enchantment glinting through her eyes. "But what do you think of our girl here? Pretty awesome, right?"

Randall nods.

And Riley wants to pull out her hair and scream. Besides being embarrassed by Samantha's hard sell, she feels like a shrinking violet next to the woman's ebullience and beauty. She feigns interest in someone walking by, fusses with her hair.

"So, would you happen to live nearby, Randall?" Samantha asks.

Oh, for crying out loud.

"I do. I moved here a few years ago."

"Excuse me," Riley interrupts, wild insecurity billowing through her, "but I need to run to the restroom before we go out on the patio. I promise not to be long."

Randall nods, then he and Samantha continue chatting.

In the bathroom, she checks herself in the mirror. She runs a brush through her hair, reapplies some lip gloss, then assesses the effort.

Better. I think?

She comes back, ready to escape this stifling crowd and Samantha's overbearing role as Cupid in exchange for fresh air and nice conversation. Standing beside Randall, Riley looks at him, but he seems different; in fact, he avoids her gaze.

"Well, it was great meeting you," Randall says, nodding to Samantha. He does the same to Riley, then walks away.

Riley looks at Samantha. Samantha's jaw drops open.

Randall is already halfway across the room and beelining it toward the bar. He orders a drink without bothering to give Riley a glance . . . and clearly without a second thought.

"What was that all about?" Riley asks.

Samantha shakes her head and in a bewildered tone says, "I have no idea."

"Did he say something?"

"Not a word."

Did you say something?

Couldn't be. She was practically throwing Riley at the man. A swell of disappointment overcomes her. Before she can speak, Samantha is doggedly marching straight toward Randall, still at the bar and chatting with a buddy. The friend walks away, and Samantha steps into his place. From the distance, and through a noisy crowd, even Samantha's booming voice doesn't carry enough to make out what she's saying, but Riley can tell the conversation isn't the least bit pleasant. Samantha's face screws into an angry scowl. It looks as if a serious ass kicking has bulleted down the chute, and Riley thinks, *Wow. She's livid. She's really stepping up for me.*

Randall shakes his head and tries to speak, but Samantha cuts him off. Her hands fly up. Her face is bright pink, then she repeatedly stabs a finger toward the exit.

Randall places his drink on the bar, and then he's gone.

Samantha stomps up to Riley. With arms across her quaking chest, she says, "They mess with you, they deal with me. End of story."

The show is over.

In so many ways.

"Doing okay there?" Samantha asks, giving Riley a compassionate look while she gathers up her press releases, price lists, and show statements.

"If you mean alive and breathing," Riley says, "then yes."

"Things will get better. You'll see."

"You don't know that."

"I do."

"How?"

"Because now you have me. I'll be there for you."

"I'm still confused. One minute he was completely interested in me, and the next, *poof*, he was gone."

Samantha looks as if she's having difficulty deciding what to say.

"There's something else," Riley says. "Tell me what it is."

Samantha releases a dispirited sigh. "He recognized you."

"What? With this new hair?"

"I guess." Samantha shrugs. "He figured it out after you left for the restroom."

Riley looks off to one side, looks back at Samantha. "But when I asked, you told me he didn't say anything."

"At the time, he hadn't. The ass-hat told me after I went to the bar and unloaded on him."

Riley doesn't remember seeing Randall get a word in between Samantha's reprimands. But they were far away, and people were walking past and blocking her view.

"Wh-what exactly did he say?

Samantha vacillates for a few seconds, then, "He said he wasn't interested in dating a child killer."

The comment is like a knife to Riley's heart. She's fighting back tears.

"Oh . . . sweetie . . ." Samantha steps closer and massages Riley's shoulder. "Don't be sad. He doesn't deserve you, so I made him disappear. Forget about the guy. Men come and go, but you'll never have to worry. I'll always have your back and make sure the bad ones never hurt you. Even though we had our disagreement the other day, I still love you."

Riley's head jiggles with confusion. She thought they'd already moved past that. Why is she even bringing it up?

"We're like family," Samantha elaborates.

"Samantha, that's complicated for me. "

She tosses up a shrug. "Life can be complicated."

A gust of heat fires through Riley, but she tells herself to calm down, that she's upset over Randall and overreacting, that what Samantha just said is an extremely common phrase, and that her echoing Patricia is just another coincidence. Besides, she prompted Samantha by saying the word first.

Pain takes another jab at her stomach. Riley grimaces. This feels different from what she experienced the other day at work, more intense.

"Hey," Samantha says, "are you okay?"

"Yeah, fine. Just a little stomach trouble. Probably something I ate." She thinks about the yogurt she stole from Samantha's fridge yesterday. Did she remember to check the date?

"We should get you something for that. I'll run to the drugstore."

"No. Don't. I have stuff at home."

"You sure? I'm worried."

"Yes, I'm sure."

"Okay, but I'm here if you need me." Samantha steps in closer. "For whatever it is. I mean it."

"I know you do, but I should probably head home."

"Right. Of course." Samantha picks up the glass sitting on a table next to her. She drinks the rest of her wine.

"This is going to be so much fun, you and me. Just wait," Samantha says.

If tonight is an example, Riley's not so sure she's up for the ride.

53

"Hi. Is Riley home?" Erin asks, poking her head through the doorway and searching the apartment.

"Very funny."

Erin pulls down her sunglasses, looks over the rims to further scrutinize Riley's hair.

"Would you like to come in and have dinner?" Riley asks. "Or do you prefer to stand in the hallway and judge me?"

Erin dummies up. On the way in, she catches sight of the fire engine–red brackets mounted to both sides of the door, a matching crossbar propped against the wall. Though Erin doesn't say anything, Riley can practically hear the warning bells going off in her sister's head. Since their disagreement over how Riley handled her intruder problem, apartment security has tumbled into the Off-Limits folder.

Or she'd thought so. But Erin takes a seat at the dining room table and revives the discussion. "Okay, so I have to ask. What's up with Red Iron Will over there?"

"Nothing." Riley busies herself with food prep in order to avoid her sister's analytical stare. "It's an added security measure."

"*A security measure,*" Erin repeats as if that sentence has no place in the English language. "Seems a bit extreme. Seems like a lot more work than picking up your phone and calling the police."

"Can we please not do this again?" Riley says, suspiciously eyeing the green-handled butcher knife next to her on the counter.

"Okay, okay. I'll stop."

"The added security is just until I move, anyway."

"What? Move?"

"You didn't think I was going to stay in this town, did you?

"Actually, I did. Where are you going?"

"There's a better life waiting somewhere. It's part of my plan."

"What plan?"

"To move on."

"But what's wrong with here?"

"Here won't work."

"I don't think this is a very good idea, Riley. I don't think you're ready for anything like that yet."

Riley smiles. "We'll see . . ."

Erin holds her concentration on Riley for a moment, then crooks her neck and tries to steal a glance at the bedroom. Riley knows she's attempting to see if Clarissa's clothes are laid out on the bed.

"Would you please knock it off?"

"Fine—" Erin raises her hands in surrender. She goes back to Riley's hair.

"You hate it."

"Hate is a strong word. I just wasn't expecting to see a dark-haired woman open my sister's door. But if you're soliciting my opinion, it seems pretty drastic. So, what's the deal?"

"I'm creating a new beginning for myself. Rewriting my story."

"Yeah? How's that working for you so far?"

"It's still early," Riley allows, serving Erin her favorite dish, corned beef with cabbage. She puts a plate down for herself and takes a seat. "Are you done slamming me?"

"Oh, Riley, lighten up. I'm kidding around. You know I always support you." Erin takes a stab at her food. "I just don't always understand you. But joking aside, what gave you the idea to go from light to dark?"

"A friend suggested it."

"A friend? You made a friend and haven't told me? What's her name?"

"Samantha, and I didn't know I was required to check in with you while forming new relationships."

"Riley," Erin says with enough inflection to convey annoyance, "I didn't mean it like that." Then she sighs. "Can't I be interested in your life? We used to tell each other everything. For crying out loud, I was the one who gave you advice on boys in junior high. I really miss us."

Then stop trying to micromanage my life.

Riley offers a flimsy nod and focuses on cutting her meat.

"I'm right here," Erin says, delivering opposition to her sister's avoidance tactic.

Riley looks up at her.

Erin asks, "When did you meet her? This new friend."

"Several weeks ago."

"Where?"

"At a restaurant."

"So, tell me all about Samantha," Erin says, forcing levity into her voice.

"What would you like me to tell you?"

"I don't know . . ." Erin throws in her lackadaisical, lawyerly shrug. "Like, what does she do for a living?"

"She's an artist."

"Interesting. What kind?"

"Bronze statues."

"Of?"

"Dark stuff."

"Such as?"

"Things with wings. Oh, and fangs, too."

Her sister winces.

"They're emotional metaphors," Riley tries to explain. "Very dramatic."

Erin takes a bite and shrugs. "Whatever you're into, I guess."

Footsteps sound in the hallway. Riley jumps, her head spinning toward the door. But the sound fades.

Erin looks there, too, looks curiously at Riley, then pauses for about three seconds before asking, "So, what's happening with your therapist? How's that going?"

Here it comes.

"Fine," Riley says.

"Been feeling okay lately?"

She looks down at the table. She scratches her head and says, "Erin, is there a particular reason why you want to discuss my mental condition right now?"

"Well, if I'm going to be honest, you seem edgy and irritable. And it looks like you're losing weight again."

"Translation: crazy again."

"Did I say that?"

"What exactly *are* you saying?"

"Damn it, Riley. For once can you not think I'm criticizing you? I'm concerned for your well-being. That's it."

"Okay. Fine. Go on."

"Well, for starters, you're jumping at noises outside, and there's the Crown Jewel Protection Plan on your door over there, then there are the binoculars and chair by your window. Yes, I noticed them. Are you watching for something in particular out there?"

Riley tries to come up with an answer that won't make it sound as if she's turned into a stalker. She fibs. "I thought I saw someone trying to break into my car the other night."

"And were they?" She's entered into cross-examination.

"No. It was a false alarm."

Erin nods and says, "I see. And did it take a long time? This false alarm?"

"It happened very quickly. In less than a minute."

"Then tell me, why did you need to pull that chair up to the window?"

Busted.

"Okay, Erin. You've got me. I didn't want to tell you, but I've taken up bird watching."

"Don't toy with me. You know I don't like it. This isn't funny."

"What's not funny is you treating me like one of your courtroom witnesses instead of your sister."

"Riley, you've been laying out your murdered daughter's clothes on the bed each day, and except for putting bars on the windows, you've got this place locked down like a prison. Now binoculars and a chair? What do you expect me to say? I mean, what comes next? The thirty cats?"

Riley looks at Erin, dumbfounded, and with a slow, disbelieving headshake, feels her eyes well up.

The familiar silence is back.

"You don't have to be funny all the time," Riley says, her self-esteem fractured by heartbreak, by a wound that's been ripped open too many times. A tear drips from her nose. Then softer, "Damn it, Erin. Sometimes *funny* hurts."

"I'm . . . I'm sorry," Erin jumps in. "I—That remark was way out of line. I didn't mean to—"

But it's too late. The cruel remark has already been made. And in that moment, it feels to Riley as though the wall between them has become thicker and taller.

54

Riley is rinsing off dishes after her lunch, but when she hears someone knocking on the door, everything tumbles into the sink.

For a few moments she freezes and wonders what to do. Feeling a sharp pang of fear, she carefully pads into the living room, careful not to step across the peephole's light.

It sure isn't Wendy.

She checks the security bar, then decides to put an ear to the door but hears nothing.

Knock, knock, knock.

She jumps back and in the process collides with the umbrella stand. She fumbles for balance.

"Riley? Was that just you?"

What in the—? Samantha? Really? She's got to be kidding me.

"Riley? Was that just you?" she repeats.

Riley darts into the living room to once again remove the chair and binoculars. Back at the door, she lifts the security bar and unlocks the dead bolt. As soon as the door opens wide enough, Samantha allows herself in.

"What the hell, Samantha?" Riley says, placing a hand against her chest, heart still thrashing. "Have you ever heard of calling first?"

"I know, and I'm really sorry, but I got so excited I just had to come over. Riley"—she takes Riley's hands in hers—"I found her!"

"Found who?"

"Rose!"

Riley braces her body.

Samantha whips out her phone, punches in the security code. "I know you weren't crazy about the idea. But I've felt so bad for what you've gone through, and I really didn't expect to find anything on the internet, but here it is." She holds up the screen and aims it at Riley. Riley squints, then takes the phone. With shaky hands, she zeros in on the picture. It's a young woman who looks as if she's accepting some award. The date says it's from about six years ago.

"Well?"

She looks up at Samantha, hands the phone back, and unsteadily says, "It's her."

"I know! Name's right under the picture. It didn't even take that long. I was able to narrow it down super fast. So check this out. It says here she's in San Diego. I don't know if she's still there, but I've got friends in the area who could investigate and hopefully track her down, then we can—"

"Samantha, do you remember what I told you? I don't think this will do any good. Nobody believed me then, and they won't now. Besides, I'm not sure I'm emotionally prepared to deal with Rose all over again. Just the idea of it makes me nervous."

"And I told *you* life is different because you have me, and I meant it." Riley doesn't speak.

"Besides," Samantha goes on, "what's the harm in taking this as far as we can? If we don't find her, then we don't find her."

"And if we do?"

"If we do, this time we'll put the bitch behind bars. I'm very good at getting what I want done."

No lie.

"And I know a lot of people. So what do you say? Let's do this?"

Riley looks at the phone in Samantha's hand for a few seconds, then up at her. Samantha raises both brows.

Riley pokes her tongue into her cheek, then says, "Fine."

"Great!"

"I'm just warning you in advance, the cops won't be helpful, and the woman is as slippery as they come."

"Let me be the optimistic one, and then you'll see, and you'll finally find the justice you wanted. How do you like that?"

"Okay . . . I guess."

"Awesome. I'll put my friends on it. I'm telling you, Rose Hopkins has just met her match."

55

Two days pass, and Riley's avoided reaching out to Samantha. No matter how much she steels herself, she's not sure she wants to hear her talk about Rose or see how this plays out.

The sign on Patricia's door says she's having a session. But according to her watch, Riley's is supposed to start right now. She sidles up to the door and hears voices inside. She stares at her watch, stares at the door. Patricia must be running a little late. So she waits.

But after about ten minutes, the door is still closed, and the people inside are still talking.

This is getting ridiculous.

She walks up to the door again and gives it two solid raps. She waits. It opens, then Patricia appears and says, "I'm very sorry, Riley, but I'm running a few minutes late."

At first, Riley can't believe what she sees through the doorway. She rubs her eyes with the hope that doing so might, in some way, change the picture.

It doesn't.

"You've *got* to be kidding me!" Riley shoves the door open wider, then pushes past Patricia. *"Samantha?"*

Patricia's gaze ping-pongs between the two women, and her face blanches.

Riley can't work past her dismay—but that doesn't seem to be the case for Samantha. Lounging comfortably on the couch, she looks up at Riley with bright eyes, almost as if an old friend has surprised her by stopping by for a visit.

Riley doesn't feel the joy, and Patricia's still not looking so great, either. Is this some sort of payback because she hasn't called Samantha for a couple of days?

"I'll just go ahead and wait out in the car," Samantha says, transparent in her attempt to escape the tension in a room where, all of a sudden, everyone but her is dumbstruck.

Samantha jumps off the couch and exits the room, leaving behind a trail of repressive silence. Patricia seems to be coming down from her discomposure, but something weird is going on here. Riley hasn't a clue what it is, but it's bristling her already inflamed nerves. Without another word, she bolts from the office in pursuit of Samantha.

"Riley! Wait!" she hears Patricia say from inside, but Riley is already marching toward Samantha's car in the parking lot.

When Riley arrives, Samantha is singing along with the radio as if nothing ever happened.

"Samantha," she says through the passenger's window, trying to control her outrage, "what was that about?"

"I know, right? Super awkward."

Riley looks over her shoulder at Patricia's building, then back at Samantha. "Why are you seeing my therapist?"

"I just thought it might be fun for us to—"

"No," Riley cuts in.

"Huh?" Samantha scratches her cheek, and with a perplexed smile, leans in toward Riley.

"No, this isn't about what you want to do, and no, you don't get to start seeing my therapist. It's invasive and weird, so, no, just plain no."

"But I was—"

"Please don't tell me you're not understanding this. Please tell me you aren't that stupid!"

"Wow," Samantha says, overenunciating the word. She looks away, then through an indignant laugh adds, "Just wow. I do everything for you, and this is what I get?" Samantha's eyes start to glisten. Her chin quivers. "Scorn? Name calling?"

Riley doesn't back down. She tightens the grip on her keys, and with a glare, firm and unwavering, holds Samantha responsible for her actions.

Samantha says, "You really need to settle down about all this. You're acting completely paranoid."

"No . . . unh-uh. Don't throw that word at me. And *I* need to settle down? You're the one acting rude and inconsiderate!"

"Again with the name calling?" Samantha crosses her arms. She's tearful. "Why do you hate me so much?"

"I don't hate—"

"Oh yes! Yes, you *do*! You hate me, and you act like it all the time. I went through all this trouble to help you find Rose, to show I care, and here you go again, abandoning me."

"What? How did I abandon you?" Riley finds herself staring at Samantha's burned fingertips, still in the process of healing.

"The way you're yelling at me now, and like the time when we were at the salon. And you said you hated my hair!"

"This is crazy! We already worked that out!"

"Then . . . then, I spent a fortune buying you new clothes." Samantha's voice is ramping up, her face turning blotchy with anger. "And all you did was complain!"

"How did I complain?"

"About the stupid money. And what about the job I got you when nobody else was the least bit interested? How about that? Your thanks was to call me a liar? For real?"

"Why are you blowing that out of proportion? I only wondered if—"

"Wondered what? How cruel you could be?" Samantha isn't just loud anymore—she's practically screaming. People in the lot are staring. "I keep trying to be close to you. I keep trying to be the new daughter you want, but I can't. You know why? Because you're a horrible mother!"

Riley rounds her eyes at Samantha.

Samantha adds, "You're awful! No wonder Clarissa died!"

Now her temples burn with anger, nails biting into palms. Through a venomous growl, deep, scornful, and gritty, she says, "You will *never* be half the daughter Clarissa was. NEVER! You're a hundred steps down from her. No, you're worse than that. I told you how horrible Rose was, and here you are, acting crazy just like her!"

"*I'm* crazy? Take a look at yourself." Samantha cocks her brow, and through a bare-toothed smile, she says, "Guess I missed the part when you were rude to the waiter."

Patricia's warning about Samantha. Now spoken *by* Samantha.

Riley's stomach turns.

What have I gotten myself into?

Through her fright, her insurmountable shock, Riley says, "I think we're done."

"No! Stop! Don't! I didn't mean it!"

But Riley is already walking away at a fast clip.

"I'm sorry!" Samantha yells, shredding under the pressure of torment. "Please! Don't walk away from me! Don't destroy me the way my mother did! I'll die if I lose you!"

Riley keeps walking, and in the distance hears Samantha say through heaving sobs, "Come back! You need me!"

56

Riley passes through the hallway, body still shaking from her encounter with Samantha, when Wendy pokes her head out the door.

"Holy . . . ," Riley says. "You scared the daylights out of me!"

"I'm sorry." Wendy surreptitiously looks up and down the hall. "I need to talk to you about something."

Riley comes closer.

Wendy says, "That woman. The one who was here the other night?"

"Samantha."

Wendy says, "I don't like her."

More abdominal discomfort strikes Riley. She holds in a breath for a few seconds, tries to conceal the pain burning through her, and says, "I know. She's an extremely troubled young woman."

"It's worse than that. She's dangerous."

They lock gazes. Wendy's jaw clenches and her temples hollow.

"Where are you getting this?" Riley asks.

"I've learned to trust my instincts. That woman is bad news. Be very cautious around her."

Riley takes a step back, and Wendy nods with grim certitude, then shuts her door.

At her apartment, Riley puts a hand on the keys in her purse and notices the phone is displaying a notification alert. After going inside, she finds a message from Patricia. She lifts the phone, listens to it.

"Hi, Riley," Patricia says in an unfamiliar tenor. "There's something I need to discuss with you. Please, give me a call, but if I don't hear back, I'll try later . . . It's extremely import—"

Riley pulls the phone away to examine the screen. There must have been a bad connection. She dials Patricia, but the phone rings and rings, then goes to voice mail. She leaves a message.

Two hours pass, and still nothing from Patricia, even after Riley tries several times to call her. She thinks about why she might have phoned. Was it to smooth the rough edges and explain herself after that awkward meeting with Samantha?

She reconsiders Wendy's warning.

Or was this *about* Samantha?

57

Nearly fifteen hours have passed since Patricia's call yesterday afternoon, and she still hasn't phoned back.

No longer is Riley just curious—she's concerned. Patricia said it was important they speak, so why wouldn't she respond to Riley's calls?

Something about this feels terribly wrong.

She decides to swing by Patricia's office on her way to work.

Patricia's car sits in its usual place, another parked a few spaces down, probably a patient's. She pulls into a parking spot for a look inside Patricia's car. She cups a hand over the side window. A nearly empty coffee mug sits in the holder. On the passenger's seat are a few issues of *Psychology Today*.

So far everything appears normal.

But it still doesn't explain why Patricia hasn't called back—in fact, this makes the situation more confusing. Maybe even irritating. So Riley walks up to the entrance. She looks at the closed blinds and a sign on the window that reads, SHHHH! IN SESSION. PLEASE, NO

DISTURBANCES! She looks at both cars in the lot, and her worry cycles into disgruntlement. Patricia failed to return Riley's calls, but she obviously has time for other patients.

She takes out a notepad and pen from her purse, angrily rips off a sheet, and writes:

Patricia,

What's going on? Stop ignoring me!

Riley

She slides the paper under the door. She marches off.

Leaving work, Riley feels another unforgiving shock of pain to her stomach, this time fiercer than the others. She grimaces and pulls open her car door, but stops when she sees a small gift-wrapped box in the center of the driver's seat. She checks her surroundings, then studies the box. Someone has been inside her car, and she has a good idea who it was. Guilt gifts seem to be Samantha's typical response to disagreements. She takes the box and gently removes the wrapping to expose a blue, velvety box that feels lush in her hands. She flips it open, and her jaw does the same. Inside is a beautiful gold chain and solitaire diamond pendant. But not any diamond. It's at least a carat with stunning color and clarity. She shakes her head with stupefaction. This must have set Samantha back about six grand. The woman is out of her damned mind.

The phone goes off and spooks her. A text from Samantha.

Gorgeous, right? Do you love it?

She reels around and scans the immediate area to see if Samantha is nearby and watching. No sign of her, but that doesn't resolve Riley's annoyance. She hops into her car, peels out of the lot, and blasts up the road toward Samantha's studio.

58

Samantha's Mercedes is parked in the building's lot.

Inside, she finds Samantha on the studio floor, leaning against the leg of a table, an empty wine bottle dangling from one hand. She looks up, sees Riley, and for no apparent reason bursts into laughter, then follows it up with a lion-size belch.

That's when Riley sees another empty wine bottle under the table.

"Hey!" Samantha says, lurching to stand. "Get in here and drink with me!"

Riley stays put.

After sloppily heaving herself up, Samantha makes a drunken attempt to navigate the studio's floor plan, then loses her equilibrium about halfway across and starts to stumble. She manages to catch herself, but not before dribbling wine onto the floor in the process. Samantha lets out a ham-fisted guffaw, which mutates into another ferocious belch. She covers her mouth with a hand and shakes her head, trying to gain control over her silent but intense laughter.

"Samantha," Riley says, "you should sit down."

"I'm fine. I do this all the time." She tries to walk, loses her balance again, then says, "Okay . . . I've got this." She staggers to the cabinet and pulls out another bottle of wine. She holds it up and says, "Want some?"

"No, and I think you've had enough."

Samantha shrugs and opens the bottle but ends up spilling some wine onto her shirt. She looks down and says, "Oh well. Men will leave, but red wine never does," then lets out another bellyful of laughter.

All Riley can do is shake her head.

"Well? Don't just stand there!" Samantha's words sound as if they've been dragged through a bowl of oatmeal. She looks down, drizzles some wine into a glass, and says, "C'mere and lemme see that one fuck of a necklace on you."

Riley stays where she is. She extends the box toward Samantha and says, "I'm not accepting this."

"Of course you are, you s-s-silly shit!"

"No, I cannot."

Samantha pokes a wobbly finger at her and says, "Don't."

"Don't what?"

"Don't start with the money bullshit again."

"I'm serious. I'm not taking it."

"What do you mean? I—" For the first time, Samantha's inebriated joy loses its luster. "I picked it out just for you."

"I said no. You can't buy me back every time you act up."

"But you have to take it," Samantha says, verging on tears. "I spent so much time looking for the right gift. To show how sorry I am for what I said. To let you know how much I love you!"

"You can't fix everything with your money."

"It's a present! You can't refuse a present! You can't!" Samantha is no longer on the verge of crying. Her eyes swim with tears. "Please! Please come inside so we can talk about it!

"I need to go."

"You bitch! I fucking *hate* you!" Samantha zigzags toward the open window. Holding the wineglass in one hand, the new bottle in the other, she tries to wrestle a leg through the opening.

"Samantha, no!" Riley yells. "Don't! You're not in any shape to go out there! You'll get hurt!"

Samantha trips over herself during a second attempt to push her leg through the window.

Riley rushes into the studio, drops the gift box on a table, then hurries toward Samantha and says, "Get away from there before I pull you away!"

"Okay, *Mom*," Samantha snarks back. "Whatever you say, *Mom*."

Riley stops to collect herself and says, "I'm not your mother, but I'm certainly not going to let you kill yourself."

Smash.

The sound of exploding glass is loud in the room.

Samantha stands freakishly still, shards of broken bottle glass scattered around her, one ankle dripping with blood. Her body writhes with frightening intensity, face set into an expression that could only be interpreted as one of raw and lethal fury.

"Samantha," Riley says, "what is it?"

Samantha doesn't speak, eyes hooded, lips trembling, a tangle of hair glued to her cheek by sweat.

"Samantha!" Riley again says. "What did I—?" She stops.

I'm not your mother.

Samantha bites down so hard that the jawbone rises beneath her skin. She moves toward Riley, leaving a trail of blood in her tracks.

"Samantha! Stop!" Riley shouts, backing away. "You're scaring the hell out of me!"

But Samantha won't stop. Still on the advance, she says, "Don't you EVER say that to me!"

"I'm sorry! I didn't mean to—"

Before Riley can finish her sentence, Samantha latches both hands onto one of the sculptures and with alarming strength slings it onto the floor. A resounding crash goes off. A bronze hand breaks off and pinwheels across the floor. Riley looks toward the door, trying to map out her path for escape.

"HOW? HOW COULD YOU DO THAT TO ME!" Samantha yells, spitting out her words as if they are blistering her tongue, thick, teary mascara running down her cheeks. "HOW COULD YOU LEAVE ME? WHY, WHY, WHY? I NEEDED YOU! YOU SELFISH CUNT!"

Riley isn't sure whether Samantha is talking to her or the mother who abandoned her. Maybe it's both. She rams her body into another sculpture. The heavy mass of bronze topples slowly onto the merciless concrete floor.

Crash. Clatter.

Samantha lets out an unearthly wail. Primal. Barely human. Riley jumps back, and for the first time notices that the blue curtain is wide open. She staggers into reverse at the sight of what lies behind it, a group of horrific, frightening statues, more grotesque than anything she's witnessed before in this studio. Although human forms, all have one connecting commonality: bestial features—horns, fangs, cloven hooves—expressions ranging from misery to agony to terror. She zeros in on one that's particularly unnerving. It portrays a man, his naked body toned and muscular. He's beautiful except for the thick tail that, upon closer inspection, is actually a monstrous snake, its barbed fangs dripping with venom, its eyes looking hungry for blood. The serpent coils around the man's legs and past a fleshy wound where his penis and testicles once were. Beside and below it, a pair of wolves with human bodies fight over what appears to be the Adonis's severed arm.

But nothing can compare to the statue at the end of the line. Samantha's latest work. The room swims around Riley and the floor teeter-totters.

A cruel statue, obviously created for Riley's benefit: a reenact-ment of Clarissa's death.

Body facedown in the grave.

Part of it covered with mud while she's being buried alive.

Riley involuntarily hurtles into reverse until her back is against the opposite wall. She tries to scream but can't, tries to catch her breath, but the air feels like a fistful of nails going down.

Then she hears a trickling sound, looks down, and sees a puddle of urine pooling around Samantha's bloodstained feet.

59

Riley flees Samantha's maniacal rage.

Now she drives into the night, muscles straining against skin, hands trembling so hard that she can barely maintain her grip on the wheel.

Her thoughts spin into reverse, mind trying to visualize what happened too fast to grasp the first time around. Samantha's violent, savage fury. Her murderous expression. She isn't just mentally unbalanced—she's a dangerous lunatic.

At a stoplight, she opens her window to draw some fresh air, then another car stops beside her, and from inside the vehicle she hears this:

"At eight o'clock, here's your top story. Investigators are looking into the murder of a Lincoln Heights therapist. Patricia Lockwood's bludgeoned body was found in her office. There are no current suspects, but police are asking anyone who might have information to . . ."

A feverish surge blasts through her body, then tears flood her eyes.

"Not Patricia! NO!"

There's something I need to discuss with you. . . . It's extremely import—

Riley never heard from Patricia again. Was she murdered in mid-sentence? Even more, is it possible Samantha walked back inside the building to kill her? She doesn't know, has nothing to prove it, but looking at the timing, the theory doesn't feel like much of a stretch.

Panic sends her foot bearing down on the pedal, and the car surges ahead at alarming speed when she thinks about the pithy note she left at Patricia's office. She was probably already dead when Riley went to check on her. Will that implicate Riley in the murder?

Just what I need right now.

Her phone dings. She grabs for it, sees a text from Samantha, but doesn't want to read it. Whatever that woman has to say will only rip at Riley's already-frayed nerves. She can't allow that to happen, has to hold it together.

About ten seconds later, the phone goes off again. Another text. Then in rapid-fire succession come three more. Her screen is littered with messages from Samantha. Her throat feels coated in toughened leather. The stomach pain starts up again with newfound intensity. She drives faster, tries not to cave while her phone continues with its *ding, ding, ding.*

She reaches her building, and the place has never looked so good. She scrambles from her car, sprints toward the entrance, flies up the stairs, her phone going off the entire way, then down the hallway and into her apartment. Inside, she locks the dead bolt, drops the security bar across her door. Then she collapses into a chair at the kitchen table, foot pumping, body shaking. Samantha's texts still roll in.

Ring.

The phone flies from her hand and clatters onto the table. As she picks it up, another ring goes off, then her voice mail chimes. Now the ringing won't stop. Riley can't take any more. She turns off her phone, rechecks her door, and makes a run for the bedroom.

She jumps into bed, clothes still on, and burrows beneath the covers, wishing all this could go away.

And regretting the day she began stalking a monster.

60

All through the night, Riley jumps at every footstep outside her apartment, every slamming door. Even the rattling pipes strike fear into her. Amid all that, she obsessively checks and rechecks her lock and security bar, worrying about how many text and voice messages will be waiting for her in the morning, not to mention trying to anticipate Samantha's next dangerous move.

The sun rises, and it feels as if the past few minutes have been her only length of sleep, then an unrelenting insomnia hangover fires off, hacksawing through her head.

She hefts her strung-out, sleep-deprived body from bed. In the kitchen her sight guardedly gravitates toward her phone, still lying on the table from last night. Maybe because fatigue has put a dull edge to her fear—or maybe simply because she knows that ignoring this horror show is no longer an option—she turns on the phone to find thirty text messages and twenty-five phone calls, every one from her enemy. She begins scrolling through the texts. In the first four, Samantha repeatedly begs for forgiveness, albeit in an utterly frenetic, crazed way.

It was all a simple misunderstanding!

I had too much to drink!

I didn't mean any of it!

I love you so much!!!

She feels a fraction of relief that the woman hasn't gone on the war-path after her. But that relief falls into a rapid decline as she reads on.

I hate you! Don't ever leave me!

How dare you treat me like this!!!

STUPID WHORE! I'M CALLING YOU! PICK UP THE MOTHERFUCKING PHONE!!!

And worst of all:

I'M COMING OVER IF YOU DON'T ANSWER!!!!

Thankfully, she didn't, but Riley decides to abandon the remaining voice mails. She can't afford to let Samantha take over her emotions more than she already has.

She walks to her window, looks at Samantha's Mercedes in the lot, looks up at Samantha's building, and a fusion of nausea and terror overcomes her.

Samantha is almost a stone's throw away from me right now.

Riley has to pull it together. This is no time to skip her meds, so she goes into the bathroom, but as she pours the Olanzapine into her hand, an abnormal, abrasive mark on one of the pills catches her interest.

What the . . . ?

She spills the rest of the bottle out onto her countertop, begins sorting through the remaining white tablets. No scratches, but they do have one feature in common. All identifying letters and numbers have been rubbed off.

She checks her Lexapro, too—which was almost identical to the Olanzapine—and gets the same result: all markings are gone.

Would it be okay if I use the little girls' room right quick?

She sure did, but it wasn't to seek relief from that large coffee she drank.

Riley pours the second bottle's remaining contents onto the countertop and zeros in on one pill that Samantha apparently missed. She lets out an infuriated laugh. This would explain why her stomach has been causing so much trouble lately.

Aspirin. I've been taking six damned aspirin a day instead of my meds.

Samantha has been trying to make Riley lose her mind again. But why? To manipulate her judgment and cause dependence? Then there was the new job. The shopping sprees. All were attempts to buy Riley. To own her.

Randall's strange and unexpected departure at the art showing after she came back from the restroom, then Samantha's explanation that didn't quite add up.

DIE MURDERER! keyed across her car door after their lunch together.

BITCH! furiously spray-painted in red across her apartment door, directly on the heels of Samantha's supposed apology and subsequent pill-switch.

She's been out to get me from the start. Probably planned on killing me, too.

Her clothes feel itchy on her skin. Again, she races to the window and rechecks the parking lot.

Is she hiding out there? Is she coming after me?

She goes back to the table and sits. More thoughts, more disturbing conclusions.

The burned fingers along with yet another explanation that didn't fit.

The hair-salon fight.

Samantha's colossal mental breakdown in the studio.

That's her MO. Samantha cries out for attention anytime someone rejects her, just as her mother did.

Now Riley starts to wonder about the break-ins and whether Samantha was responsible for those, too.

But how did she slip in?

A loud *thud* goes off outside her front door, and she nearly leaps from her shoes. She's on it. She makes a break toward the door, looks through the peephole, and her pulse taps down. Just a pair of workers moving equipment for some final hallway repairs.

The fire.

She picks up the phone and dials Erin's number.

61

"I could really use your help, sis," Riley says, breaths huffing despite her best efforts to conceal them.

"You sound funny," Erin replies.

"I'm in a crisis."

"I don't think I like the sound of that, either."

"I'm in serious trouble."

"Oh no, Riley. What is it this time?"

"It's Samantha. The woman is crazy. She's dangerous and trying to destroy my life. And I think she might have murdered Patricia."

"Whoa, hold on a minute. The gal from the hair salon is trying to destroy your life and murdered your therapist?"

"She's not from the salon! She took me there. Erin, please!"

"Okay. Fine. Tell me what's happening."

Riley explains about the friction rising between her and Samantha. How Samantha became increasingly needy and possessive. How last night she exploded and became violently unhinged.

And her suspicion that Samantha could have been the one breaking into the apartment.

"*Breaking,*" Erin repeats.

"Huh?"

"You said *breaking* in the present tense. As if it has continued since the first time we spoke about it."

Riley offers no reply.

"You've got to be kidding me. More lies? Really?"

"Because telling the truth turned into a fight last time, and I didn't want that to happen again, so I've been trying to handle the problem myself."

"There is no such thing as lying for a good reason, but I'm guessing this call is because you've figured that one out.

"Something like that. Yes."

"You should have told me in the first place."

"I know."

"Then I could have helped you."

"Erin! Can we please discuss all that later? I'm scared out of my mind!"

"Okay, okay! But my God, you sound bananas. It's worrying me."

"I need to figure out if Samantha's the one who's been breaking into my apartment!"

"But the first incident with the headboard happened before the two of you even met. Riley, that doesn't make sense."

"I told you! I'm trying to figure this out!"

"Let me rephrase that. What proof do you have?"

"That's why I'm calling! I need your help finding it!"

"Okay. Let's just back it up here for a moment. What was her motivation? Do you even know that? Was she stealing?"

"No. It's not like tha—"

"Trying to frame you for something? Planting evidence, maybe."

"Erin! Just for a minute, would you stop being a lawyer?"

"I *am* a lawyer, Riley! And being a lawyer, it's hard to ignore the fact that you're tossing out allegations left and right with nothing to support them. If I'm going to be honest, you sound more paranoid than logical. So once again, tell me why you think this woman is stalking you. Do you even know that?"

Riley pauses, then, "Well, no. Not yet."

"See? None of this makes sense!"

"How about if you listen instead of judge?"

Riley hears Erin take a deep breath.

"Fine. Go."

Riley takes in her own breath. "All I'm trying to figure out is whether Samantha was able to get her hands on the new key after I changed my lock."

"What makes you think she did? And multiple times?"

"I'm starting with the most obvious incident, okay? If I can figure that one out, maybe I can find links to the other times. So, the fire happened a day or two after I called a locksmith. Not long after that, the doll started moving."

"The *what*?"

"It . . . it's a long story," Riley says, rebuking herself for letting out information she didn't mean to. "The point is, I think Samantha might be the one who started the fire and made it look like an accident. Maybe she snuck into the neighbor's apartment and dropped a lit cigarette in his bed while he was passed out."

"Okay . . . ," Erin says, stringing out the word and not sounding one bit convinced.

"So, after the flames were extinguished, I think I might have left the door unlocked when I went outside and talked to a firefighter."

"*Might* have?"

"Well, yeah. I must have."

"Conjecture."

"I'm putting pieces together! But with all that upheaval, it was the perfect opportunity for Samantha to sneak into my place and steal one of the spare keys. I was hoping that maybe you could look at the fire report. You know, use your skills to see if you can find anything suspicious."

"Except that you haven't shown me a sliver of proof this woman set fire to your apartment building. Did you try speaking to the guy with the cigarette whose unit it started in?"

"No, because I'm just now figuring this out. Besides, I don't want people knowing what I'm up to."

"Oh hell. I'm sorry, but I'm not doing this."

"It's important! I'm in danger!"

"Then call the freakin' police like I told you!"

"I can't! They're part of the problem! They're after me too!"

"And here we go again with the paranoia . . . Riley, this isn't ten years ago. And every police department in Northern California isn't out to get you. Not one thing has happened to indicate that. You haven't even seen any sign of Sloan since we left Glendale."

"That doesn't mean she's not still out there watching me."

"Oh, for crying out loud. Don't you see? Your fear isn't real! It's all in your head!"

"History is my proof, and that's good enough for me."

"It is *not* proof. It sounds screwy."

"So you're calling me crazy."

"No, but you're giving me another migraine." Erin groans. "Look, I seriously doubt there's anything of substance here, but I do know a gal who works with the fire department. Maybe she can check into it for me, but *just* to quiet you down."

"Thank you."

"In the meantime, could you please do me a favor?"

"What?"

Erin makes her voice solemn. "If this Samantha woman is as dangerous as you claim, you need to take precautions to protect yourself. Put aside your unfounded fear of the police. Get in touch with them and make a report."

"Okay."

But when they end the call, she's thinking, *You'll have to forgive me, sis, but I can't do that.*

62

Riley will take precautions to protect herself—just not the way Erin wanted.

She gives serious thought to moving. Someplace with better security. Someplace not right under Samantha's nose. There's only one problem. She doesn't have the money to do it. She's living from paycheck to paycheck.

She feels stuck.

She pulls down every blind and closes every curtain in the apartment. She repeatedly checks the security bar, which she obviously can't engage after leaving her place. She's got to find a way to keep Samantha out when nobody's here.

Aileen won't change the lock, and she's given Riley a stern warning not to, but this is no time to worry about that. Safety comes first.

She calls the locksmith again for a re-key and, while he's at it, also has him fortify the door frame with a stronger strike plate to prevent it from being kicked in. Samantha probably isn't powerful enough to do that, but Riley isn't taking chances.

But she needs to do more. She visits the hardware store and picks up a portable door alarm, which only costs about thirty-five bucks. It won't alert the police, but it will make a lot of noise if Samantha tries to break in. She also grabs a can of Mace. The law forbids her from buying a gun because of her psychiatric history, but she'll spray the shit out of anyone's eyes who comes too close.

At home, Riley sits in her self-made fortress and finds a whiff of measured relief.

At least for the moment.

Before work, Riley stops at Wendy's apartment. She commits two raps to the hollow aluminum door, then waits.

And waits.

But if she's learned anything about her isolated friend, it's that she's not a quick responder.

Riley knocks a few more times, shouts, "Wendy! Please come to the door! It's really important!"

"What's happening?" Wendy at last answers.

"I'm in a mess and . . ." She stops to slow her mind. "And I can't talk to a door. Could you open up?"

Wendy must sense her anguish, because she immediately pulls her door open wider than ever before. For the first time, Riley is able to see her from head to toe. She's a tiny woman, even smaller than Riley realized. Sympathetic eyes look back at her. Pretty blue eyes, in fact, that shed an entirely new light on the woman. Wendy doesn't say anything; instead, she waits, giving Riley time to sort through her thoughts.

"This isn't how it was supposed to be. This isn't how I planned it," Riley says.

"Planned what?"

"You see, I had a strategy . . ."

Get out. Stay strong. Trust your truth.

"And I was going to make it work. I was going to take care of things, but they started going haywire. And you were right about Samantha. I should have listened. The woman is bad news. I didn't realize how dangerous she'd become. Now I'm caught in the middle and can't find my way out of it."

"You can."

"How?"

"Riley, you're one of the strongest people I've ever seen. Look at what you've been through. I wish I had half your courage."

"Yeah, so much of it that all I want to do is go back behind Glendale's locked doors where I felt safe and protected."

"You don't."

Riley doesn't answer. She looks away with disgust.

"You do not," Wendy again asserts. "Trust me. Closed doors don't give you safety—they just make you their prisoner, squeeze the life from you. Then one day you wake up and ask yourself, 'Is this it? Is this what I was meant to do? Live one meaningless minute after another inside these screaming four walls?'"

"Why should I believe you?" Riley says. "How can you possibly know that life is better on this side of the door when you never walk through it?"

Wendy raises her brows. She reaches out for Riley to take her hand.

Riley does.

Then, as if walking an unsteady emotional tightrope, Wendy takes steps, slow and wobbly, through her doorway until she's standing in the middle of the hall. After a shaky breath, she gazes at Riley.

"Believe me now?" she asks.

The two women look at each other while contentment builds across their faces.

And somehow for Riley, in some small way, the world outside Wendy's door feels a little less weighted, a little more secure.

63

The feeling doesn't last.

Trouble is back. Not that she ever really left.

Riley's trying to work, and her phone is again blowing up with texts and calls from Samantha. It's not just frightening—it's completely disruptive, and Francine is shooting her dirty looks.

The phone rings again. Riley's jaw clenches.

Enough is enough.

Fear and patience take a back seat to irritation. She hoofs it out into the Pancake House parking lot, fumbles for her phone, and shouts, "LEAVE ME THE HELL ALONE! STOP CALLING. I MEAN IT! DO YOU HEAR ME?"

"Riley?" Erin says, alarm so tangible that it nearly sends a charge down from the cell towers.

Shit.

"I didn't have a chance to look at the number," is all Riley can come up with.

"I—I was calling to let you know I'm out here in the parking lot."

She looks off to the right and sees her sister waving through the car's windshield.

"How perfectly random of you," she quips. "Hang on. I'll be there in a minute."

She looks through the restaurant window, sees Francine trooping off to her office, then slips away to see Erin.

"Are you checking on me?" she asks.

"Given the way you answered my call, somebody should be. What's wrong now?"

"It's Samantha." Riley does a cursory skim of the parking lot, then turns back to Erin. "She's been calling all day. She won't leave me alone."

"Did you file that complaint?"

"Not exactly."

Erin slaps her hand against the steering wheel. "Oh, for fuck's sake, Riley. It's a black-and-white sort of thing, kind of like being dead or alive. Either you have or you haven't."

"I haven't."

Erin's disapproving hush says it all.

"So, want to tell me why you're here?" Riley asks, sounding clumsy while trying to dance around a volatile topic on the verge of a cataclysmic explosion.

"Well, in addition to my persistent worry about you, I came to give you some information. I spoke to my girl at the department."

Riley leans in closer toward the window. "What did she find out?"

"Nothing."

"Huh?"

"Absolutely nothing. The tenant even admitted to investigators that he fell asleep with a burning lung dart in his hand. Textbook case of an accidental fire. It doesn't get any more slam dunk than that."

"But Samantha still could have used the opportunity to steal a new key, right?"

"Riley, stop."

"Stop what?"

"Stop jamming your gears. Let this go."

"I can't!"

Erin sighs. "I'm not asking this again to irritate you. I'm asking out of love. Are you sure you're feeling okay?"

"I've got the she-hound from hell on my tail, so the answer would be no."

"I'm not talking about that."

"What, then?"

"Don't take this wrong, but our conversation last night had me worried, and you sounded absolutely hysterical just minutes ago when I called."

"With good reason."

"Riley, it's not like all this is new. Your behavior has been strange for a while, and it keeps getting stranger. It started with you lying about those bare spots on your headboard. When I later pressed you on that, the story changed to an intruder who carved a nasty message on it. But you couldn't even tell me what that message was."

"You think I was lying about it?"

"Did I say that?"

"You don't have to. I know the way you say things without saying them." Riley feels the heat of anger spread across her face. "It said, 'Child Killer,' okay? Are you happy now?"

Erin grimaces.

Riley says, "And as I've already explained, I think that intruder was Samantha."

"Do you? With the arson theory put to rest, you've got nothing."

"She went wacko on me. Isn't that enough?"

"No, it's really not. In a court of law, that wouldn't fly at all."

"But we're not in a courtroom. We're two sisters, talking."

"And as your sister, I listened and tried to help by gathering more information."

"I thanked you for that."

"Then I saw the chair shoved next to the window with a pair of binoculars, and you gave me an improbable story about someone trying to break into your car."

Riley's not sure how to respond. What can she say? That she used the binoculars to spy on Samantha? That she's the one who created this mess, which has spun so far out of control that she can no longer stop it?

A few brisk knocks go off behind Riley. She zips around and through the restaurant's window glass, sees Ms. Pancake Dictator herself, head wigwagging, hands bolted to her boney hips and, of course, with that disapproving glare splashed across her puss.

Riley holds up her index finger. Francine gives Riley the stink eye.

"And another thing," Erin adds, "how come I've never met this Samantha woman?"

"Would you please stop referring to her as *this Samantha woman*?" Riley says, still distracted that Francine hasn't left her roost behind the window. "It's very condescending and implies that I'm making her up."

"I'm starting to wonder about that, too."

"She's real! And you haven't met her because I didn't feel compelled to introduce you. My God, Erin! I'm trying to create my own life. How can I do that when each step of the way you misinterpret my every move? Look, I appreciate everything you've done for me—I do—but that doesn't give you the right to make judgments about my mental state. I was seeing a shrink for that. If there were a problem, she would have been the first to let me know."

"Except she's dead, and she only knew what you told her. I'm seeing you in real time."

"Damn it! I was released from the hospital for a reason! Because the doctors think I'm well enough. I'm trying to find my place in this world, but it's been hard. *Really* hard . . ." Riley chokes back tears. "I'm doing the best I can, so please, stop looking at me cross-eyed every time I pick up a pair of scissors!"

"I haven't done that, and you know it!"

Francine pokes her head out the door and calls, "You've got about ten seconds to get in here and keep your job. Comprende?"

Riley gives Francine a fast nod, then looks back at Erin, who says, "I care about you. I'm concerned, okay?"

"Here's an idea. How about finding a better way to show it?"

"Riley . . ."

"Look, I have to go. Bitch for a Boss has crawled so far up my rear end that she may puncture a lung soon."

"Will you please give me a call after you're home so we can talk some more?"

"Fine. I'll call you."

Erin starts her car, then leaves the parking lot, and Riley turns to go inside.

"HEY, BITCH!"

Her feet stop moving, then her hands shake and rattle like jingles on an old tambourine.

When she wheels around, Samantha stands before her.

64

Riley looks into the eyes of a madwoman but can't speak. She can barely move, paralyzed by bloodless terror.

"I was totally playing with you!" Samantha says through a boisterous laugh. She slaps Riley's back. "Damn, girl! Don't be so sensitive!" She doesn't seem angry at all; in fact, her joviality is so convincing that, for a fleeting moment, Riley wonders, *Is she crazy, or am I?*

"Wha-what are you doing here?" Riley says, words catching on their way up.

"What do you think, silly?" Samantha lets out an innocent giggle that drives a chill into Riley's bones. "Did you forget already? I'm picking you up to go shopping. Oh! And I found a new mall to try this time, since you couldn't find anything you liked the other day."

The other day? What is she talking about?

"Westland, I think it's called?" Samantha rambles on. "Or something like that. Have you heard of it? Westland?"

Riley adds being freakishly dumbfounded to being scared out of her wits.

Samantha has entered a strange new state of mania. One that sends nerves prickling beneath Riley's skin like tiny dancing stilettos. And that hyperanxious look on her face. The kind that could burst into menacing hysteria at any second. All Riley knows for sure is that she's in danger. This woman is a ticking time bomb, and Riley has to avoid doing anything that might set her off, which means getting as far away from her as possible.

She opts for the Abrupt Departure Strategy: she reels around, but with daunting speed, Samantha digs her thumb and forefinger into Riley's clavicle, squeezing so tight that it induces tooth-gnashing pain. All Riley can do is close her eyes, let out a shivering moan, and pray for a solution.

"WHATDIDIJUSTSAY?" Samantha isn't just speaking—she's growling her words through gritted pearly whites. Her anger is volatile and tactile, a different kind, the likes of which Riley hasn't yet witnessed. Anger that totters dangerously close to combustion. Anger that, if provoked, promises to be hotter than melting steel.

Riley's body trembles beneath the inescapable death lock. The pressure ratchets up. Her agony hits a fever pitch.

"Please! Stop!" Riley cries out. "You're hurting me!"

Samantha releases her hold, and a grin cracks across her face, then she moves right along as if nothing ever happened. "So what do ya think? Shopping? Yes? Then lunch? Maybe our favorite coffee shop after that. Lovely, right?"

It's a lose-lose situation no matter how she answers. Unless . . .

"You know what? Why not?" Riley says, checking the restaurant window. Francine has momentarily stepped away. She looks back at Samantha. "I've finished my shift, so let me go grab my purse from the car, and then we're off."

Samantha claps and claps, rubs her palms together, and says, "Yay!"

Riley pulls the keys from a pocket on her way to the car. Inside, she slams the door, starts the ignition, and jets into reverse, leaving Samantha alone on the black tarmac, body motionless, face robbed of expression.

65

Riley blows along asphalt at a rate fast enough to make any traffic cop's head spin. Several feet ahead, a red light pulls her to a stop. She checks the mirror: no sign of Samantha, but that may only be temporary.

"Come on, come on, COME ON!" she yells at the light, pounding the wheel as if doing so might cause the signal to change.

It changes. She takes off, then hears this on the radio.

"We have new information for you today about the murder of a Lincoln Heights psychologist found bludgeoned to death in her office a few days ago. A confidential source tells NEWS One Hundred that Patricia Lockwood's face and body had been beaten so badly that the medical examiner had to use dental records to confirm her identity."

Riley swallows hard against what feels like a golf ball–size lump in her throat. She didn't need to hear that. She turns off her radio and, for a moment, considers calling in a tip about Samantha being Patricia's killer.

Don't.

Too risky. She'd love to put Samantha behind bars, but the effort could backfire in a huge way. She doesn't have proof that the woman actually did it, and authorities are probably already looking at Riley as a potential suspect. By now, they've figured out that she was Patricia's last appointment for the day. Then there's that troubling note Riley left. Detectives will soon come calling with questions. Offering a tip would bring her worst fear to life even quicker, moving the spotlight of suspicion directly over her.

Nope. Steer clear of the police.

Keeping her mouth shut is imperative to survival—that and doing everything possible to avoid becoming Samantha's next victim.

Riley sees a Mercedes logo in her rearview mirror.

Son of a bitch!

Seconds later, Samantha is driving right alongside Riley's car. Her stalker unveils the smile of a psychopath, glacial, confident, beaming with menace from corner to corner. Then Samantha falls behind Riley, and she knows vengeance is chasing her.

And this busy road is a hazardous place for it. Samantha has raised the stakes, and from here this situation can only take a turn for the worse. Riley needs to make a fast getaway—her life depends on it—so she jams her foot into the gas pedal and juts forward, leaving her follower several feet behind.

The move only buys momentary relief. In addition to having a lead foot, Samantha's got a powerful engine to match. She catches up and is soon on Riley's tail again. Too close, in fact. With mere inches separating their bumpers, traffic snarls, and she finds herself trapped, unable to change lanes or escape Samantha's road rage. She taps her brakes several times in the hopes that the flickering warning lights will make Samantha back off.

They do not. The action only seems to inflame Samantha's anger, fueling her into a more aggressive attack. She surges forward enough to give Riley's car a good *thwack*. Retribution is Samantha's wheelhouse, and her gears are spinning faster than a weather vane in a Texas tornado.

They hit the parkway, and traffic speeds up—so, too, does the danger, along with Riley's surging nervous system. Samantha keeps on her tail, and now they're both moving entirely too fast for safety.

Crunch. Crunch.

The Mercedes slams once, slams twice into her car, with neck-jerking force. Riley cranks the wheel to the right, and her car skips into the next lane.

But the effort proves futile. Samantha keeps up with her, and they're at it again, courting jeopardy in a perilous game of hawk-dove. Other than maintaining a hazardous speed, she doesn't know how to free herself from this death derby.

In a feeble attempt at self-preservation, she checks her mirror, but the psychotic huntress has vanished from view. She pokes her head through her window, checks the blind spot, but doesn't see the Mercedes, which only elevates her consternation. As she's quickly learning, Samantha is more dangerous out of sight than in it. All she can do is drive on, but it feels like waiting for the other shoe to drop—although in this case, *slam* might be a better word.

SLAM.

The hit comes from behind again, this time so powerful that it hurls Riley's car into a reckless shimmy. Her vehicle breaks into an out-of-control spin, barely missing another car while it ferociously skids and screeches and whirls toward the roadside. A blur twirls around her in double time as if she's flying through a Technicolor tunnel.

THUD, THUD. CRUNCH.

Her car skips onto the shoulder and keeps going. She tries to apply her brakes, but speed and a carpet of ice plants make a deadly proposition, lubricating her tires at a time when she least needs it and sending the vehicle into a wicked rate of acceleration. Sweaty palms keep their gorilla grip in place on a steering wheel that has nowhere safe to take her. Up ahead, a concrete bridge column looms directly in her path, moving toward her at an alarming and inescapable rate.

This is it. Right here. This is how it's going to end.

She tries to scream but nothing comes out.

She's about to crash head-on into the column of death when she sees a potential safety net. She wrenches the wheel and rockets front-end first into a brambly tangle of shrubs.

66

Riley's car chugs into her building's parking lot like a rolling train wreck.

Her tailpipe belches black smoke. Her mangled rear bumper dangles from one end, barely clinging on. Lengthy scratches run along the passenger's side panel, a mottled array of twigs and leaves sticking out from almost every gap wide enough to allow them.

She tries to straighten the bumper, but . . .

"Ouch! Shit!"

A jagged piece of metal cuts the side of her wrist.

Her phone dings.

It's a message from Francine, and Riley hardly needs to check it to know she's been fired. Now she doesn't even have a job to finance her car repairs. But the vehicle—and her wrist—have nothing on her mental state. Death came knocking in the form of a flipped-out woman bent on destruction, and were it not for that heavy patch of tall shrubs, the effort would have been a raging success. Her hands won't stop shaking. Her stomach feels lodged in a throat so dry, so tight, that it would take a crowbar to pry loose.

Samantha is nowhere in sight, but that makes Riley's nerves sky-rocket. The woman is an expert at surprise attacks. Today's failed attempt will only make her a bigger threat.

She looks out at the parking lot as if it were an active minefield. Rows of densely packed cars can provide great hiding places, which makes the threat of danger more potent at every turn. She rubs her aching clavicle, a threatening reminder of worse dangers that may lie ahead. She considers grabbing a tire iron from the trunk for protection, then nixes the idea. Too dangerous. Too many opportunities for Samantha to go on the assault while Riley searches for it.

She leaves her car and advances across the parking lot, ears tuned for the sound of approaching footsteps, eyes sifting through every shadow for Samantha's Mercedes. She knows her life has evolved to the place where, from here on, she'll live in constant fear, fleeing from the wrath of a dangerously warped mind.

The sound of tires scratching pebbly asphalt goes off behind her, and she reels around in time to see taillights on a black sedan peel out of the parking lot.

A banging sensation detonates in her throat. She decides to cut and run.

Several feet before the entrance, she looks up and stops so fast that she almost trips over her own feet. The lights are on inside her apartment, but that's not the problem—she left them that way before leaving for work. But the open sliver in her curtains? That's a problem. Samantha has already proved herself masterfully adept at bypassing locks, so without hesitation, Riley goes to Aileen's unit. Aileen calls on one of the maintenance guys to escort her upstairs, but after searching each room, he finds that everything appears normal.

Aileen pokes her head through the door to appraise the situation.

Maintenance Guy reports there's nothing out of the ordinary.

Aileen's eyes practically roll up into the back of her head. She walks away.

Great. I'll end up being the dead girl who cried wolf too many times.

She locks and secures the apartment, then collapses into her living room love seat, at last succumbing to the exhaustion of running for her life. She studies the barely opened drapes, the new lock, the door frame with its fortified strike plate, and the alarm with its green flashing light.

She looks back at the drapes. Did she leave them open and not notice? Is she, in fact, becoming paranoid, as Erin accused her of being? She doesn't know. Her judgment seems knotty, her senses too much on overload to trust any longer.

She hears a noise outside. She hustles to the window, pulls her curtains open wider, and stares into a night as black as pitch. She's about to pick up the binoculars when a bright light goes on in the watcher's apartment across the way. A dark figure brazenly walks up to the window. In this bright illumination, she can see that the person's head is indeed covered by something.

A welding helmet.

Samantha pulls it off and shakes out her hair. Although the distance between them is significant, Riley can feel the woman's eyes searing feverish holes through hers. Samantha waves, but there's nothing cordial about it; in fact, the action feels like a warning. Like a silent, mortal threat.

The thickening sensation in Riley's chest intensifies into a burn. She yanks her curtains closed, and as she backs away from the window, feels something brush against her foot. She looks down, leaps up.

Off to one side, two Mary Janes stick out from under the drapes.

I'm not going crazy. I'm not going crazy. I'm not going crazy.

Not again.

After checking and rechecking every lock and window in the apartment, she drops into bed, hoping exhaustion and sleep will pave a temporary escape from her growing fear of the unknown.

As she dozes, she gives one last thought to Samantha.

She'll never leave me.

"I'll never leave you," she hears just as she did during her old days on the streets, then stirs and rolls over.

"Clarissa? Is that you?" she drowsily mumbles, then again drifts off into sleep.

67

Sleep that doesn't last.

About an hour later, she awakens and sits straight up to the sound of commotion outside her apartment. She leaps from bed, grabs her robe, then through a dizzying haze and a pounding head rush, springs toward the living room. At the door, she looks into the peephole, and that's when a black, ephemeral shadow drifts past the glass. She dodges away from the door, presses a hand against her chest, and feels it rise and fall with each rasping breath.

When she peers out again, whoever it was seems to be gone, but she's not taking chances. She unlocks the door and takes hold of the security bar, tightening her grip around it. She opens the door, advances a few paces into the hallway, and looks both ways. Nobody in sight.

But as she steps back over the door's threshold, her heart again picks up speed when she sees a folded sheet of paper at her feet. The security bar falls from hand to floor. She feels a little dizzy, a little lost inside her head. She opens the paper, hand shaking so hard that the sheet noisily rattles. It's a letter.

Written in blood.

Mother,

We both know the truth.

Our truth.

We are connected by blood.

Our blood.

I'll never leave you.

Clarissa

A thin, wayward trail of dried blood runs from the end of Clarissa's name to the bottom of the page. A spatter of goose bumps breaks out across Riley's arms.

I'll never leave you.

The only person she discussed Clarissa's words with was Patricia. How could Samantha possibly know about them?

A sharp and fiery sensation twists through her, and for the first time she considers a different scenario—and this one is more frightening. The only way Samantha could know is if Patricia told her.

This might be much worse than I thought.

She feels panicked, rocky. She grabs the doorknob for stability. Out of anger or helplessness or—she doesn't know what anymore—she lets out a scream, loud, fearful, and powerful enough to resound through the apartment.

She stops. Samantha could be outside, hiding somewhere.

Without further thought, and most definitely without a moment of hesitation, she grabs the green-handled butcher's knife from the counter, then bounds through the door.

A few minutes later, she stands outside in the middle of the parking lot but can barely remember how she got there. Her mind races with a strange mix of confusion and anger. She throws her view up to the darkened window where Samantha's been watching Riley's life fall apart for a second time. She grits her teeth, gnawing against outrage, and with everything left in her, shouts to the apartment, "COME ON, BITCH! COME DOWN HERE AND GIVE ME EVERYTHING YOU'VE GOT! I'M READY FOR YOU. DO YOU HEAR ME? I'M READY!"

"Riley?"

She turns around, but it's not Samantha standing before her. Erin takes in her sister from head to toe, eyes wide like half dollars.

The fixed panic.

The tattered robe.

The bare feet.

She recognizes her sister's reaction all too well.

"This isn't what it looks like!" Riley shouts.

But she knows exactly how it looks—it looks like ten years ago, like her sister's worst fear again unfolding before her.

"Don't do this to me. DO NOT!" Riley implores. "Let me explain! It'll all make sense! I promise!"

With eyes acutely focused on Riley's right hand, Erin starts backing away. Riley looks down toward the butcher knife.

Erin's fear tells Riley this is indeed the same scenario all over again. Not just the part where she's crazy.

The part where Erin doesn't believe her.

68

This crisis is no longer snowballing. It's an official whiteout.

The two sisters sit across from each other at Riley's dining room table. Nothing said yet, but the strain between them is so tight and unyielding that it could snap at any moment.

Erin notices the cut on the side of Riley's wrist, then looks up at her.

Riley says, "Don't worry. It was an accident. If I wanted to slit myself again, I'd pick a much better spot."

"That's not funny, and it's not what I was thinking. I was just concerned."

"What are you doing here anyway? It's ten thirty at night," Riley says, hand wrapped snugly around the cup of decaffeinated tea that Erin gave her—an obvious attempt to settle her down.

"You were supposed to call me after work, so I got worried. And why weren't you answering your phone?"

"I went to bed early."

"Riley, what on earth were you just doing outside?"

She gives Erin a long, contemplative look. She shoves the blood letter across the table and says, "Left under my door by Samantha."

Erin starts reading, and with each passing second, her mouth opens wider. "What the . . . ?" She drops the letter onto the table, looks up at her sister. "Please don't tell me you believe this woman could possibly be . . ."

"Oh, come on, Erin! Would you give me some credit? Can you imagine for a second that I have a little bit of sense?"

"You were wandering around outside and screaming in your bathrobe with a knife in your hand."

"Do you want the actual truth, or do you want to sit there and keep treating me like I'm nuts?"

"Okay." Erin sets her hands, palms down, onto the table. She looks at them for a moment, as if she's trying to calm her thoughts, then raises her gaze to Riley. "So what's this letter all about? Does she believe you're her mother or something?"

"She's been trying to make me one."

"But why would she pick *you*?"

With an impatient huff, Riley says, "I don't know."

Erin studies her. She appears doubtful again.

"If you don't believe me, take a look out the window at my car. She tried to kill me today."

Erin goes there, catches sight of Riley's car in the parking lot, and her expression deflates.

Riley says, "And she's not going to stop. That's what I've been try-ing to tell you."

Erin walks back to Riley. She exhales through her nose and says, "I want to believe you—I really do."

"Then why don't you?"

"Because it's been hard! You keep throwing all these disjointed theories at me, and then there are all the lies . . ."

Riley doesn't speak, but her eyes are pleading.

Erin looks back at the window for a long moment. As if she's thinking on it, maybe even trying to bend her beliefs in Riley's direction.

"Okay," Erin at last says. "So, we have to figure out a way to stop this . . . Samantha."

"Except she's an emotional vampire who won't unhinge her jaws from my neck."

"Luckily, your little sister knows quite a bit about that particular topic. So, here's how this will play out. First, we file a restraining order, then—"

"Hang on a minute. No. I'm not involving the cops!"

Erin gives Riley a sour look, and her bottom jaw juts out. "They don't have to be. Not unless she violates the order."

"But by then it'll be completely useless. There's not a cop in this town who would respond to a call for help from me." Riley balks. "They'd probably give Samantha a police escort right to my door."

"Would you relax? Please? Look, I offered a suggestion about how to protect yourself after the apartment break-in, but you thumbed your nose at it. Now that you've got no other choice, maybe you'll finally listen and dump this . . . *policiophobia* that's been occupying a giant space in your brain. Do you honestly believe I'd allow any of that shit to happen? That I wouldn't stand up and rip into anyone who violates your rights?"

Riley doesn't answer.

Erin says, "Give me twenty dollars."

"What for?"

"Just give it to me."

Riley opens her purse, roots around for her wallet, then hands over the money.

"It's official." Erin shoves the bill into her back pocket. "That was my retainer fee. I'm representing you."

"Can you do that with your sister?"

"There's no law saying I can't. It's not completely advisable, but I don't see any conflict of interest. And you know, desperate times."

"You think you can stop her?"

"Maybe you've forgotten my professional reputation in this town. I'm a vulture. I rip out intestines and eat people for lunch while they're still kicking and screaming."

"Okay." Riley blows out a fast breath. "Good."

"Trust me. I'll come down so hard on that woman's ass that they'll need a crane to pluck it out of the ground."

69

Erin has established belief that Riley may not be crazy, after all.

Or at least it seems that way.

But this morning Riley knows her troubles continue. She sits on the floor outside Wendy's apartment but doesn't knock—she needs to be here. She could . . .

"I could use a friend right now . . ."

"Then you've come to the right place." Wendy's soothing tenor is very much what Riley needs.

She looks at the door and says, "Would it be possible if—could I come in? Even just for a moment?"

The door opens. Their eyes meet: Riley's tearful, Wendy's compassionate. She's about to put a hand on Riley's shoulder but—as if all at once remembering that her personal boundaries take precedence over emotional closeness—stops short of making contact.

Time stands still.

Until Wendy says, "This is a one-time offer, so don't blow it. Either step in or move on."

Riley laughs a little through her tears while entering the apartment. Behind her, she hears Wendy closing the door and a dead bolt engaging. She looks around: the apartment is immaculate, everything neatly in place, not a speck of dirt to be found. And decorated quite nicely. It's kind of unexpected.

"We're not *all* a bunch of sloppy hoarders who collect boxes of strings," Wendy says, as if catching Riley's thought in midair.

"Clearly."

Wendy points to the couch and says, "Sit."

Riley does.

"I have iced tea," Wendy informs her. Riley can only assume that this is her version of *Can I get you anything?*

Wendy pulls a pitcher from the refrigerator, and Riley continues perusing the apartment until she stops at a framed photo that rests prominently on top of the entertainment center. It takes a moment to realize the picture is of Wendy—a different Wendy—from quite some time ago. A pretty woman with silky blonde hair and high cheekbones. Arms wrapped around a handsome young boy. Both smiling, probably giggling, actually, the resemblance between them unmistakable. Looking at this photo is like peering through the window at Wendy's once-normal world, a beautiful one. She wonders why it never occurred to her that Wendy wasn't always trapped in this dungeon called life.

A glass of iced tea clacks on the side table, startling her. She turns from the photo, then stutters a thank-you.

Wendy lowers herself into the love seat so they're facing each other and nervously twists a ring on her finger. A beautiful ring, featuring a moderate-size emerald-cut stone the color of green sea glass, so brilliant it nearly takes Riley's breath away.

"My son gave it to me as a Mother's Day gift," Wendy tells her. She holds up her hand as if admiring the ring, but it's not pride Riley sees—it's something else. A momentary stab of joy, of unmistakable love. Wendy adds, "He worked and saved for a whole year."

"It's beautiful," Riley says, then goes back to the photo.

"That's him."

Riley nods.

"He was fifteen in the picture."

The same age as Clarissa.

"After his dad left, we got closer than ever." Wendy looks as if she's grinning at a memory. "Such a little joker, that kid. And ornery?" Through a repressed giggle, "Good Lord, he was always causing trouble."

"You look so much alike."

"We *did*." Wendy stares vacantly at the photo.

Riley wrestles to speak, but all that comes out is, "You . . ."

"I lost a child, too. I did."

Riley had wondered what horrible event could have happened to make Wendy quit life. To hide away from the world. But never once had she imagined it was because the two share a similar kind of pain.

"His name was Sean," Wendy says.

"When did he die?"

"Ten years ago. The day after that picture was taken."

Riley lowers her head and closes her eyes for a long moment. Wendy's life fell apart around the same time hers did.

"It was his birthday."

"Wendy, I'm so . . ."

Wendy's voice is coarse, and her eyes glisten when she says, "One of the best days we ever had. Followed by the absolute worst."

Riley sees a box of tissues on the coffee table and hands it to Wendy. Wendy takes the box, pulls one out, but doesn't use it, as if refraining might keep her tears from coming.

Riley says, "How come you've never told me? I could have helped . . . or at least listened."

"Don't like talking about it." Wendy points to the door. "Out there I may have to, but in here I don't."

"I can understand that."

"I imagine you would," Wendy says, looking out through her window at some faraway place.

"We don't have to talk about it if it makes you uncomfortable."

"You know . . . it's kind of strange, but for the first time in a very long time, it feels okay, like you're the only person I know who understands—*really* understands—what I'm feeling. What I've felt."

If a smile could be both happy and sad at the same time, Riley's would be the image of it.

"It happened right in front of me," Wendy says.

Something else we have in common.

"What I wouldn't give to wipe that memory from my mind."

And something we don't.

"But it's a part of me—the memory—like a sick, putrefying organ. Every damned day it kills me a little more."

"What happened?" Riley asks gently.

"A maniac happened. A madman. He walked into Burger Palace with three guns strapped to his back and opened fire on a crowd of innocent people. One minute we were all enjoying lunch, and the next we were scrambling for our lives. People hid under tables, ran for the exits. A guy at the rear of the restaurant crashed through one of the windows and bled out onto the sidewalk. The parking lot looked like a bomb went off, littered with injured people, blood, and broken glass. After he was done, twenty were dead and twenty others were injured. The whole incident was so terrifying that it felt like it couldn't possibly be real. It was all over the news, one of the biggest mass murders in California history."

Riley remembers now.

"I jumped on top of Sean—on top of my baby—to cover his body, to protect him," Wendy says as if each word is being squeezed out of her. She's clutching the armrests, trembling. "But I wasn't fast enough." Her voice falls into a ruptured whisper. "I . . . I couldn't save him."

I couldn't save her.

How many times has Riley echoed that statement? How many times has it punished her? She looks out the window, too, seeing Wendy's world from a brand-new perspective. A world that, on so many levels, has betrayed this woman in the worst of ways. A world so horribly damaged that Wendy can no longer face it, let alone be a part of it.

A world that Riley knows all too well.

"My baby didn't stand a chance," Wendy says, wiping her wet face, barely able to finish the sentence.

Riley reaches across to put a hand on Wendy's knee and leaves it there. She can hardly draw oxygen, can't make her voice work, and even if she could, she wouldn't know what to say. There are no words for this. Nothing to comfort a mother going through this level of suffering.

"Our situations may be different," Wendy says, trying to clear her throat, "but our pain is much the same. Know what I mean?"

"I do."

"So this is my life. Constantly living on edge, jumping out of my skin every time a car backfires or some jackass sets off fireworks outside. Can you imagine? To always be looking over your shoulder. To see every person as a potential danger. To . . ."

"To lose faith in everyone and everything," Riley says, hearing her raw helplessness. And she does know. She's living it.

Wendy looks at her through the tears and nods.

The room grows quiet, but at this moment silence feels so much bigger than any words could ever be.

Wendy says, "You don't know how many times I've wished that bullet had hit me instead. I'd give anything to be the one who died that day—anything—and in a way, I did."

Different situations, same outcomes, Riley thinks.

"So instead," Wendy goes on, "I live inside this self-imposed jail, terrified that if I walk out the door, what happened to Sean will happen to me. It's not that I mind dying—Lord, I wish every day that I could—it's about what happens before that, being forced to relive the horrific nightmare. To see my child die all over again. I . . ." She hugs herself, folds over, and bursts into tears. Almost begging, "I can't. I just can't do it again."

Riley moves to sit beside Wendy. No conversation between them, but none is necessary. Their mutual and tragic histories are the bonds that connect them in a most profound way, are all that matter during this heartbreaking moment.

But Wendy is only telling half the truth. There is no difference between the two sides of that door. Riley knows. Each day, she wanders between both worlds, and each day pain and anguish travel right along with her. Clarissa will indeed never leave her, nor will the painful memories that are left in her wake.

But that doesn't mean Riley has to remain a victim of her own mind.

Not anymore.

70

Get out. Stay strong. Trust your truth.

She's ready. All she needs to do now is get the gears spinning.

Each day, without fail, the daughter I lost still lives on, she said to Samantha during one of their first meetings.

"This one's for us, Clarissa," she says now.

She's dressed and ready to go. She peers out between the drapes. The Mercedes is in its spot below. A few minutes later, Samantha appears in the lot. She steps into her car and drives off to work.

Riley punches the security code that will grant access to Samantha's building. Then she strolls through the lobby as if she owns it.

After letting herself into Samantha's apartment, Riley heads straight into the office and picks up where she left off last time, digging through files on the hunt for any information that will give her a leg up on Samantha.

In a filing cabinet beside the desk she finds a folder marked *RH*. When she opens it, the oxygen scuds from her lungs.

Samantha had been building a dossier on Riley for a long time. Inside is a boatload of newspaper stories about her, including the recently leaked info that Erin had mentioned, detailing Riley's progress and expected release. This one was dated five months before she got out.

Mother Accused of Burying Daughter Alive Improving at Psychiatric Hospital. May be Released in a Few Months.

And this one.

Riley Harper to be Discharged from Glendale Next Week.

She shuffles through the folder, pulls out two sheets of paper. One is an online brochure, detailing Glendale's Hospital Release Housing Program with one interesting section.

List of locations currently booked.

Riley's building is the only one available, and it's circled with a black marker.

Samantha was definitely on a mission to find information. The next few pages are notes from either a visit or call to the hospital after inquiring about treatment for the father she no longer has, then about housing assistance upon his release.

Who's been following whom?

Samantha was obsessed with figuring out where Riley would live before even *Riley* knew. Talk about the lengths some people will go just to be loved.

Her gut twists like a nine-strand rope. Had Samantha gone so far as to stalk Erin while she visited Riley's apartment complex to make living arrangements?

She digs deeper, comes across a billing statement, which illustrates a string of unpaid visits to Patricia that began shortly after she and Riley met.

Then she thinks about the time Samantha found that appointment card on the floorboard during their drive. Riley didn't walk in on Samantha's first visit with Patricia. She'd been seeing the therapist throughout the entire friendship. No wonder Patricia looked so blown away. She had no idea she'd been treating Riley and Samantha at the same time. And look: Samantha used a different name.

Christina Henry.

The same initials as Clarissa's.

If that isn't a sign she was trying to replace my deceased daughter, I don't know what is.

She slams shut the drawer. As she walks toward the doorway, she slows; she can feel a slight bump beneath her feet. After pulling up the corner of the swanky shag rug, she finds a stack of yellow loose-leaf pages filled with writing. She takes a look at the first page, and a grin blossoms across her face.

I've got you.

She shoves the papers into her waistband and leaves as unobtrusively as she came.

Outside the building, she steps up her gait, periodically glancing over her shoulder. Nobody's watching, and she's relieved.

Until a hand, firm and harsh, clamps onto her arm.

71

The nemesis stares Riley in the face.

Not Samantha. The other one.

Detective Demetre Sloan doesn't say anything, but there's no need to. Her presence, her flinty stare, her unforgiving grip on Riley's arm, say everything.

"Let go!" Riley shouts. "You're hurting me!"

"I wouldn't have to grab it in the first place if you watched where you were going." She lets go of Riley's arm after practically shoving it back, a small and sensible gold hoop swinging from each ear. "You almost plowed right into me."

Riley rubs her forearm, mindful not to let the papers in her waistband under the jacket make noise. She looks at a dark-colored sedan parked several feet away against the curb. It's identical to the one she's seen spying on her. She points a finger at Demetre and says, "It's been you all along! *You're* the one who's been creeping around my parking lot!"

Sloan cocks a brow. "Sure it wasn't one of your imaginary friends?"

"Bitch," Riley says.

"Watch it."

"I will when you stop persecuting me."

"I'm doing my job. You know, investigating leads. Solving crimes."

Riley nods toward the dark-colored sedan, looks toward her own parking lot, and says, "You sure have been investigating lots of leads within a confined perimeter. Don't they let you out to travel the streets like a big girl?"

Sloan tilts her chin toward the top of Samantha's building. "I'm thinking that unless you've inherited some serious green—or robbed a bank—you can't possibly afford a place like this. So I'm curious what you're doing here."

"Wow. Not much has changed. Still chasing after the wrong suspect."

"Am I?" Sloan says through a smirk as rotten as spoiled vinegar. "I bet Patricia Lockwood would beg to disagree."

"What's that supposed to mean?"

"It means you're under the microscope. It means we know you were the last patient to see her before the murder."

Riley's teeth are clenched so tight with anger that her jaw aches. She pulls the phone from her pocket and says, "Detective, are you arresting me? Do I need to call my sister?"

"Not this particular moment, but you may want to keep her on speed dial."

Riley says, "Is there anything else you need from me, Detective?"

"Not yet."

"Is there anything else you need from me *right now*, Detective," she says, but this time it's not a question—it's a stern warning to either put up or shove off.

"Nope. That is, unless you finally got smart over at Glendale and want to fess up."

Riley walks away, blowing off the woman like a horrid stench.

When she comes back to her apartment, she pulls out the papers she found under Samantha's rug, pages torn from Patricia Lockwood's consulting notebook, which Samantha must have stolen after killing her.

Notes from both Riley's and Samantha's sessions.

The further she reads, the more her neck stiffens with mulish tension, followed by revulsion that sends blood pumping through every vein in her body like searing magma. She skims the notes from Samantha's visits with Patricia.

Patient has trouble expressing grief over daughter's murder. Never allowed herself to. Suppressed anger. Anxiety with depression.

Samantha changed the circumstances so well that Patricia would have had difficulty making the connection.

A penetrating shiver ticks over every bone in her spine. Page after page, it's the same. Samantha claiming ownership of Riley's feelings purely as a data-mining effort, to learn all the right words, to have all the right reactions, to cultivate trust. To dominate.

Riley then reviews Patricia's notes from her own sessions, which only lead her deeper into another stage of frightening comprehension.

Used example to describe Samantha—If someone is nice to you but rude to the waiter, they are not a nice person.

What Samantha parroted to Riley during their scuffle to try to rattle her.

Another mystery solved.

But one more still remains. Why did she kill Patricia? To eliminate anyone who could corroborate Riley's story? Or was it pure rage after she and Samantha got into that fight outside the office?

Or was it something else?

A product of Samantha's deadly possessiveness? Riley saw the way she acted when she found the appointment card from Patricia that day. Was it raging jealousy because someone other than her was getting close to Riley?

Her skin crawls just thinking about the lengths Samantha went to intrude in every part of Riley's life.

Another thought slides in over the last, and this one is just as troublesome. Samantha's invasiveness probably hasn't stopped there.

Angst returns. Vulnerability magnifies.

Her sight flits around the apartment.

Could Samantha have the place bugged? Or even worse, have put in hidden cameras?

It's conceivable. After all, Samantha already gained access to this apartment those other times.

The thought is mortifying.

What about her food? Is it possible she put something in it?

"Okay . . . okay . . . okay . . . calm down." She places both palms against her thighs, blows out a series of short breaths. "I might be overreacting."

Then she immediately goes on the hunt for recording devices. She looks under every piece of furniture, looks behind pictures on the wall, even looks inside vases big and small.

After an extensive search, she finds nothing, then Patricia's murder comes crashing through Riley's mind.

I could be next. I have to go on the attack before she does.

72

Riley sits on a coffee shop patio a few miles from her apartment. Her dark hair is gone, replaced by the original flaxen color with scattered accents of strawberry. What once flowed past her shoulders now barely covers the tops of her ears.

Her intent is purposeful. It's strategic. She knows that the only way to beat Samantha at her game is to play it. Putting herself in plain sight will be the first step. The next will be to take back the control she lost. This is an extremely dangerous effort, and she's nervous, but hopefully, being in public and in close proximity to others will keep her safe.

She does a quick inspection of her surroundings. No sign of the enemy yet, but that could soon change.

In the meantime, she makes herself look busy by drinking coffee and scrolling down the screen of her laptop. About ten minutes later, she notices someone standing still behind her in the screen's reflection. The face is blurred, but she can make out the long, dark hair, the white T-shirt, the jeans.

She found me.

She prepares herself, turns around toward Samantha, but Samantha isn't whom she finds—it's a young woman with her friend waiting at the service counter. She holds a cup of coffee in one hand, and with the other points to an empty table several feet away. When the girl notices Riley staring, she offers a neutralizing, sorry-just-trying-to-get-settled smile. Riley smiles back, then takes her wary gaze around the patio.

"Looking for someone?"

A whumping pulse pumps through Riley's veins, and she whirls around. Samantha sits directly across the table. She smiles a jolly smile. Riley tries to speak, but shock prohibits it. She was expecting the Female Antichrist to show, but not like this. She should have known better.

"Hate the hair," Samantha remarks with a snort.

"Figured you might," Riley says, then crosses one leg over the other.

Slap, slap, slap.

Samantha glares at the red pump snapping on and off Riley's foot—the same shoe Samantha stole from the store and Riley subsequently stole from her.

"They looked better on me," Samantha says, flicking her gaze away and toward another table. She comes back to Riley and, without missing a beat, says, "So, I'll go first. After careful consideration, I've decided to give you a second chance."

For obvious reasons, the offer provides Riley with not a sliver of relief.

"You know," Samantha goes on, "take the high road. Forgive and forget. It's the right move to make, and I'm thinking with a little work, you and I can move past all that ugly stuff. We had something special that most moms and daughters can only dream of. Let's not throw it all away."

She's got to be kidding.

Samantha brings her hands out from under the table. She rests them on the surface, fingers intertwined, locked . . . and clad in a pair of latex gloves. She blinks and smiles. Blinks and smiles again.

Riley tries her best to conceal the fright jackrabbiting up through her esophagus.

Samantha extends her gloved hands across the table and says, "So what do you say, Mom? Forgive and forget?"

Riley hoicks her hands out of reach and tries to channel calm, despite the spiny heat that, like a hungry flame, spirals through every part of her.

"Come on now, Mother. Don't be like that," Samantha says, her pout of disappointment both playful and sinister, latex-clad fingers wiggling like worms at Riley.

Don't let her intimidate you. Do not.

Riley pulls from her purse Patricia's billing statement. With a flat look, she holds it up.

Samantha's grin is flippant.

Hold steady. You're doing fine.

"That's all you've got for me? That's your big"—Samantha makes air quotes with her fingers—"game changer? Damn it, I was hoping for a lot more fun than this."

Riley regards the paperwork. "I can have you arrested with these."

"For what? A little maintenance therapy?" Samantha snorts. "No crime in striving for self-improvement."

Riley pulls out Patricia's notes. "This doesn't look like self-improvement. This looks awful suspicious, like a desperate act to hide something."

She can see Samantha trying hard not to show a reaction, but her wretched vulnerability plays like a chink in the armor. She flaps her attention away and says, "I've never seen those notes before in my life."

"They came from your place."

"Prove it."

Riley doesn't know how to prove it, and telling the cops she broke into Samantha's apartment to steal them certainly won't fly. So she punts with a bluff. "I'll let the police do that. It won't take long for them to figure it out."

"Be careful what you wish for, Riley."

"What's that supposed to mean?"

"It means you were Patricia's last appointment for the day. It means *I'm* not the one holding that nasty little hot potato in my hands. If they suspect anyone, my guess is that you're stuck dead center in their crosshairs."

"You set me up for the murder."

"Say you love me and I'll *unset* you. Come on. How about it? Some of that awesome mother love?"

"I am *not* your—"

"*Bup, bup, bup, bup,*" she interrupts. "Do not finish that. You know what happened last time. I've got skills you haven't even seen yet. Don't make me use them."

"Is that what you're calling all those atrocious personality disorders these days?"

Without warning, Samantha snatches away the notes, shoves them into her purse, then seizes Riley's wrist. With the gloved hands, she begins mercilessly twisting.

Riley tries to yell for help but chokes on air, skin burning to the command of torqueing latex. All she can force out is, "You're . . . hurting . . ."

"Not nearly as bad as you've hurt me," Samantha says, sounding grisly and deep—deadly, even. The tips of Riley's fingers are purple and throbbing. Samantha's eyes water, but there's no sadness in them. All Riley sees is unadulterated anger. With her free hand, she latches on to Riley's ring and pinkie fingers and, with the other, adjusts her grip around the next two.

"So many ways to break you," Samantha says, pulling the sets of fingers apart. Then through gritted teeth and a blazing-hot stare that could burn down a city, come these snarling words: "Say you love me."

The pain is unbearable. Tears crawl down Riley's cheeks, but in her belly there is nothing but base fury when she says, "I am NOT your mother!"

That's when she feels the *crack* between her middle and ring fingers, but a silent scream is all she can get out.

"Fine, have it your way," Samantha snarls as she releases Riley's wrist. "I'm going to crucify you."

Riley finds her voice, lets out an excruciated groan. Holding one hand with the other, she rocks in writhing pain. People are staring. One guy snatches up his cell phone, probably calling for help. The madwoman rises from the table and grins.

"Do you ever think about how your husband really died?" she asks.

Riley is filled with horror and despair. Through her pain, she manages to say, "No, Rose. I know you killed him, too."

73

Riley waits more than six hours at the clinic, nursing an agonizingly painful and throbbing hand until someone can see her. When the examination and X-rays are done, the doctor diagnoses a fracture between the middle and ring fingers.

She goes home with a cast on her hand, a sizable medical bill to add to her debt, and smoldering anger in her gut. The hand may be broken, but her determination is not; neither is her robustly bitter taste for retribution. She will destroy Rose Hopkins, no matter what the cost.

Now she stands before Clarissa's grave. Not once since the funeral has she come here. It isn't because she doesn't care or that it's too painful—it's because her daughter doesn't live in that box of bones beneath the plush lawn and crumbled granite. Clarissa's light shines aboveground and through Riley.

And she didn't come here to visit. She came to evade Rose's surveillance. This is likely the last place the woman would look for her. Clarissa's gravesite is also well hidden behind a mausoleum and surrounded by tall bushes. For added measure, she made sure Samantha didn't follow her here, so hopefully, she'll be safe.

Erin pulls up and parks next to Riley's car on an adjacent frontage road. She gets out and turns stone-statue still, eyes traveling from Riley's changed hair to the cast, then back to the hair.

"Whoa . . . ," she says, "I'm not even sure where to start, but let's hit the most pressing issue first. What happened to your hand?"

"Samantha."

"Are you kidding me?"

"I keep telling you she's dangerous."

"Did you call—" Erin stops herself short of saying *the cops*, then changes topics. "Why are we having this conversation at Clarissa's grave, anyway?"

Riley looks to her left, looks to her right. "Privacy," she whispers, then motions for Erin to come closer.

Erin sends her perplexed gaze around the cemetery as if she's trying to find a perceived enemy off in the distance. When she comes back to Riley, it looks as though someone snapped a towel in Erin's face.

"She's getting more dangerous," Riley says. "I need that restraining order wrapped up."

"Yeah . . . so, about that."

Riley steps in closer to her sister.

"I did some research before filing the order to see what I could dig up on Samantha."

"And?"

"Samantha Light doesn't exist."

"What do you mean? Of course she exists."

"Not on paper. No driver's license. No registered vehicle."

"What about her apartment? I know she laid tracks there."

"None that I could find."

Riley withdraws.

"Still with me here?" Erin asks. "Because I almost filed a restraining order on a phantom."

"She's not. She's real."

"Then explain this."

Riley stalls, then says, "Samantha Light is an alias."

"You're kidding me, right? Withholding information? Again? I'm tired of this. Either tell the truth or I walk." Erin starts to walk away.

Riley latches on to Erin's sleeve, pulls her back, and says, "She's Rose Hopkins."

"Oh no . . ." Erin looks down at the lawn, puts a palm against her forehead. "We are not really doing this all over again, are we? Riley, listen to me." She treads past the headstone, knits both hands through her hair, then looks back at her sister and says, "Rose Hopkins did *not* kill Clarissa, and I don't for a minute believe she's returned to terrorize you under this Samantha Light persona. Do you even realize how ludicrous that sounds?"

"It's not! It was real. It happened. She even tried to throw me off track with a phony southern accent, then claimed she'd found Rose by pulling up some old photo of herself before the plastic surgery."

Erin flinches. "The *what*?"

"She already admitted she got a boob job; it's no stretch to guess she altered her face, too. But that doesn't matter now. The point is that Rose turned our lives upside down."

"You had nothing to prove that!"

"I tried!"

"And brought me to a vacant house! And the more you explained, the less it added up!"

"What did you want from me? Sworn affidavits? How many times did I have to tell you? The only other person who could support my story was Clarissa, and she was already dead. And while we're on that, Rose killed Jason, too."

Erin's head rattles. "Every piece of evidence at the scene—every shred—pointed to an accident. An *accident*, Riley. He tripped on a rock. He wasn't killed by a little girl. And that little girl hasn't come back as a new person with a new face."

"Maybe she put the rock there."

"Again, where's the proof?"

"Look at this." Riley produces the bill she stole from Rose.

Erin spares her sister a cryptic glance before taking the paper. When she reads it, her posture deflates. "How did you gain access to confidential patient information? Please don't tell me you broke into Patricia's office, which, incidentally, would make you a suspect in her murder. Please don't tell me that."

"I didn't take it from Patricia's office."

"Thank heavens."

"I took it from Rose's apartment."

Erin's spine stiffens as if someone has ordered her to straighten her posture. "Wonderful. Now you're breaking into people's homes?"

"That's not what's important here!"

"But what does this prove?"

"That she killed Patricia!"

Erin blinks twice. She tries to compose herself and says, "All it demonstrates is that you were both seeing the same therapist."

"She used a fake name. I also found Patricia's session notes in Rose's apartment. She stole them after killing her."

Erin holds out a hand. "Let me see them."

"I don't have them anymore. Rose took them when she broke my hand."

"Riley! This is a damned shell game. Nothing you've said is tracking. I need evidence!"

"I'm telling you what happened!"

Erin pauses to gape at her sister, then says, "Who are you right now? Do you even realize how paranoid you're sounding again?

Stop bending reality. Stop seeing people who don't exist. Tell the truth!"

"I am!"

"Are you?" Erin looks at her sister with anger for a few seconds, then, "Riley, were you fired from your job?"

"I don't see why that has anything to do with—"

"Were you fired from your job?"

"Okay, yes, but how do you even know that?"

Erin nods toward Riley's car. "You shouldn't leave employment circulars sitting on your dashboard. When did it happen?"

"Wednesday."

"I came to your place that night. Why didn't you tell me then?"

"Because there were other pressing matters. Like the letter written to me in blood? By an extremely dangerous woman who nearly killed me on the freeway?" Her volume is rising. "Why does it matter?"

"Because it illustrates your continuing pattern of omission."

"Here we go again. We've landed back in Erin's Courtroom."

"I'm just saying that if we were in front of a judge, your lack of accountability would get you torn into microbits."

"What am I doing on the stand in the first place? Why aren't you being my sister instead of—"

Erin's phone goes off. She silences it, takes in a breath through her nose, then says, "So where were we?"

"Check your notes, counselor. I think you were exposing my *pattern of omission*."

"Tell me something else," Erin says, ignoring the snipe. "Besides you, has anyone you know ever seen Samantha?"

"Patricia did."

"A witness who also happens to be dead."

"Wendy saw her, too."

"And Wendy is?"

"My neighbor. My friend."

"Great. Someone else I've never heard of."

"Are we really going back to your suspicion that Samantha isn't real? You said you believed me!"

"That was before all this," Erin mutters. "What else have you not told me?"

Riley starts to speak, then stops herself.

"What?"

"I can't."

"Why not?"

"Because you're one of them. You won't believe me about it, either."

"Oh, great. Now here comes the persecution complex."

"Well? Ever since I left Glendale, you've been monitoring my mental competency, analyzing everything I do. And all these pointed questions and doubts? Those aren't a beaming vote of confidence, either." It's Riley's turn to scrutinize Erin. "And since we're going there, tell me something. Do you remember how many times you came to visit me at Glendale?"

"I don't exactly remem—"

"Three times."

"But the first time they made me leave because you were having hallucinations that I'd killed Clarissa! I wasn't allowed to come back until they stabilized you."

"And the rest of the two years?"

Erin doesn't have an answer for that one.

"*Three,*" Riley says, "while I sat there staring at cracked walls and breathing the smell of people's filthy urine."

"I'm pretty sure I came more than that."

"And I'm sure you didn't," Riley says, eyes filling with tears. "And I know exactly why."

"Okay, this is getting completely bananas."

"Because not once during those visits—or anytime before or since—have you told me you believe I am innocent of killing my daughter."

"You should know that I—"

"I'm not a damned mind reader!" The tears are no longer filling Riley's eyes—they're falling down her face, dripping from her chin. "Dammit, Erin! I needed to hear it!" Riley takes a gasp of oxygen so sharp, so deep, that it feels as though it could be her final breath. And, at last, as if she's opened a mighty floodgate, her emotions come surging through in full force. A fearless tide of agony, of intense suffering, so raw, so real, that she collapses onto Clarissa's tombstone as if it's the only thing that can hold her up, body swaying to and fro, trying to rock away the punishing sorrow.

Erin tries to place a wavering hand on her sister's shoulder, but just as fast, Riley shoves it away.

"My daughter was murdered!" Riley says, but it comes out as though she's begging to be rescued. "And as if that wasn't excruciating enough, they accused me of killing her! Me! The person who loved her the most in this world! They destroyed me." Riley breaks into racking sobs. "But you did worse, Erin. So much worse. Can you even imagine what it felt like to realize that my sister might actually believe I killed my own daughter? Then you refused to talk about it. You left me alone, Erin! When I needed you most!"

"I never thought any of that. I never thought you killed her!" Erin says, nearly choking on her tears. "I swear I didn't!"

"Then why didn't you ever tell me that?" Riley says in an angry whisper. "Why did you leave me to fall apart in that place?"

"Because I was scared! Because after I saw you bleed out on your kitchen floor, and after I had you rushed to the hospital so they could save your life, and after I had to commit you to Glendale, you stopped connecting with me. You disappeared. And . . . and I thought you were angry. Angry at what I'd done!"

Riley doesn't respond. Not because she doesn't want to—it's because she can't. And the worst part: she's not sure if it's sadness or anger that throttles her words and holds them hostage. Maybe it's both. Maybe it's even more complicated than that.

"I was never angry at you," Riley says at last. A voice fractured by anguish, and in it there is so much regret. Regret that drills deep into her until it hits marrow.

"It was like all of a sudden this giant wall shot up between us, so tall and thick that I couldn't figure out how to tear it down," Erin says, wrapping her arms tightly around herself. "And it kept getting worse, and everything felt bigger than us, and completely destroyed."

"You could have tried."

"I didn't understand you anymore!" Erin sniffles and wipes her nose. "I'm not even sure if I know who *we* are. All I do know is that it feels like there's nothing left of us."

Both women fall into heartbroken silence.

"And the worst part?" Erin goes on, trembling. "The worst part is that I'm not sure if either of us knows how to find our way back."

She walks away, leaving Riley alone beside her daughter's grave.

74

Riley catches up to Erin's car just as she's about to drive off.

"Wait!" Riley says through the open window, face stained by tears and trying to catch her breath. "You're not leaving that easily. You don't get to just drive off now."

"I'm done here." Erin angrily shoves the shifter into park, then looks up at her sister. "There's nothing left to say."

"I'm not losing it again, and I'm going to prove it to you."

"Damn it, Riley! Don't you get it? This is no longer about proving something. This is about damages. Broken feelings can heal. Broken relationships? Not as often."

"We aren't broken."

Erin waves off the comment.

"We're *not*. All that ugly stuff has been brewing in us for too long. It needed to come out. And as difficult as that was, I feel better now."

"I don't."

"You will. Think of it like vomiting."

"Wow. *There's* a lovely visual to help this along."

"It always feels gross when you purge bottled-up emotions, even for a short time after. Then it gets better."

"Great. Now I'll see throw-up every time I think of you."

Riley almost grins, then she becomes serious. "Erin, we're going to make it through this. We are. We've been through the tough stuff before and survived it. Remember when Mom's cancer finally took hold and she was put in hospice? How, during her last days, you and I held each other up?"

Erin's pinched-up face softens a hair. "It was the closest we'd ever been."

"We were there for each other then. Please, be here for me this time," Riley says. "Can you get into the car with me?"

"Why?"

"To prove I'm not going nuts again."

"Where to?"

"To meet the woman formerly known as Rose."

Erin stares sightlessly out at the cemetery and says nothing.

Riley tells her, "Maybe I need to see she's real, too."

Erin turns. "Now *you're* having doubts she exists?"

"Not that. Maybe this is more an attempt to gain some kind of footing on my life. To feel anchored. I guess doing it with you feels like a safe place to start. It always has."

"Not always. Not anymore."

"It was never gone. We just couldn't see it beneath all the garbage that came after losing Clarissa."

Erin doesn't look at Riley this time, but her eyes, wet and softened, seem to speak what she can't say.

"I still see her sometimes." The comment comes out as if free of Riley's will, as if she's been waiting so long to tell her sister this.

"I know," Erin says with so much sadness. "I see her all over the house, can almost hear her, then, when I turn to look, she's not there, and I realize it's one of many haunting memories from when she'd stay with me . . . and it hurts so much."

Riley struggles to speak through the grief that squeezes her heart. "In the moments when I see her, I feel like I can reach out and touch her, smell her beautiful scent, and it's comforting, Erin, so damned comforting. But then she disappears, and my world collapses, and it's like having to watch my beautiful girl die all over again." She stops and tries to keep the hurt from knifing her in the heart. Then, in a ragged voice, "I miss her so much."

"Me too," Erin says.

75

They park in Riley's lot.

Erin exits the car and, with a stunned look, says, "Please don't tell me she lives right in your building."

"Relax. Don't you think I would've told you? No, wait. Let's not do that one again." Riley points to the other complex. "She's over there."

Erin looks at the place and, with mocking approval, says, "Nice digs."

"She's loaded."

"An artist who makes a great living? Never heard that one before."

"The statues didn't make her rich. Her father did. She gave me some made-up story about how he abused her mother, who ended up killing herself, then he died of a heart attack. But none of that ever happened. The mom ran off with some guy, and Rose probably killed her dad for the inheritance after they moved away."

Erin doesn't comment, but at least she's not questioning Riley's accusation or Rose's existence. It's a start. A delicate one, but nevertheless a start.

At the wrought iron gate, Riley mindlessly punches in the keypad numbers. Though Erin doesn't comment, it seems evident that dubious thoughts are entering her mind, most likely a product of Riley's confession about breaking into the apartment.

The buzzer goes off. Riley opens the gate and gestures for Erin to walk through. At the building's entrance, Riley again punches the code. This time Erin looks as if she's pretending not to notice. But once they're inside, there's no way to avoid what she sees.

"Holy Moses on a pony," Erin says, sight bouncing in every direction. "This place is way over the top."

At the apartment, they look skittishly at each other. Rose's door is open about four inches, and all that's beyond it is a swath of darkness.

"I don't like this," Erin says. "Not one bit."

Riley takes hold of the knob to keep the door steady, then knocks her cast against it a few times.

No answer.

"This feels like a trap," Erin urgently whispers. "We need to get out of here."

Riley can't argue the point. Rose has demonstrated exceptional prowess, always one step ahead, and in every situation savoring the shock value. She could be inside, waiting to leap out and attack.

"Let's go," Erin urges.

Before Erin can say anything else, Riley gives the door a good shove, and it swings open.

"Riley, stop!"

"Stay out here if you want, but I'm going in," she says, one foot already through the doorway.

Erin groans and follows. Inside, an inkwell of darkness surrounds them. With timorous hands, Erin clutches Riley's shoulder.

A few feet later, Riley finds the light switch and flips it on. Recessed floodlights ignite the living room. Both scan the apartment with wide, incredulous eyes.

"Riley . . ."

"It—This can't be . . ."

The entire apartment isn't just empty—it's immaculate, not a sign anywhere that someone ever occupied the place.

"She moved out, probably to keep me from breaking in again or sending the police!"

Erin examines Riley, and clouds of doubt return, drifting across the plains on her face. With hot-blooded pigheadedness, Riley grabs Erin's hand and pulls her toward the door.

"Riley! What are you doing?"

"Come on. Rose has been manning another apartment as an observation area to keep tabs on me."

Erin pulls her hand away and, as if staring at a stranger, says, "Please. You have to stop this. Right now."

"Stop *what*?"

"Can't you see it? This is your pattern! The same thing happened ten years ago when you brought me to an empty house, trying to prove your theory about an evil child named Rose who you believed had killed Clarissa. Now here we are again in an empty apartment, still chasing after her damned ghost."

"I'm not! You have to believe me!" But her voice is the epitome of what losing ground sounds like. Once again, she's drowning in a sea of doubt and suspicion, which, once again, Erin has thrown her into.

Desperation sends her sprinting down the hallway.

"Riley!" Erin shouts, chasing after her. "Stop before this gets worse!"

She jumps into the elevator without answering.

When Erin catches up, her sister stands before the other apartment, paralyzed by bafflement and watching while an older couple leaves.

"She—she must have been breaking in. You've got to believe me!"

"Come on," Erin quietly says, owned by sadness so physical you could poke it with a fork. "Let's go home." She takes hold of her sister's good hand, sweaty and trembling, then says, "We'll find you some help. It's going to be okay."

"It's *not*." Tears flood Riley's eyes. She yanks her hand away and says, "Haven't you figured that out? It never *has* been. It never will be."

76

It only takes one look at Riley's cast, her teary, bloodshot eyes, and her new hairstyle for Wendy to move away from the door and clear a path to enter.

"Go sit," Wendy says. After a final check through the peephole, she locks her door.

Riley takes a place on the couch. She pulls a tissue from the box on the table, wipes her face, and grapples for composure. Wendy is in the kitchen pouring ice tea. She brings a glass into the room and puts it on the table. With eyes fixed on Riley, she feels for the seat cushion beneath her and tentatively lowers herself onto it.

"The dark-haired lady did that," Wendy says, pointing to the cast.

Riley drops her face into the good hand, and through it comes a timorous whimper.

"What is it?" Wendy says. "You can tell me."

Riley looks up. She strokes the front of her neck, body and mind crumpling to despair. "I'm drowning. I'm sinking. And each time I reach for the lifeline, she pulls it farther away."

"Who does?"

"Erin. My sister. It's like I'm not here anymore," she answers, anguish crushing her voice. "It's like she doesn't see me. Doesn't hear me." She looks away and sniffles.

"Riley . . . ," Wendy softly says, "look at me."

Riley shakes her head.

"Riley, please . . . just look at me." When she does, Wendy continues, "Now listen, okay?"

Riley takes in a deep, sustaining breath.

"I see you," Wendy says. "I will always see you."

Then, as if they've waited the past ten years for this moment to land, a connection is made. Light fills in darkness, making it disappear. They surrender to the companionable hush, each fully aware of what the other is thinking, what she's feeling.

Bang.

Wendy launches backward into the chair cushion. She throws both hands over her ears, trembling.

Riley moves quickly to her friend's side and gingerly pulls one hand away. Instilling calm in her voice, she says, "It was the rear door of a truck. Everything's fine."

But it isn't fine. Like a frightened child, Wendy looks up at Riley. All that comes out is, "I—I'm . . ."

"You don't have to be embarrassed about anything when you're with me." Riley takes Wendy's quaking hand in hers and holds it.

Wendy lets out a fainthearted laugh.

Riley tips her head toward the door. "You know, you won't die out there."

Wendy's hands are still shaking.

Riley observes her for a moment, then, "You feel safe around me, right?"

Wendy nods.

Riley asks, "Safe enough to take a risk?"

"What—Where are you going with this?"

"I want to lead you out of this apartment."

"I already did that the other day."

"Farther this time. Let's take a walk down the hallway."

Wendy looks at the door, then at Riley. She shakes her head quickly and says, "I don't think I can."

"But you said you'd give anything to be out in the world."

"It was figurative."

"I don't believe it was."

Wendy gives her a look.

"Listen for a moment, okay? We don't have to go far. To the staircase and back. I'll help you do this."

Wendy contemplates the door again, both palms stuck firmly to the seat cushion as if her stability were contingent upon it.

"I'll be right beside you," Riley encourages. "I won't let anything happen." She stands, then reaches out to Wendy. In what feels like the most delicate of moments, she sees burgeoning trust looking back at her.

Wendy rises.

As though crossing thin ice that may crack at any moment, the two friends tread hand in hand across the room, Wendy's perspiring grip so snug that it nearly cuts off Riley's circulation. Right before the doorway, she pulls to a jerky stop and looks at Riley. Riley nods her reassurance. Wendy faces down the doorknob as if she's staring into the mouth of a bloodthirsty monster.

"Let's do this," she says, "before I pee my pants with terror."

Riley laughs.

Wendy pulls open the door, then looks at her guide for support. Bound by trust well earned, by faith, they walk outside.

Little by little, they advance down the hallway, Wendy's wide-eyed gaze bouncing from the walls to the ceiling to the floor. She places a loose hand against her chest, then looks at Riley. With tears falling down her cheeks, mouth quivering, she can't speak. But there's no need to. Riley sees the mix of amazement and joy drifting across her friend's face—so physical she can almost breathe it in—and now she, too, holds back tears.

Slam.

Wendy whirls around, face ashen, chest rapidly rising and falling.

"It's just a noisy neighbor closing a door from around the corner," Riley assures her. "We're good."

They walk forward.

Four feet to the staircase. Three feet, then two.

They make it. Wendy places her palm flat against the wall, and for several seconds stares at it as if trying to validate the reality of this moment. She inhales a ragged breath.

Ten years, Riley surmises. That's how long it's been since Wendy has walked this hall. Ten years of fearing the external world instead of embracing it. Ten years of intense, inescapable agony that, no doubt, felt irreversible. Of mourning her son's tragic death the only way she knew. By disappearing from life and from herself.

Wendy falls into Riley's arms and breaks into tears. The two women cling to each other as if they're holding on for life. And Riley needs it, needs it just as much, because she's never felt so lost, so irreparably unconfirmed.

"We did it," Wendy very quietly says.

"We did." Riley pulls away with a tearful grin, and from somewhere deep inside comes an implicit message of mutual, restorative healing.

Brilliant sunlight spills through a hallway window. Wendy stares at it, transfixed, face reflecting the wonderment of a child who's experiencing something magnificent for the first time.

"I don't want to lose this feeling again. Ever," Wendy says.

77

Wendy, in the fullness of time, got her chance to enjoy the taste of freedom, but Riley couldn't be further away from it.

She can't stay here any longer.

Rose has gone into hiding, which makes her more deadly. Riley knows her enemy is tightening the screws, and with each tick of the clock, this apartment becomes more of a death trap. Staying at Erin's place is no longer an option; the chasm between them feels wider than ever. She has to figure out her next move.

She goes to her fridge and finds a small dose of consolation waiting there. The last bottle of water—of anything, really—stands front and center. She takes it to the living room, collapses across the couch, drinks greedily.

And falls fast asleep.

She wakes with a giant, heaving gasp and a hard, cold surface beneath her body. She's groggy, and her back aches. As body awareness expands, so, too, does her grasp on her surroundings. She's crammed into a confined space. Claustrophobia hits. Panic strikes.

Where am I? Where on earth am I?

Her autonomic nervous system kicks in, throwing her body into an upward thrust, but a viscous liquid beneath her counters the move. She looks down, looks around, and a firestorm of disarray torpedoes through her. She's lying in a bathtub. Not any bathtub—it's hers, and it takes a few additional seconds for her mind to grasp that she's partially submerged in a pool of blood.

Oh no, oh no, oh no! I'm bleeding out! But from where?

Her mouth is so dry she could spit sand, and a hard knot of fright sits lodged in her chest, granting barely enough oxygen to keep her from passing out. Feverishly, she sends both hands searching her body for wounds while the coppery smell of lifeblood sends her stomach contents sloshing into a virulent wave of nausea. She looks to her left but only finds another source of wretched horror waiting there. More blood. Dried blood, ribbons of it, running down the tile. But nothing can prepare her for what she sees after following those ribbons to their source: a bloody pair of toes dangles above her, and as her vision climbs higher, a hanging corpse comes into view—so, too, does comprehension.

This isn't my blood.

Terror ricochets through her. A faint, slow-moving mewl worms up her throat, gathering sound until it transmutes into an unyielding, unearthly scream that could crack tile. She tries to stand—tiny, frantic moans escaping between ice-cold lips—but the pool of blood beneath her won't permit it; her feet slip and give way, plunging her back into the red liquid. Only after grabbing hold of the nearby toilet seat with her good hand does she manage to hoist her body over the rim of the tub and flop onto the floor. She slowly rises, her clothes dripping crimson, cold and wet. The moment she looks toward the shower wall, the floor seesaws, and the room curls in around her.

A crucified human hangs across the shower wall like some barbaric and bloodied drape. A thick metal spike penetrates the center of each hand and the perforated tile behind it. The head lolls to one side. The mouth drops wide in an eternal scream. And where the eyes once were are two deep, vacuous holes, darker than pitch.

Written in blood across the tile above is the haunting question.

WHY MOMMY? WHY?

A knife handle protrudes from the center of the chest: Riley's butcher knife with the green handle. There's so much blood covering the face that it's unidentifiable, hair a congealing, stringy cluster. But the ring on one hand, with a sea-glass, emerald-cut stone, tells her exactly whose body hangs over her tub, and whose blood she's been bathing in.

That wave of nausea no longer makes a threat to explode. It delivers.

But nothing stacks up to the merciless pain in her shattered heart as she reconciles herself to her dear friend's murder, the murder of a damaged and defenseless soul who, in the cruelest way possible, was forced to die by her worst fear.

"NOOOOOO!" Riley yells, the word barely distinguishable through her racking wails. Her knees buckle. She collapses and sobs.

"Well, hello there, little sleepyhead!"

Riley's head flies upward, and a flare of white terror explodes, clouding her vision. When it clears out, Rose Hopkins stands in the doorway, her bloody latex-gloved hands wrapped around a steamy mug of coffee.

"Well!" Rose says, appraising her bloody creation on the wall. "That was a lot of work!"

The tendons in Riley's shoulders are tighter than overwound rubber bands ready to snap, while legs that feel boneless clumsily struggle to rise.

"Guess your little friend won't be of much help to you anymore, what with her new vision problems. Oh, and being dead." Rose speaks with feverish excitement and eyes a-glimmer. She raises her cup. "There's more in the kitchen. Want some? You're probably still a bit groggy after that calming drink of water. A little java? Yes?"

"Wh-why?" is all Riley can muster.

"You know *why.*" Rose's neurotic and merry facade dematerializes into a pernicious glare. "Because you've ruined my life. Because you're a horrible, evil mother!" She advances closer. "And because you deserve this."

I'm not your mother. Riley doesn't dare speak the words, but Rose must know she's thinking them because she hurls her cup of coffee onto the tile, and it explodes into pieces. Shards of porcelain and scalding coffee go everywhere. Rose's surgical-shoe covers drip brown liquid. Her bare ankles turn hot pink, but she doesn't react; her pain is detectible only in the voice that reflects her craze-driven emotions, spinning toward violent hysteria. "How could you do that? How could you abandon me?" Rose asks, lips puffing in and out with each breath as she moves closer, each step ratcheting up the danger.

Riley doesn't respond. She can't, vocal cords entering an abrupt state of paralysis, and even if she could, it would only feed Rose's gathering psychotic hailstorm.

With tears of anger dripping down her face and the whites of her eyes showing, Rose unleashes a frightening, unhinged laugh and says, "Somewhere in your narrow, STUPID mind, can you even comprehend the agony you've caused me?"

Riley glances toward the crucifixion. This situation is about to blow, her only hope for survival, the knife buried in Wendy's chest. If she can just get her hands on—

"LOOK AT ME WHEN I TALK TO YOU!" Rose shrieks.

Riley snaps her gaze back to the lunatic. Rose's head drops. "Why, Mommy, why?" she says in the voice of a little girl through weak, plaintive sobs. The same question hanging above Wendy's bloodied, mutilated corpse. "Why couldn't you just . . . just . . . love me?"

"I tried!" Riley attempts to say earnestly, persuasively, hoping to stabilize a madwoman going madder, in order to save her own life.

Rose's head rises unnaturally slowly. Lines of wet mascara crawl down her cheeks like the tears of a homicidal clown. And in a tone deep, thick, and husky, she says, "Do NOT lie to me." She moves even closer. Mere inches separate the two women's faces, and Riley can almost see venom leaking from the corners of Rose's mouth.

This is it. This is what she's been working for. I'm her final victim.

Not if Riley can help it. She closes her eyes, prepares to lunge toward Samantha, but stops when she feels warm breaths against her neck.

"It's your turn to be crucified, my love," Rose whispers into her ear.

Riley opens her eyes. A tear falls.

Rose licks it off her cheek and says, "The taste of your fear inspires me."

Then, without saying anything else, she exits the room. Riley hears the front door close, leaving her alone and helpless in the middle of a murder scene.

About a minute later, she hears sirens wailing up the road and coming closer.

78

Riley's apartment is a working crime scene.

She watches from the hall, supervised by a uniformed officer while investigators come and go, ducking beneath yellow tape that stretches across the doorway like a heady threat. Her bloodstained clothes have been bagged and tagged as evidence, but she at least had enough foresight to bury the knife inside a planter near her bedroom before the cops showed up. Leaving it out would have been the final nail in her coffin, sure to land her in the middle of a murder charge that already seems imminent. The only concern is whether the cops will find it. Then a gust of worry hopscotches through her when she realizes that Rose could have planted other incriminating evidence in the apartment. There's nothing she can do about it. Nobody needs to tell her how bad this looks—the writing is on her bloody bathroom wall. All she can do is watch helplessly while authorities build their case.

Footsteps approach behind her. She whirls around.

Great.

Demetre Sloan.

Oh, for the love of—Erin, where are you?

She should have known the viper would come slithering in. This is Sloan's dream come true, her euphoric moment, her golden opportunity to throw Riley behind bars. She did it once—she can do it again.

"Ms. Harper," Sloan mutters while passing by, sight fixed on the crime scene as if it were a sumptuous banquet.

Riley slides down the wall until her ass hits the floor.

I'm screwed.

She steals another look inside. Investigators are still busy working the scene, Erin has yet to surface, and Riley's stomach is kicking up one hell of a twister.

Sloan comes out of the apartment.

Make that a monsoon.

"Here's how this is going to work," she begins. "You've got two choices. You can come down to the station for questioning, or we can begin our investigation and draw our own conclusions, which, I assure you, would not be in your best interest."

Riley glances down the hallway and wonders why Erin isn't standing at her side.

"Looking kind of nervous there, Ms. Harper," Sloan remarks.

Got that right. Riley checks the empty hallway again.

"Ms. Harper? Is there someplace else you need to go?"

As far away from you as possible.

"I'm not talking until my lawyer gets here," she instead says.

Sloan shrugs. "Erin's welcome to join our party."

"Sorry, Detective. The party's over."

Sloan and Riley spin around.

Like a soldier storming the battlefield, Erin marches up, lips pursed and arms swinging. Locked, loaded, and ready to give Sloan what for.

"What took you so long?" Riley asks Erin while they wait in a corridor at the police station.

"I got called to the jail to meet with a client. They don't love it when phones go off there."

Riley lets out a ruffled sigh, then asks, "So what have you found out?"

Erin looks in both directions. Nobody is within earshot. She puffs her cheeks full of air, blows it out, and says, "This doesn't look good. From what I've heard, there's some weighty evidence stacked against you."

"But I'd never hurt Wendy! She was my good friend!"

Erin looks pointedly at Riley, then says, "Nobody saw Samantha, or whoever she is, enter or exit the building."

"That doesn't mean she wasn't there!"

Erin studies Riley but doesn't say anything.

"You know, for a lawyer, you've got a lousy poker face." She walks a few feet past Erin, turns back. "At least Sloan had the nerve to say it, so why don't you pony up? Come on. Get it all out."

"Get *what* out?"

"That you don't believe Samantha, or Rose, exists. That you think I'm making all this up. It's like Clarissa all over again!"

"Don't you go to that again. Don't you dare!" Erin looks up at the ceiling. Then, in a diminished voice: "Riley . . . please. I'm trying to help you. For once, can you stop judging everything I say? Can you listen to me? With your history of mental health issues, they'll find a multitude of ways to discredit what you say. I'm only trying to prepare you for that."

The two sisters look at each other, their silence wealthy with tension.

"Ms. Harper," Sloan says, poking her head out through the door, "we're ready for you."

79

Erin and Riley sit side by side in the interrogation room.

Sloan looks down at the table as if putting facts together in her head.

"So. Ms. Harper, from the beginning, please. What happened in your apartment?"

Riley keeps her focus on Rose as the suspect, explaining about the spiked water, passing out, then waking up in a tub full of blood with Wendy's corpse hanging overhead. That Rose—who now calls herself Samantha—has been stalking her, killed Wendy, and is trying to frame her for the crime.

Sloan rubs her temple, rubs it again, and says, "You do know how familiar all this sounds, right? A murder and no memory of it?"

Erin clears her throat and levels her gaze on Sloan.

Sloan takes the cue, then to Riley, "Here's what I don't understand. You claim that, after committing a gruesome murder, this Rose-Samantha-Stalker-Woman had time to hang around for a while. To chat." She emphasizes the word *chat* as if it's positively ridiculous.

"And here's another strange thing: besides your bloody footprints all over the apartment, we found no others. Thoughts?"

"She had on those surgical-shoe covers."

"*Shoe covers* . . . surgical ones . . ." Sloan stares at Riley as if trying to figure out a bad joke, then shakes it off and says, "Continue, please."

"She had on latex gloves, too."

"Of course she did."

"Anyway, I wasn't able to see the murder because I was passed out from whatever she put in my water bottle. Are you even going to test that for drugs?"

"It's been sent to the lab." With a lazy shrug, "But you could have just as easily put something in it to throw us off."

"That doesn't make a bit of sense."

"Quite frankly, a lot isn't adding up—that's why we're having this conversation."

"But you're wasting time picking apart everything I say when the real suspect is probably on her way out of town."

Sloan holds off on saying anything for about five seconds, but everything about her reeks of skepticism. She asks, "Any idea what the phrase *Why Mommy, why?* might mean?"

"It's the same message Rose left as a kid when she was stalking us. Before she murdered Clarissa."

"We're not going back to that theory again, are we?"

"I'm answering your question."

"And the broken coffee cup in your bathroom?" Sloan asks. "How did that happen?"

"Rose threw it down."

"So you were awake for that part."

"Yes."

"Why'd she throw it? Didn't she enjoy the coffee you were serving?"

"Detective," Erin chimes in, emphasizing each syllable.

Sloan settles.

Riley says, "I didn't *serve* anything. She helped herself to it."

Sloan looks at her notes so fast that reading them would be impossible, then says to Riley, "You've got some heavy-duty security hardware inside that apartment of yours."

It's not a question, so Riley doesn't provide an answer.

"Is there a particular reason why the place is locked up tighter than Fort Knox? Been trying to hide a few things in there, maybe?"

"Okay, Detective." Erin jumps in again. "If you have accusations to make, make them. Otherwise, stop badgering my client."

"We don't all have the luxury of living in safe neighborhoods," Riley tells Sloan. "My apartment has been broken into several times. By Rose."

"Do you have any evidence to support that?"

"No, but—"

Sloan cuts in. "No reports filed on the alleged incidents?"

Riley hesitates. "No."

"Because?"

Because I don't trust you or the people you work with.

Riley can't say that. It will just make this worse. But now she appears even less credible.

"So," Sloan goes on, "with all those security measures in place, how do you suppose the Rose-Samantha-Stalker-Woman's been able to gain access to your apartment?"

"I was never able to figure that out, but she's been doing it for a while now."

Sloan cocks a brow. "No signs of forced entry after the murder. Are you sure this Samantha-Rose-Stalker-Woman is exactly real?"

"Detective." Erin jumps in again. "Where exactly are you going with this?"

"That your client has a history of mental illness, and her information could be unreliable."

"Then why even bother questioning her in the first place?"

Sloan looks down, shuffles through some notes, and says, "Just trying to keep it real here."

"It's like a sickness, that's why," Riley weighs in. "Kind of like how you got off on following me around after I left Glendale."

The muted smirk confirms what Riley suspected all along about the hovering black sedan.

Sloan aims her pen at the cast and says, "What happened there?"

"It's broken."

"Obvious. What happened?"

"Rose did it."

"That didn't happen to occur around the time of your therapist's murder, did it?"

"Detective . . . ," Erin says.

"It's a reasonable question, counselor. Could be a defensive wound."

"She already explained how it happened, so unless you can prove otherwise, reel it in and quit with the fishing expedition."

Sloan moves on. She angles her head up to regard Riley's hair. "Nice new look. Quite a drastic change. Were you planning on taking that new look someplace else?"

"Okay, Detective," Erin says, "I've about reached my saturation point with you. We're here to cooperate, but keep this up and we'll be asses-and-elbows out of here."

Sloan looks bored. She flips through pages in her notebook but does not glance up when she says, "Here's me reeling it in: a neighbor reported seeing you enter the victim's apartment earlier today. Time of death still pending, but since I've found out she hadn't formed relationships with anyone else in the building, it will likely establish you as the last to see her alive. I've also gathered that the victim was agoraphobic and never left her apartment. Since there's no blood at her place—or in the hallway—and not one person saw the victim leave—"

"We walked right down the hallway together! Did anyone happen to see *that*?"

"Since not one person saw the victim leave," Sloan reiterates, "there's reason to believe that she was forced from her residence and into yours, where she was then killed. So. Did you enter the victim's apartment before she was murdered?"

"Yes, I went in, but I did not kill her. She was a dear friend, and I was visiting. Besides, why would I crucify her in my own bathroom?"

"To make yourself *not* look like a suspect?"

"That's ridiculous."

"Believe me, I've seen stranger schemes than that." Sloan flips to a new page and writes on it. "Now let's talk about Patricia Lockwood's murder. You were her last patient for the day, and quite possibly the last to see *her* alive. Do you see the pattern here?"

It's your turn to be crucified, my love.

Killing Riley would have been too easy; instead, Rose prefers to see her squirm through a slow and painful demise.

"I wasn't the last person to see Patricia alive," Riley corrects. "Rose was. When she bludgeoned her to death."

"Come on, Ms. Harper. This Rose-Samantha-Stalker-Woman has become a worn-out cliché, a go-to for everything you're unable to answer. Where's the evidence?"

"Now you want me to do your job for you? How about finding it yourself?"

Sloan answers by pulling out a sealed evidence bag and holding it up. She says, "The note you left for Patricia."

Riley was worried that could come back to bite her. She shifts her weight in the chair, which complains with two chirpy *squeaks*.

Erin is visibly stunned.

Still holding up the bag, Sloan narrows her gaze on Riley and says, "Found inside the murder scene."

"Barely inside. I shoved it under the door. You're taking that completely out of context. Besides, I left it the morning *after* she was killed."

"Got any proof of that?"

Riley doesn't, so she gives no answer.

Sloan says, "You were pretty upset with her, yes?"

"No, I was worried."

"'What's going on?'" Sloan recites from the note. "'Stop ignoring me!'" She appears puzzled. "Am I missing something? I don't see the word *worried* anywhere here."

"Relevance?" Erin asks.

"It points to a possible disagreement between the two women. Disagreements can escalate into confrontations."

"She wouldn't have left a note sitting at the crime scene."

"Not unless she'd left it earlier, then came to confront Patricia when she didn't respond, then forgot to remove it after killing her."

"This is all conjecture! And what proof do you have that anything even escalated between them?"

"How about this?" Sloan pulls out a sheet of paper tucked away between the pages in her notebook. "Can you explain why phone records show the two of you calling each other shortly before Dr. Lockwood was killed?"

"Wait a minute," Erin interrupts. "Can I please see that?"

Sloan slides the record across the table.

Erin inspects it and says, "Got a time of death for me?"

"Estimated between the hours of four and seven."

"One of these calls was made at 7:37 p.m., which would be after the murder. How can you be sure my client was speaking on the phone to Patricia Lockwood before she was attacked?"

"That's why they call it an *estimated* time of death."

"Thirty-seven minutes seems like quite a stretch past your already *estimated* time, don't you think?"

"And look a little closer at both phone records. Patricia didn't answer that call, so there's nothing to show she was alive at the time.

Erin shakes her head and scoffs, refusing Sloan's eye contact.

"So," Sloan continues, "we have a rather angry-sounding note to the victim from Ms. Harper, sealed within the scene where Patricia Lockwood was found murdered. We've also got a witness who saw you go back to the scene of the crime the following morning. And you know what they say about that."

"A witness who happened to be you, no doubt," Riley snaps at her. "Oh, but you haven't been following my ass, so never mind."

"That one wasn't me."

"Of course not. And I supposed that witness didn't stick around long enough to see me put my note under the door *after* Patricia's murder."

"Nope."

"This is ridiculous!" Erin intervenes. "You've been throwing bullshit against the wall to see if it sticks! This isn't about guilt—it's about a vendetta that goes back to the mistrial. Unless you're planning to make an arrest, we're done here. Call me when you've got some solid facts."

Sloan effortlessly pitches Erin the kind of grin one might offer a small child who's asked where the Easter Bunny comes from. She slaps her notepad closed, stands up, and says, "I was finished anyway."

Erin waits until they're outside and far enough away from the building to tell Riley, "We've got serious problems here."

80

Wendy's body has been removed from Riley's apartment.

Erin calls a cleanup crew to wash down and decontaminate the place, but since it's getting late, they won't be able to start until tomorrow.

It doesn't matter. All the soap and water in the world can never wash away the pain in her heart, or the horrid, bloody images from her mind. Aileen's probably in the process of kicking Riley out, anyway.

Erin has offered to let Riley stay at her place for the evening until the apartment is finished. Although Riley is staunchly against reentering those turbulent waters, she has no other choice.

She decides to turn in early. She longs for time and peace to begin grieving her loss. Wendy was her only true friend, the one person who believed in her unconditionally, who understood her pain on a profoundly personal level. Just when she'd shown her friend there could indeed be safety and order outside the apartment, Rose stepped in and, in the most brutal way imaginable, stole that faith away.

She rolls onto one side, squeezes her eyes shut, and tries to control stubborn tears intent on seeping through. She didn't think her life could be any worse, and yet here she is, trapped in a world of hurt that keeps hurting harder. Suspected of two murders, and in one of them, as before, with no memory of the incident and nobody to believe her.

Two timid knocks hit the door. Riley doesn't respond. A few seconds later, it opens an inch or two, and Erin asks, "Okay if I come in?"

Riley sits up. She pulls both knees toward her, wraps her arms around them.

Erin lowers herself to the bed's edge. For a long while, neither says anything, Erin facing away from her sister and staring at a wall, Riley intently focused on the covers while repeatedly twisting them between her fingers.

"You know—" Erin stops to clear her throat, then tries again. "There's this old adage that says, 'The lesson will be repeated until it is learned.'"

Riley draws the blanket closer, stares at it, and continues twisting.

"I think that's us," Erin goes on. "We keep missing the lesson. It's like we're a broken record that won't stop playing a one-note song."

"We used to have it," Riley says. "The right song."

"But then life got messy."

"So what do you think the lesson might be? What aren't we seeing?"

Erin leans slightly forward, looks at the floor. "Maybe that when the relationship goes sideways, instead of coming together, we break apart, both scrambling to try to fix the situation instead of ourselves, both forgetting what we mean to each other."

"What if that's who we are now? Who we've become. Maybe we're different people, too different to ever come together again."

"I refuse to believe that, Riley. Because no matter how much we disagree, how much anger, how much utter frustration we feel toward each other—and no matter how hard tragedy tries to drive a wedge between us—there's one thing I know is true."

The two women look at each other.

"We've got fierce love between us." Erin's eyes well up with tears. "You know that, Riley, you have to. It's not gone." She breaks from their gaze. She looks down at her empty hands, shakes her head. Then, in barely a whisper, "I . . . I can't be wrong . . . I just can't be."

"You're not."

Erin looks up at her.

"You're not wrong. We've just lost our way and can't find the road back."

"I loved her, too," Erin says, voice catching on each word.

"Love."

Erin shakes her head with confusion.

"You can still love her," Riley says. "She's not gone. Only her body is."

"Right. Of course. But aren't I allowed to miss her, too? Don't I get to make mistakes?"

"Sure."

"Then let me in. Let me finally grieve her death with you instead of us doing it separately at the same time."

Riley doesn't reply.

Erin watches her.

And waits for yet another answer that never comes.

81

It's morning.

And the rain is coming back.

Dark clouds like soiled cotton balls govern the skies, while tiny drops of rain spit against the windows of Erin's house. The pavement is spotty. Wind gusts pick up speed.

Figures.

But the gloom doesn't only live outside—it lives inside Riley, consuming her.

Erin's blow-dryer starts up in the other room.

Riley snaps to. Hoping to avoid another awkward moment between them, she pads toward the front door on a trail of eggshells. In her car, she takes the Road to Absolutely Nowhere. The apartment will be clean later today, but *safe* is a whole other concern. She told Sloan that Rose could be on her way out of town, but that was just an attempt to urge the detective into action. Hurricane Rose is coming, still on a course of destruction, and whipping a path straight toward Riley.

So she drives with vigilance, keeping one eye trained on the road, the other on her rearview mirror. Comfort food is about the closest she'll get to any comfort, so she stops at a greasy-spoon diner. Looking over the menu, she cringes at photos celebrating all the disgusting pancake dishes, each stack with a different topping sloppily thrown on and bleeding down the sides.

Post-traumatic pancake stress.

She opts for the scrambled eggs.

The waitress delivers Riley's meal, but she spends a good part of the time staring out her window on the lookout for Rose. Though she makes a valiant effort to eat, she knows that's not going to happen. Not today. It isn't that the breakfast is so bad—it's that her nerves are on a fast climb. She drops her fork and gives up. No relief to be found here; in fact, she feels worse.

When the bill arrives, she digs through her purse but then stops, surprised to see her phone screen lit up with a voice-mail message and a string of missed calls. Then she remembers: desperately in need of sleep last night, she put the phone on "Do not disturb" in case Rose decided to call and brag about her latest victory . . . or worse. For a moment, she hesitates before opening her messages.

The calls are from Saint Francis Hospital.

She puts the phone to her ear, listens to the message.

"Ms. Harper, please call the hospital immediately."

She does.

Erin has been rushed to the trauma unit.

82

The storm flexes its muscles.

On her way to the hospital, Riley pushes safety aside by speeding up through the onslaught of gusty rain. With each hurried turn, giant puddles erupt, belting the windshield with water on a slick road that feels paved with banana peels.

What if Erin's car crashed in this awful weather, and what if her life is in jeopardy?

What if I never have the chance to reconcile with her?

And what if Riley wasn't Rose's next intended victim, after all, if she still had one more to knock down? The person who means the most to Riley.

Chased by flying sparks of red-hot anger, Riley swerves into the parking lot and leaps from her car and into the downpour, hotfooting it toward the entrance, perspiration in each tightly fisted hand.

Inside, she takes long strides down the hospital corridor, quick, short breaths punctuating her steps. Nearing the trauma unit, she rounds a corner, spots a nurse, then grabs her by the arm. The woman guides her to the nurse's station to check on Erin's information. Less than two minutes later, a doctor stands before Riley, who falters beneath his reflective gaze for a moment.

And Riley knows whatever's coming can't be good.

"Someone tried to slit her throat," the doctor says.

That statement bounces through Riley's mind, bounces hard, screams at her. Then the room swims around her, and the walls close in.

Is she . . . ?" Riley tries to push the rest of her sentence out through thick and narrow pipes but can't.

"She lost some blood, and—"

"IS SHE ALIVE?"

"Yes. Bruised up, and there's going to be a scar across her neck, but she's stable."

Riley locks both hands behind her head and releases the breath she's been hanging on to. With reassurance that Erin will be okay, the peripheral questions begin to surface, so she asks, "How did it happen?"

"You'll need to speak with the police, but from what I know, someone attacked her inside the parking structure at work."

Just didn't know you had one. A sister.

Rose knew damned well that Erin was Riley's sister—she had to. The question was an act to appear innocent and unaware while still playing the role of Samantha.

She's a lawyer.

What kind?

Defense.

Ahhh. So she's a tough one, right?

What's her last name?

An attempt to probe for Erin's current information. Riley should have seen this coming, should have protected her sister.

"I need to see her," she insists.

"Of course," the doctor says. "She's up on the fourth floor."

Riley walks into the room and finds Erin staring at a wall. A white blood-spotted bandage circles her neck, and her elbows, knees, and face are marred by scratchy bruises.

This is my fault. My sister was nearly killed, and it's because of me.

When she looks at Riley, her expression is hollow, a not-so-gentle reminder that nothing has changed between them since their uncomfortable conversation last night. Riley pushes her discomfort aside. Erin is safe, and that's all that matters. With halting steps, she approaches.

Erin averts her interest toward the foot of her bed.

Riley tries to pretend it doesn't feel as if her sister has jabbed a knife in her side. "Erin," she says, recognizing how tortured she sounds, "look at me. Please . . . look at me."

Erin does. But very slowly.

Riley sits at the edge of the bed. She doesn't speak. Erin shows no visible reaction but maintains her gaze on Riley. It's a start.

"Were you able to see who did this?"

Erin shakes her head.

No proof that Rose was the assailant, but it would be one hell of a coincidence if she weren't.

"I don't want to do this anymore. It's so . . . This is . . ." Riley drops her head. She can't cry. She cannot. She looks up at her sister. "You're right. I haven't been truthful, but it wasn't because I didn't trust you. It was something else, and I'm going to tell you. I promise, I will. Not yet. But soon. And when I do, this will all make sense—perfect sense—and you'll understand. You'll understand all of it."

"I don't know if I can believe you anymore," Erin says with a voice enfeebled by her neck injury. "I'm tired, Riley. Tired of waiting to understand what never ends up making sense. Of trying to figure out why *we* don't make sense. I . . ." Her speech falls into a barely audible whisper. "I'm dead tired."

"So you're just going to give up on me?"

Erin breathes in deeply but offers no answer.

And something inside Riley breaks apart, then shatters. Maybe it's her heart. Maybe it's her will.

Maybe it's her whole world.

She tries to speak but can't.

So she walks away.

83

Erin insists on going home the next day—the hospital warns against it, but she won't back down, so they relent, but only with a promise she'll take time off from work and immediately follow up with her primary physician.

But there's not a doctor on this earth who can fix Riley's problems.

It's your turn to be crucified, my love.

Rose's latest threat still echoes through Riley's mind, louder than ever.

Out of sight is nowhere near out of mind where Rose is concerned. She's gone back into stealth mode, is probably preparing to stage her next attack, and if history repeats itself, Riley stands a good chance of unwittingly landing right back in the woman's dangerous and deranged hands.

Riley's work isn't done yet, either.

Get out. Stay strong. Trust your truth.

Infuriation replaces fear, determination shatters trepidation. She made her share of mistakes after leaving Glendale; the biggest one was letting Rose gain control of their relationship. But this is the part where Riley takes back the power.

You don't mess with family.

She folds Clarissa's shirt to put it away for the day, movements quick, exacting, and decisive. "Rose messed with you, baby. Now she's tried to do the same to Erin. But this is where it ends. It will be her last mistake. This time, I'm writing the story."

She digs out her green-handled butcher knife from the planter, cleans it off, then holds up the razor-sharp blade to study it.

It's time.

Time to step into action.

Kill her dead.

Goal set. Plan in place. Her logic is simple: one of the best ways to lure an enemy is to become the bait. There's one victim left on Rose's list, and Riley knows she's it. The woman will show up here—it's not a matter of *if*, just *when*—but Riley is ready. All it will take is some waiting and patience.

She checks the clock. She takes down the mirror in her living room, hangs it on the opposite wall.

The storm beats its chest, hurling down an onslaught of weightier showers. A flash of lightning explodes through the sky, followed by strident thunder.

She shores up her grip on the knife: Rose isn't coming over for a chat—she's coming to kill, and this time Riley will happily exchange roles, switching from prey to predator. She unlocks her door, then hides in her darkened kitchen and sits tight.

A few hours later, through her relocated mirror, Riley watches the front door handle rotate silently. Then the door cracks open. Then Rose's face appears in the gap. Like a hungry hunter searching for her kill, she peers through, eyes sliding from side to side. She sneaks into the apartment with a canvas sack slung over her shoulder and a hammer protruding from it. When Riley hears the jingle of metal spikes, her heart punches hard and fast.

Rose turns her body to gently close the door. That's Riley's green light. She charges forward, the knife in her good hand, and with the other slings a hold around Rose's neck and starts ratcheting up the pressure. Rose coughs, gags, and struggles to break free while Riley push-walks her deeper into the apartment.

But Rose retaliates with unexpected, roaring power. She reaches over her shoulder and digs her nails into Riley's cheek. Riley brings the knife around, but Rose's arm flies up, knocking the weapon out of Riley's grip—it sails through the air, then *clanks* to a hard landing on the kitchen tile several feet away. Rose is about to break free from the arm hold when Riley jacks a foot into the back of her calf. Rose's knee buckles and caves.

Rose chatters with pain. Riley scrambles forward to retrieve her knife, but the other woman quickly recovers and cannonballs a knee into Riley's lumbar. Pain blasts up Riley's spine as her body surges forward and she makes a facedown landing hard on the floor. Her lip is busted—she tastes blood—but that's nothing compared to Rose's crushing weight when it barrels down onto Riley's back, chasing the wind from her lungs.

Harnessing everything she's got, Riley labors to flip onto her back, but Rose maintains the upper hand and holds her firm to the floor. Riley jerks her head to one side and finds the knife; it's a few feet out of range. Before she can stretch to reclaim it, Rose hitches both hands around Riley's neck and squeezes. Keeping her completely immobilized and glued to the floor, Rose throws her whole body into the action, repeatedly and rhythmically grunting while she steps up the compressions. Riley fights for each languishing breath. The room whirls into a dizzying spin, and her eyes feel as if they're going to explode in their sockets. This could be the end if she doesn't act fast.

Outside, a shock of lightning goes off, setting the night on fire. Thunder cracks and pops like the sharpest of whips, and well-placed rage sparks unexpected power. Riley's good arm springs up. She grabs hold of Rose's bicep, giving herself enough leverage to throw a sucker punch into Rose's abdomen with the hard and weighty cast. As Rose falls off to one side and squeals with pain, Riley's foot sails into the other woman's stomach, sending her body into a tumble across the floor. Riley recaptures the knife, then rises to her knees.

Rose rises, too, but not fast enough. Riley launches herself on top of her, then, with all the strength she can muster, plunges the blade into Rose's chest.

Rose lets out an ungodly scream, then gurgles and chokes on her own blood. Riley stabs her again, this time in the neck. Cartilage crackles, blood spurts, and Rose's mouth pops wide open with lethal alarm.

She keeps stabbing as Rose's blood spills across the floor in a slow-moving river of red. The woman is near death, but now fury holds the knife, and it won't let Riley stop. Each time the blade pierces flesh, memories of Clarissa's murder whipsaw through her mind.

Memories initially lost. But they aren't gone—they resurfaced while Riley was at Glendale. Since then, she's kept them secret from the world, waiting for this day with only one plan in mind: sharp-toothed revenge.

Get out. Stay strong. Trust your truth.

Like frames in a fast-spinning film reel, the images from that horrible day storm through her mind.

Stab.

On their way home from school, she and Clarissa have an argument. The disagreement escalates. Riley almost misses a distant and fleeting glimpse in her rearview mirror of a pink bicycle crossing the road.

Stab.

Dark skies turn darker. Clarissa's tantrum explodes.

Riley flies off the handle. She stops the car, orders her daughter to walk the remaining distance home.

Stab.

Several minutes later: Clarissa still isn't home, and Riley begins to worry. She grabs her coat, grabs her scarf, leaves her house, and hits the sidewalk running.

Stab.

On her way, a wicked downpour drops from the heavens like a sheet of lead, followed by an electrical storm. Lightning explodes. Thunder roars and booms.

Stab.

She arrives at the spot where she let her daughter out. A stiff gust blows.

Clarissa screams.

Riley twists around to look.

Oh no! Oh God . . . NO!

Rose is dragging Clarissa's unconscious body away from the road and out of sight of traffic. One of Clarissa's sneakers falls off and hits pavement near the curb.

My baby! My precious girl!

Stab.

I have to save her. I HAVE TO SAVE HER!

She tries to dash across the road, but the speeding cars create a formidable blockade. Wind and rain only add to the problem, making visibility difficult. She helplessly watches Rose drag Clarissa's wilted body toward the cemetery. Toward the already-open grave.

Traffic opens up. Like an arrow racing toward its target, Riley takes off across the road. Nearing the middle of the street, she can see Rose hefting Clarissa to the grave's edge, then, with a foot, she shoves her in. Consumed by visible, naked fury, she shouts into the grave, "You don't get to have her! *I* get to have her!"

At the curb, Riley scoops Clarissa's bloody sneaker up into her hands.

Stab.

Screeeeeech.

She looks up. A car rounds the corner at vicious speed.

"NO! STOP!"

The vehicle swerves close, dangerously close, hurling an aggressive swell of water her way. She tries to dive off the road, but wet, slippery pavement betrays her. She loses her footing, skates forward several feet, and in the process, connects eye to eye with Rose. In that unnerving moment it's as if time freezes: Rose shocked, Riley racked with distress. Then Riley collides with a roadside boulder.

A powerful wind rips the scarf from her head and sends it sailing through the air. It snags on a tree branch. That's the last thing she sees before thick black ink spills across her world.

She's out.

Thunder brings her back around.

What—Where—How long have I . . . ?

She's lying on the ground in the middle of a ruthless rainstorm, has no idea why or how she got here. Her clothes, her body, her surroundings, are soaked. Spearing pain pulsates from her head.

There's something in my hand. Someone has put something in my hand.

She looks down, sees her daughter's sneaker with streaks of watered-down blood running through the canvas. She touches a finger to her forehead, inspects it, but finds no blood.

Oh no! No, no, no, no, no! Clarissa's been hurt! How? And where? I have to find her! I have to help her!

But her mind is woolly, her memory nonexistent. She clambers to stand, tries to negotiate for stability with the earth but slips and falls. She tries again. Slips and falls again. Then finds success and launches down the road through wind and rain. She hysterically calls out Clarissa's name to no avail.

Another burst of lightning opens the skies.

Boom.

More rain, harder now, mercilessly pelting her face, her neck . . . everything. She doesn't even know where she's going.

Where am I going?

She keeps running anyway, then . . .

Is that—?

An oncoming police car drives directly toward her. Before she can raise a hand for help, the cruiser's lights spin, tossing a red-and-blue glow across shiny, wet pavement.

"HELP ME!" she yells with a voice that sounds as if it's scraping over bedrock. "PLEASE! HELP ME!"

She sprints faster toward the vehicle, almost tripping over herself along the way.

The squad car's door flies open. The cop piles out. He gets a fix on her, sees the swelling bruise on her forehead. He snatches the radio from his shoulder, calls for help.

"Someone's hurt my daughter!" she tries to explain. "SHE'S BLEEDING, AND I CAN'T FIND HER!"

The statement pulls him to a standstill and paints confusion across his face while he observes the bloody sneaker Riley holds.

"Ma'am," he says, "is that your daughter's shoe?"

"Yes!"

"Where did you find it?"

"I . . . I don't know."

He reexamines the bruise on her forehead, seems to make a connection, and his expression shrinks.

Stab.

Riley straddles Rose's bloodied, lifeless body, her face, neck, chest—everything—perforated with so many holes that the woman is unrecognizable. Riley looks to the right, sees the knife clenched in her hand, poised and ready to stab again.

She lets out a scream but doesn't know why.

The apartment door flies open and smashes into drywall.

She looks up to find Erin standing in the entryway, stunned into silence and staring at a floor covered in so much red that it's nearly impossible to see what's beneath it. Then she sees the body, and through a sickened and breathless whisper, says, "Oh, Riley. What have you done?"

"Justice," Clarissa calmly says, moving out from the room's shadowy corner.

84

"Riley, please," Erin says. She's backing away, staring at the bloody weapon. "Put down the knife."

Riley looks toward the corner and speaks to Clarissa. "Come here, sweetheart," she says, soothing. "No more hiding."

Erin looks in Clarissa's direction, too, and turns alabaster white.

Clarissa gives her aunt a nod. Riley gently lowers the knife onto the table.

Erin lets out a sigh of relief, but she's trembling as she takes in Riley's face, her hair, her clothes, all covered in coagulating blood. She glances at Rose's maimed corpse, then all at once becomes animated, covering her mouth and gagging.

A joyous smile emerges beneath the blood on Riley's lips. She points to Clarissa and triumphantly says to Erin, "See? I told you it would all make sense. This is it. This is what I couldn't tell you all along."

Erin stops gagging. She takes the hand away from her mouth, and in a quivering voice, says, "W-what?"

"We can explain everything," Riley says. Clarissa takes soft, soundless steps toward her mother. She stands beside Riley and takes her hand.

"We had to keep this quiet," Riley continues. "Until everything was finished."

"I don't understand," Erin weakly says.

"Our plan," Clarissa says. "Get out. Stay strong. Trust your truth." Then, to Riley, "Mom, the bus is leaving soon. We have to get you cleaned up and out of here."

"I'm not going anywhere until I explain this."

"Then explain it!" Erin says, mind on the fast track to its breaking point.

"I AM!" Riley shouts at her sister.

Clarissa grabs hold of her mother's arm. "Mom, calm down. This is all a shock to her."

Riley nods. Striving for composure, she says, "One night during my stay at Glendale, I woke up to the sound of footsteps. I flipped on the lamp and at first couldn't believe it. There she was. My angel. My beautiful daughter, and it was amazing, Erin. It was so damned amazing."

Erin's about to speak, but Riley interrupts her with a raised hand. "Stay with me for a minute here, okay? I promise, it'll all come together."

Erin closes her mouth.

"From that day on," Clarissa continues with the story, "I came to visit her."

"*Secretly,*" Riley elaborates, smiling at her daughter. "Together, we sat in my room and worked to recover the lost memories. Clarissa would repeatedly tell me the story, then, the next day, see if I still remembered. For a while, I couldn't, but then the memories started to stick. Eventually, I was able to recall everything, but I kept quiet about it after my release from Glendale in order to move forward with our plan to kill Rose."

"*The cops will just get in the way,*" Erin slowly says, repeating Riley's comment from when they drove home from the DMV that day.

"Exactly." A grin of acknowledgment spreads across Riley's face. "Now you're following. That's why I fought you so hard about calling the police."

"*I still see her sometimes . . . ,*" Erin says, comprehension widening.

Riley gazes lovingly at her daughter. "We knew Rose would come after me the moment the news reported I was leaving Glendale, hoping to continue a relationship that never began in the first place. Trying to make me her mother. She thought she could evade me with the phony plastic surgery, but right away I saw through it.

"She wanted to replace me then, and she wanted to now," Clarissa says. "She even dyed her hair the same color as mine, and that walk . . ."

"Still trying to imitate that, too, as a way to get my attention. She knew I'd recognize that confident walk anywhere."

"The only way she'd stop was if *we* stopped her," Clarissa says.

"And we wanted revenge for her ruining our lives. We had to kill her."

"So we decided to set her up."

"All this time," Riley says, "the hound thought she was hunting the fox, but it's been the other way around."

"Except the situation started to backfire. Our plan was for Mom to slowly work her way into Rose's life, then go in for the kill, but she got ahead of us with her own plan, and that one ended up being dangerous. We had no idea how much more deranged and violent she'd become in the last ten years."

"She got unmanageable in a hurry," Riley agrees, "and it took some time to gain the upper hand."

Erin's growing comprehension looks as if it's morphed into a full-body chill.

Riley nods to her sister. "I get it. I'm in serious trouble, but you don't need to worry. I've got an escape strategy. I'll be far away and long gone before the cops are onto me. It's been my plan all along."

"Here won't work . . . There's a better life waiting somewhere." Erin again echoes Riley's words.

Clarissa checks her watch, then looks at her mother.

"I know," Riley tells her. Then, to Erin, "Leave now. You have to leave before you're implicated. Hopefully, nobody knows you were here. We have a few things to take care of, then we'll be gone, too." Back to Clarissa, "Right, baby? Go to my room and change into the clothes I laid out on the bed."

"Riley," Erin says, voice weakened by tears, "who are you talking to?"

"Who do you think? The only other person here is Clarissa."

Erin shakes her head.

Riley takes hold of Clarissa's hand. She raises it into the air, lets it drop. "Are you blind?"

Riley looks at Clarissa. Clarissa shrugs.

"Riley," Erin says, "Clarissa isn't here. You think she is, that you're seeing some kind of . . . ghost. But she's not real."

Riley backs away, head shaking. "I swear, Erin, don't do this to me again. Do *not*. Stop gaslighting me. Stop treating me like I'm crazy. That has to end right here."

"We need to get you help," Erin says. "We have to get it right away."

"For crying out loud! She's your niece!" Riley points to Clarissa. "How can you just stand there and not even acknowledge her presence? Why won't you even look at her?"

"Because she isn't here. She is gone," Erin says with so much sadness, so much grief, while she blinks away more tears. "We lost her ten years ago."

"No! She is not gone! She's not! She came back to life again!" Riley shouts, but it comes out like a desperate plea for affirmation. She's hyperventilating, her stomach sucking in, sucking out. "LOOK AT HER, DAMN IT!"

Erin won't.

"I SAID, LOOK AT HER!" Riley shouts, louder this time.

But when she looks to Clarissa for support, Clarissa is no longer there.

"Now you've done it," Riley says to Erin. "You hurt her feelings." She angles her head to see toward the bedroom. "It's okay, sweetheart. Come back out . . . Clarissa? Erin didn't mean to—Where did you go . . . ?"

She feels a little light-headed, her perception a little fuzzy, and stumbles as she steps toward the bedroom—then more images *whoosh* through her mind. Images she doesn't understand. Are they other lost memories?

She watches herself going into the bedroom to put away Clarissa's clothes for the day. She thinks about Rose and how much pain she brought into her life.

"Child killer!" Clarissa shouts in outrage, reading her mother's thoughts.

Riley's anger ignites, too. She takes off, storms down the hallway, ducks into the apartment under repair, steals a nail from the carpenter's bag, runs back to her place, and uses the sharpened tip to scratch her daughter's angry statement into the headboard.

She sees herself with Clarissa, who pulls the green-handled butcher knife from the dishwasher. She holds it up for Riley to see, then puts it back, leaving the pointed tip sticking up as an angry reminder that Rose must die.

Erin comes over to help unpack, and Riley accidentally pricks her finger on the knife.

"What's going on with you?" her sister asks. When Erin leaves, Riley panics. She hides the knife under her pillow.

At the breakfast café, Riley intentionally drops Clarissa's photo while passing by Rose's table, then moves on toward the restroom. Inside, her daughter waits, sitting on the sink's countertop. With legs playfully swinging, she smirks, then gives her mother a colluding wink before Rose walks in.

After Riley's lunch with Rose, Clarissa yells, "DIE, MURDERER!"

Riley runs to her car, takes out her key, then scratches Clarissa's comment into the passenger's side door. After finishing, she shouts, "QUIT HIDING AND BRING IT ON, YOU COWARDLY ASSHOLE! I'M READY. DO YOU HEAR ME? I'M SO READY!" as people on the street stare at her in confusion.

Rose comes to Riley's apartment and apologizes for her behavior at the disastrous hair appointment.

"Bitch!" Clarissa shouts after the woman leaves. Riley grabs an old can of spray paint from under the sink, uses it to furiously write Clarissa's sentiment across the door, then tosses the can down her hallway's trash chute. A day later, she flies into a huff because nobody has removed the ugly graffiti, then does it herself.

Clarissa plays her game, moving the doll around Riley's apartment, then, as her final joke, hides it behind the curtains.

Riley grabs the butcher knife off the counter, digs the blade deeper into the cut on her wrist to draw blood, then uses it to write while Clarissa dictates: "Mother, we both know the truth. Our truth. We are connected by blood. Our blood."

"Riley?"

Erin has been speaking, but Riley didn't hear a word of it. She tries to regain her focus.

"Riley," Erin again says, eyes flooding with tears, "Clarissa is gone. And that's not Rose. You killed someone, Riley, but it's not Rose."

"I killed Rose!" Riley shouts. "Her body is right in front of you, and you still don't believe me?"

"Just listen!" Erin pleads. "It's what I was coming here to tell you. Samantha Light wasn't Rose—she was a woman named Christina Henry. She was an artist. Samantha Light was just her professional name."

"Christina Hen—No, no, no, no, no." Riley shakes her head vehemently. "That's just a fake name Rose used with Patricia. She used Clarissa's initials to mock me!"

"She wasn't Rose," Erin reiterates. "Rose Hopkins was killed in a car wreck." She takes a step forward, pleading again, palms up. "I'll show you the obituary."

Riley, with tears streaming, stares vacantly at the body, then at Erin.

Erin's own tears are falling. "Rose was headed for Glendale Hospital on the day of your release. It was the destination on her phone's GPS. The cops never understood why . . . but I do." Erin looks at her with an aching heart that almost seems visible. "I should have listened. I should have believed you when you said that Rose killed Clarissa. I . . ." Her voice breaks. "I should have been a better sister. I'm just . . . so sorry."

Erin pulls her phone from a pocket, hands shaking so much she can barely hang on to it.

"NO! What are you doing?" Riley asks, a riptide of worry rising through her. "Who are you calling?"

Erin gives her no answer as she unsteadily dials 9-1-1.

"DON'T! DON'T DO IT! YOU'RE GOING TO RUIN EVERYTHING!"

Clarissa has returned to her side, and they embrace, Riley holding on tight with hands coated in dried blood, the two of them rocking hard, rocking fiercely, and feeling the warmth of each other's embrace.

The sound of blaring sirens outside grows louder.

"Don't worry, Mom. I'll never leave you," Clarissa whispers into her mother's ear.

Riley closes her eyes and keeps rocking.

85

A balmy trade wind blows from the east, effortlessly pushing fleecy dove-white clouds across turquoise skies. Up ahead, waves tumble forward and kiss the glistening sun-bleached sand before falling back to their rightful place: an ocean so transparent you can see straight to the bottom.

Riley readjusts her floppy yellow hat, lolls in her beach chair, and digs her feet into the snug and toasty sand. After sipping her mai tai, she savors the curaçao liqueur still on her lips, then, with a contented grin, breathes in the fresh, salty air.

"This is so amazing, isn't it?" Clarissa asks.

Riley gazes lovingly at her daughter and says, "It is. Everything is amazing. You . . . me . . . this. I've never been happier in my life."

The two lean back in their chairs, sunlight heating their legs before the breeze sweeps in to cool them off.

Riley pulls off her hat, shakes loose her long, thick hair, then leans back into the chair again. She draws in another relaxing breath, relishing the delicate ocean spray that washes across her face.

"I've missed us, Mom. I've missed us so much."

"You won't have to again," Riley assures her.

"I'll never leave you." The drifting gale carries Clarissa's beautiful voice over the ocean waves, where it washes away.

"I know that, sweetheart," Riley says. "I know." She smiles tenderly at her daughter, but that smile begins to fade when, over Clarissa's shoulder, something on the beach demands her attention. And as Riley zeros in, her fading smile opens into fear. An angry whirlwind takes off, grains of sand whisking and twirling until they reveal what lies beneath. As if risen from the sweltering ground, a barren wooden cross sticks up, its inscription across the top bearing a name.

RILEY HARPER

"I'll never leave you," she hears again. But this time it's not Clarissa speaking.

Riley's toes curl. She buries her face in both hands and screams into them.

Two pairs of footsteps echo on concrete, along with two voices, growing louder.

Riley sits straight up, throws both arms around her knees, and hears, "What happened with this one?"

"Riley Harper? She butchered some woman she believed murdered her kid."

Two men appear, then vanish, their footsteps and voices dissipating.

"Did she kill the kid? The dead woman?"

"That's the kicker. Harper was stalking the wrong woman, but the victim turned out to be even crazier than *she* was."

An image of the stabbed and bloody corpse flashes through Riley's mind.

Then through crackling speakers, she hears, "Attention all prisoners. Lights out."

Slam.

Her eyes flash open into near darkness.

ACKNOWLEDGMENTS

This book almost didn't happen—that's because *I* almost didn't happen.

Back in 2015, shortly after the release of *Twisted*, I was on my way to a book signing and found myself caught in a nasty car accident. I had no idea that very moment would end up being the greatest gift of my life. During a routine scan, doctors accidentally stumbled upon a stage III malignant thymoma aggressively moving into my heart.

In the blink of an eye, I was fighting for my life.

Shortly after the major chest surgery, and the five weeks of daily radiation treatments, lightning struck twice when I was hit with a debilitating neuromuscular disease called myasthenia gravis.

What followed would be my new reality: a two-month hospital stay, the news I had a cerebral stroke, and the possibility of a life dependent on breathing machines and wheelchairs. During that time—among the many ups and downs—*What She Doesn't Know* became an off-again, on-again possibility. But despite my body's fierce protestations, I was determined to complete my fifth novel. So many times I could barely lift my fingers to the keyboard or, for that matter, my head to see the screen. Still, I was determined. Between daily physical therapy sessions where I learned to walk again, and during the moments when I felt strong enough, I did my best to work on the manuscript, much of that time from a hospital bed.

Now, three years later, here we are.

What you've read is the final result of my stubborn struggle, and I hope with everything I've got that I've given you something of which I can be proud. Not only because I fought the good fight but also because a satisfying novel is—and always has been—my first and foremost goal for you, the amazing readers who mean everything to me. Thank you for waiting. Thank you for still being here.

I can say with the utmost confidence that I couldn't have written this book without the help of people who held me up during my struggles. To them I'll be forever grateful, appreciative, and downright humbled.

I'm so thankful to Gracie Doyle, Megha Parekh, and the publishing team at Thomas & Mercer for their unfailing and tireless support. Added thanks to Gracie, who patiently waited while I wrestled to finish this book, repeatedly extending my deadlines. One can only hope for an author/publisher relationship like ours, but I don't have to, because that's exactly what we have.

Caitlin Alexander was my developmental editor for *Twisted*. We worked well together then, and we're even better now. Thanks for your thorough attention to detail. You treated my work as if it were your own, and I'm grateful.

To my agent, Scott Miller in New York, you've been with me from the start of my mainstream publishing career, and I couldn't be happier about it. You do your job so well, and with such dedication, that I sometimes wonder how I got so lucky. I truly enjoy working with you and hope we can continue our teamwork for many years to come.

Forensic psychologist Cynthia Boyd joined my team of consultants during *Twisted*, but in working together, we also discovered a wonderful friendship. Thank you for visiting me regularly (with baked goods, no less) during my seemingly endless hospital stay, and thank you for being the wonderful person you are.

I'd be remiss if I didn't mention the nurses, doctors, and physical therapists at Scripps Memorial Hospital. Thanks so much for your dedication, knowledge, and hard work. Without it, I wouldn't be standing on two feet today or, for that matter, writing these words. Each day you selflessly—and sometimes thanklessly—save lives, and I'm eternally grateful to you for it.

To the people I call My Tribe, the intimate circle of friends whose love and support are the fuel that keeps me going . . .

Kelley Eskridge at Sterling Editing started out as my personal editor way back during the indie days, but after six years, you are so much more to me than that: you're my friend, my publishing touchstone, my breath of fresh air when the pressure of writing becomes too overwhelming. Thanks for untangling my confusion when I need it most.

Jessica Park, my protector (a.k.a. Tinkerbell). Thanks for your love and for being the voice of reason during times when there was little to be found in my life. I've enjoyed your style advice, our marathon phone chats, our dinners out, and the fiercely close friendship we've shared.

Deb Brada, I've known you since our college years when dreams were big and the determination to reach them was even bigger. Since then, we've seen many come true, along with the tragedies life threw in our paths along the way. Those are what we cannot control, but there's one thing I know to be the absolute truth: I'm so damned grateful to have taken this journey with you and for the understanding that it's the one thing that will never change.

Jill Sniffen is another college friend who has come to mean so very much to me. Thank you not only for your psychological expertise on the book but for your amazing friendship, for taking me to countless doctors' appointments when I was too weak to drive, and for the hours of ceaseless and refreshing laughter that became my true medicine. Thanks for being one of the most caring and selfless people I've ever known. I feel truly blessed to have you in my life.

Barbara Richards, thank you for the dinners filled with cheesy goodness and great laughter. They've meant more to me than words can ever describe.

LJ Sellers, I've treasured our author-to-author talks and our clandestine chocolate indulgences. I'll never forget the times when, without so much as a second thought, you hopped on planes from Oregon to San Diego just to care for me during and after my hospital recoveries. Your instinctive desire to help those in need is beyond admirable and one of many things I admire about you. I'm beyond grateful to call you my friend.

To Linda Boulanger: Your friendship is a gift. Thank you for giving it to me. Thank you for your light, love and laughter.

To my father: I'm so thankful for the close relationship we share, which, over the years, has only deepened. I'll always treasure those special moments we shared during my recovery as you drove me from one place to the next, and our dinners filled with great conversation.

To my mother: I miss you terribly, and although you're no longer here in the physical sense, the most important part of you, your light, still shines as brightly as ever in my life.

And by no means last, to you, my readers. Thank you for giving me years of pleasure by providing a place to tell my stories, and for the literally hundreds of get-well wishes you sent during my fight to stay alive. Not a single moment passes when I don't feel extraordinarily grateful to have you in my life.

ABOUT THE AUTHOR

Photo © 2016 Cara Vescio

Andrew E. Kaufman is the author of the novels *Twisted*; *The Lion, the Lamb, the Hunted*; *Darkness & Shadows*; and *While the Savage Sleeps*. He is also a contributor to the Chicken Soup for the Soul books, where he's written about his experience recovering from cancer. After receiving his journalism and political science degrees at San Diego State University, he became an Emmy-nominated writer/producer. He now lives in Southern California with his two Labrador retrievers, who think they own the place. Visit www.andrewekaufman.com.